What people are saying about
The Empty Confessional . . .

The Catholic Church once again made headlines with the recent news that former Pope Benedict XVI had repeatedly mishandled sexual abuse cases by Catholic priests. This came as little surprise to author and former professor of religion Tom Hogan, who has been writing about pedophilia within the Church ever since his article about the subject for Newsweek in 2003. Now Tom takes readers even deeper into the Church's culture of coverup in his new novel. *The Empty Confessional* uses the thriller format to take the reader behind the scenes of a horrific event, educating them on the workings of the Church while they follow twists and turns. A frighteningly realistic, compelling tale of retribution.

    —Premier Guide Miami

Hogan writes with the acumen of someone who has been on the inside of an institution capable of turning a blind eye to heinous acts.

    —The Table Read

The Empty Confessional plunges readers into the dark workings of the Catholic Church and its tacit policy of protecting pedophilic priests.

    —Keep the Faith

A gripping thriller that will keep you guessing all the way to the end. Tom Hogan doesn't shy away from difficult settings and thought-provoking topics and his latest book is no exception.

    —ELIZABETH CVETIC

The Empty Confessional, a gripping new thriller from Tom Hogan, compels a moral person to ask an important question: Just how far would I be willing to go—what level of violence am I personally be prepared to undertake—if I knew I could stop a network of pure, unadulterated, and unapologetic evil?

    –JIM DECKER

Can a man of the cloth exact vengeance with righteous anger and still maintain his faith? In his latest crime thriller, Tom Hogan makes his main character and the rest of us question how much is too much when it comes to protecting the most vulnerable of our communities.

    –TRACIE DUDMAN

A captivating tale of morality and responsibility told from the perspective of a young, idealistic priest, *The Empty Confessional* takes the reader on a compelling ride through questions of morality, responsibility, commitment, honor—and what to do when a protector becomes a predator.

    –AMANDA ILES

A chilling thriller that delivers an intense solution to a social depravity. The engaging characters, unique Pittsburgh setting, and knowledgeable story line bring forth a fast-paced finish.

    –CINDY LOPER

In Hogan's excellent new thriller, you'll meet the most interesting priest since Father Damien in *The Exorcist*. The difference? Gabe takes justice into his own hands—right up until the keep-you-guessing conclusion.

    –LAURENCE NORTON

THE EMPTY
CONFESSIONAL

THE EMPTY CONFESSIONAL

Tom Hogan

LAUGHING DOG PUBLISHING • AUSTIN, TEXAS

Dedication

*In memory of my father, John Hogan (1916–2001),
and my mother, Peggy Hogan (1919–2021).
They were wonderful parents
in so many ways.*

ISBN: 978-1-7369436-3-2 Paperback
ISBN: 978-1-7369436-4-9 eBook
Library of Congress Control Number: 2022906123

Published by
Laughing Dog Publishing LLC

For bulk orders or permission to make copies of any part of the work
email your request to Tom Hogan: Tom@CrowdedOcean.com
BISAC: FIC031010 FICTION / Thrillers / Crime/ FIC030000
FICTION / Thrillers / Suspense
Names: Hogan, Tom, author.
Title: *The Empty Confessional*

Editing by Melanie Mulhall, Dragonheart
www.DragonheartWritingandEditing.com
Cover design by Maya Hogan and Bob Schram
Interior design by Bob Schramm
www.BookendsDesign.com

First Edition
Printed in the United States of America

Prologue

Pittsburgh 2000

THE PRIEST WHISTLED TO HIMSELF a big band song from a bygone era. Slight of build and in his late thirties, he wore Dad jeans and a short-sleeved collared shirt with a Roman collar. His face, small-chinned and dominated by a hatchet nose, slid into a smile as he looked around the living room one last time.

The room still held the faintly fresh odor of the paint job one of the parish parents and his crew had completed in one busy day a month back. The IKEA furniture, an aging collection of ash and chrome—assembled by his fellow priests years ago in one beer-fueled and frustrating weekend—was arranged in a loose square, the center of which had been the focal point of that night's gathering. The coffee table had been pushed over to the far corner to free up the center, but his departing brethren had forgotten to put it back. Frowning, he walked over and, bending at the knee, pulled and shimmied the table to its proper position.

Trash bag in hand, he made one last circuit through the living room, gathering the remaining pizza boxes and napkins. He crossed to the front door and set the bag down, leaving it for the housekeeper who would be there in the morning. Nodding at the results of his efforts, he keyed in the security code and stepped out onto the covered porch.

It was as if the night couldn't make up its mind. When he had arrived at the cottage to set things up earlier that evening, it had been humid, the sky almost dripping. By the time the first guests arrived, the damp had turned to rain—not heavy but steady, enough to impel him to run out to the arriving cars with his umbrella. Now, with the evening concluded, the night air was crisp and the stars were out.

As the door clicked behind him, he stood for a moment and breathed in the crisp taste of the evening. Off in the distance he could hear a car with a bad muffler gargling its way down the street. He heard the neighborhood turning in: men picking up their beer cans from the stoop and shuffling inside; mothers gathering up the older kids, calling back inside to the younger ones; the odd whistles calling dogs home. The priest smiled to himself. Things felt right, in their place, as if he'd stepped back in time to a fifties sitcom.

His smile broadened as he thought back to the evening's events. It had been one of their most successful and enjoyable gatherings. The regulars had all played their roles, taking their places and joining in the activities without coaxing. The sole first-timer, a girl of seventeen with Botticelli looks, had stayed on the sideline at first, viewing the action with curiosity but unsure of where she fit in. But eventually, with the encouragement and coaching of one of the veterans, she joined in, at first cautiously, then enthusiastically. Those moments for the scrapbook made it all worthwhile.

The priest stepped lightly down the steps to the front walkway, which led to the driveway and the parish car, a late-model Cutlass. With the faint porch light not extending beyond the front steps, he had to negotiate his way to the car in the semi-dark. But it was a calming dark, a warm gray that had the feel of a blanket at the end of a good day.

He took a shortcut across the lawn toward his car. His shoe moved from concrete to the soft reassurance of grass. As he felt it shift from grass to the gravel driveway, he stopped to let his eyes get accustomed to the dark, made heavier by an overgrown wall of shadow, high hedges, and ivy lining the far side of the driveway.

He took out his phone, flipped it open, dialed a number, and held the phone to his ear, his free hand reaching for the car keys. "Kevin? Jeff. Yeah, sorry about the last-minute notice. You know how it goes. With everyone so busy, you grab the moments when you can." He listened and nodded, moving around the back of the car and stopping at the driver's door. "We had the same thought about a schedule. From here on, it'll be the first Friday of every month." He listened some more. "Uh-huh. The regular crowd plus a newbie. Remember that girl who had the lead in Grease last fall? Yeah, that one. She was hesitant at first, but you know how Jerry is with rookies." He listened and chuckled. "Yeah, the 'teen whisperer.' Okay. See you next Friday then." He pocketed the phone.

He was still smiling to himself when a black-clad figure moving with stealth and purpose stepped silently from a hollow in the bushes lining the driveway that hadn't been there earlier. His left hand gripped the priest by the shoulder and spun him around. In a blur of flesh, bone, and motion, he drove three fingers into the space right above the Roman collar. The priest's throat spasmed once, a rhythmic flow of muscle and flesh, then collapsed, closing off speech and breath. The throat muscles spasmed once more before beginning to regain their shape, but the ability to speak was gone and breathing was only partially restored.

The priest's knees buckled, but before he could collapse, his assailant caught and dragged him into the hollow. It was dark and dense, with the feel of a cave. The two figures disappeared into it at the same time. Crossing his ankles, the figure in black slowly lowered himself and his cargo into a sitting position, a graceful motion that resembled an origami exercise. The assailant cradled the stricken priest in the crook of his arm and patted his cheek gently with that hand while the other rested lightly on the priest's throat, a gentle but powerful reminder of who was in charge.

The figure in black lowered his head until his mouth was right next to the priest's ear and said in a calming voice, "I know you can't speak, Father, so I'll say your confession for you. I'll try not to get anything wrong." His voice deepened slightly. "Bless me, Father, for I have sinned. My sins are: I have violated the trust and the bodies of children, damaging them for life. Including earlier tonight."

Disconcerted by the sudden violence followed by the gentle voice in his ear, the priest tried to gather himself and assess his situation. Realizing how close he was to both the street and the church, he let his shoulders slump, as if in defeat. At the same time, he gathered his muscles to scream and thrash. Anticipating the move, his attacker stifled the shout in his throat with a strong pinch of the thumb and middle finger to the priest's larynx. His other hand reached over and pinched the nerves next to the collarbone, sapping the strength the priest was marshalling in his knees to attempt to flee.

"And did you conclude the festivities by warning the kids that they and their families would go straight to hell if they told anyone about this evening, just like the other times?"

The priest's shout slid out as a silent rush of air, the last breath of a wounded animal. The futility of that sound, as much as the total control his assailant asserted with his fingers, caused him to surrender. His body went slack, the muscles softening.

His assailant nodded at the capitulation. "Wise move, Father. Now, as for your penance, I think we'd both agree that ten Hail Marys won't cut it. Not for the damage you've done, not just tonight, but in all those evenings in the past. Damage that will last for the rest of these kids' lives, through their adult lives and to the grave. Help me out here and put yourself in my place. What would you suggest for a crime of this magnitude?" He relaxed his control over the priest's vocal cords, but no response came.

"Didn't think so." He cradled the priest, one hand resting on his forehead, a move both comforting and restrictive. With the priest completely quiet, the man whispered into his ear, "You know how at the end of the Act of Contrition, that part where you promise to sin no more? I'm going to help you keep that promise by making it impossible for you to sin in this particular way ever again."

The priest's eyes widened, but all he could make out was a masked face that blended into the leafy darkness. His eyes closed as he felt the taut forearms tighten like a vise on his neck and then squeeze. As he felt himself collapse, the darkness closed over him.

Easing his way out from under the slack body, the black-clad figure knelt over the priest for a moment, taking a final assessment. Kneeling atop the unconscious man, he spread the priest's knees with his own until the upper legs were splayed and the groin was exposed. He flexed his hands once, then he tucked his thumbs and little fingers under, turning the remaining calloused fingers into hardened instruments. Calmly and methodically, he reared back and then pistoned his arms, driving his fingers into the priest's groin in three quick strikes.

He stood up for a moment and turned to leave but stopped, turned back, and repeated the attack. The only sounds disrupting the quiet night were the dull sound of the strikes finding their home and the whisper of the unconscious priest twitching reflexively at the pain.

One

Three Months Earlier

"A PRIEST CHECKS INTO A HOTEL and says to the clerk, 'I hope your pornography channel is disabled.' The clerk looks at him with disgust and says, 'No, it's regular pornography, you sick fuck.'"

There was a momentary silence as the group processed the joke. Then the woman broke the silence with a loud, horsey laugh. Belatedly, the men joined her. The woman punched the joke-teller lightly on the arm. "That's your best one yet, Gabe. Your seminarians are really turning into yuckmeisters, aren't they?"

Gabe nodded. "They keep trying to shock me each class with a new joke, like teenagers learning to swear in front of their parents. But you're right. This is their best so far." He held up a cautionary finger. "But remember: The semester is young."

"I don't know which I look forward to more at these dinners, your students' jokes or Mike's updates from the archbishop's office." She turned to the man on her left. "Speaking of which, any new gems?"

Michael puffed himself up as the group turned to him. "You guys know St. Martin's is closing due to low attendance? The diocese isn't sure what to do with the holy water. Move it to another church? Flush it? I said, 'Since it's a sacred object, shouldn't we burn it?' Neither the archbishop nor his apostles found it—or me—funny."

Everyone smiled. None of the other three priests—or Jenny, the only nun at the table—envied Michael his job.

The group was seated at a booth in a local Pittsburgh tavern. The tabletop was heavily varnished, its surface scarred from untended cigarettes that had burnt themselves out. The dinner dishes had been cleared. Only the heavy glass pitcher with two inches of beer left in it and the mugs remained. The waitress caught Gabe's eye and nodded at the near-empty pitcher, raising her eyebrows in question. He shook his head and motioned for the check. A moment later she was back, dropping the check in front of him, motioning that there was no rush.

It was a typical neighborhood tavern: Bud and Penn Pilsner on tap and an array of bottles and cans, dominated by Iron City, in the sweating mini-fridge. Nothing trendy or imported. The food was as basic and unimaginative as the beer selection. But the TVs had sharp pictures and good sound. And the location was central to everyone at the table. Walls were festooned with posters and uniforms from the Pirates, Steelers, and Penguins. A signed Mario Lemieux game jersey held a special place of reverence behind the bar. Whenever one of the bartenders received a notable tip, he would ring a bell and touch the jersey in gratitude.

An informal support group for new clergy had been meeting monthly for the past year in the restaurant. Jim Cavanaugh, the oldest of the priests, had started the group. Jim had been at his parish for the past eight years, and he said it was the group he wished had existed when he graduated from the seminary and stepped, unprepared, into parish life with all its obligations and responsibilities. Jenny had chanced upon the group one night, and after contributing her own insights into the challenges of religious life, she'd been invited to join them.

Another reason the tavern was popular was the diversity of its menu. Jim, a lifelong burgher, and Gabe, who had moved there with his family from California during middle school, had eaten their fill of pierogis, stuffed cabbage, and jumbo to last a lifetime. The others were Pittsburgh transplants and were still delighting in the tavern's ethnic cuisine. The only thing the entire group agreed on was dessert: Klondike bars, which had been born and raised in Pittsburgh.

The most experienced of the group, Jim, was also the quietest. Soft-spoken to begin with, he usually waited for the three new priests to raise issues and ask questions instead of initiating conversations. Over the course of his ministry and primarily by trial and error, he had created a tight parish with great outreach programs to the community. His physical appearance made the parish women want to fix him, while the men appreciated his focus on comfort. His body seemed to be in a perpetual slump, the few extant muscles suffering from inactivity, and he sported an indecisive combover. His grooming and dress were so haphazard that one of the group—no one remembered who—called him "Pigpen" one night. The name stuck.

"Which Pigpen?" Jenny had asked on her first night with the group. "The Peanuts character or the keyboardist for the Grateful Dead?"

"What's the difference?" Danny had asked.

"Well, the Grateful Dead version died of alcoholism."

"Then let's go with the Peanuts version."

Gabe picked up the check and glanced at it, doing the math in his head. At twenty-six, he was the youngest in the group. According to an article about him in the *Catholic Gazette*, he was the youngest priest with his own parish in the eastern United States and perhaps the entire country. His youth was accentuated by his unblemished, unlined skin, which Jenny said most women would kill for. He had the kind of gentle good looks that men didn't find threatening and women found attractive: a slight hook to the nose, full lips, and warm eyes. His eyes were soft, almost to the point of being moist, leading the parish women to treat him as either a son or a forbidden crush. That night he was wearing a long-sleeved T-shirt, faded jeans, and running shoes.

He wore his hair loose and longish. That and his casual dress had driven his predecessor, Monsignor Keane, to distraction. Gabe took his grooming cues from the monsignor. If the old man looked up at Gabe once when he came down to join the monsignor at the breakfast table, Gabe knew his clothing was the issue. If the monsignor looked up a second time, Gabe knew it was time for the barber.

He took out his wallet and put a twenty down, then he passed the check to Danny. Although only two years older than Gabe, Danny looked like he had at least ten years on him, the results of a determined campaign on his part to look older than he was. He combed his hair back, accentuating his widow's peak, and he had thin lips and soft cheekbones, both partially hidden by the sparse beard he had cultivated since his final year in the seminary. In a final attempt at maturity and sagacity, he had started smoking a pipe, though there was no way he was going to bring it out in front of his counterparts.

In contrast to Gabe, who usually complemented his Roman collar with a hooded sweatshirt, Danny often wore what Jenny called Vatican light: unstylish black slacks topped by an equally bland black shirt. Only the white in the Roman collar broke up the monochromatic look. "Leave it to the Vatican to be the only ones who can make black on black uncool," Jenny had said. Off-duty, Danny wore clothes that Jim said were Ward Cleaver hand-me-downs, a reference Danny had to look up.

Matching Gabe's twenty, Danny passed the bill to Jenny. In her early thirties, Jenny was a beauty in everyone's eyes but her own. Gabe called her a walking milk commercial while Jim said she was right out of a Norman Rockwell painting. But her appeal came from neither her hair nor her sense of style. At work, she wore her dishwater blonde hair short and pushed back by the stiff white head garb her order required, and off-duty, it was held in check by a variety of colorful kerchiefs she wore either as a headband or in what she called her do-rag look. Her clothes were equally casual and careless: slacks and a blouse when teaching, jeans and a polo shirt otherwise.

It was her eyes and smile that everyone remembered, not her outfits or hair. She seemed to find everyone fascinating, taking them in with her chocolate-brown eyes and holding them for the bulk of the conversation. Her warm smile came easily and frequently, especially for her kids. She was the clear favorite of both students and parents at the parochial elementary school where she taught second grade.

"Speaking of the archbishop, what's going on over at St. Ambrose with Ferguson?" Jim asked.

All eyes shifted to Michael, the resident expert from the archbishop's office. Like the other priests in the group, he had joined the priesthood intent on a parish assignment. But his administrative skills coupled with his knowledge of computers—a new, mostly unused resource for the archbishop and his staff—meant he had been marked early in his seminary years for the archbishop's office. Having come to the restaurant straight from work, Michael was the only one wearing the "full Vatican," the black suit and Roman collar that was his daily uniform. With sandy hair and a slight population of freckles on his cheeks, he looked younger than his thirty years. Jenny told him she couldn't decide if he looked more like Huck Finn or Archie from the comics page.

"Ferguson's screwed," Michael said. "We found kiddie porn on his computer and we've got testimony from his victims. The idiot even kept a diary."

"What do you think will happen to him?" Gabe asked, handing the bill and pile of cash to Sheila, their regular waitress, who nodded her thanks to the group, knowing they always left a nice tip.

"Oh, a year of spiritual reflection," he said using air quotes. "Then they'll put him back in circulation somewhere out West."

"God, we're an embarrassment," Jim said. "Imagine if Ferguson were an Episcopalian. Or a Jew. They'd fire his ass and call in the cops. But not us. We protect and recycle them."

"That's not fair, Jim," Danny replied. "Sometimes we promote them as well."

"Well, I hope they string the bastard up by his tiny balls," Jim said.

The group turned to Jenny to see if she was offended. "Jim's more lenient than me," she added. "I teach the kind of kids that bastards like Ferguson target. If it were me, I'd castrate the asshole and cauterize the wound with vinegar."

"Well, aren't we the cheery group tonight," Gabe said. He looked at Jim. "I don't know about you, but I'm starting to get questions about Ferguson. Only a couple so far, but they had an edge to them. How about in your parish?"

"Same," Jim replied. "A few. But they didn't give the impression they're going away, and I'm not inclined to ask them to stop."

Gabe turned to Michael. "What's your take? How deep does this thing go?"

"No idea. But I'm going to start digging, and not just in this diocese. According to the archbishop, my job is to keep track of activities in every US diocese, meaning I can go anywhere the headlines—or rumors—take me. So I can easily justify digging into the Ferguson thing. And anything else of that nature."

"Can you do that without drawing attention to yourself?" Jenny asked.

"As long as it stays within the office, it's not a problem. The other priests there are older and practically paralyzed by what they call 'these new-fangled machines.' They barely know how to turn a computer on, much less delve into admin files." He frowned slightly. "Trouble is, we're just starting to computerize, so I'm bouncing back and forth between what's been entered in the computer and what's still on paper. I don't know if I'm going to have the time to do both. And that worries me, because I don't think that everything on paper is going to make it over into the new files."

"Deliberately or by accident?"

"Both. But deliberately, mostly."

"And you think that comes directly from the archbishop?"

"It might, but it doesn't have to. The priests I work with don't need a directive from Himself to know they should eliminate any potential embarrassments or legal exposures. Tracking down their changes file will take me hours. And that's for each file they alter."

"That reminds me," Gabe said. "You guys mind if I invite someone to this group? You know Paul Reynolds?" He looked at a table of blank faces. "You wouldn't. He's been in Rome the past ten years. But he was my—well, actually, the monsignor's—predecessor here. This was his parish. Now he's a big shot Church historian on loan to the seminary this year. I bet he could help with Mike's files, given his history in the archdiocese and his archive work."

"If he's who I think he is," Jenny said, "I've seen him around. Gorgeous guy. Looks like Richard Chamberlain in *The Thorn Birds*?"

Gabe nodded. "That's him."

"Then he's in, unless anyone here has any objections," Jenny replied.

"Anyone who's good with paper is welcome," Michael said.

"Then I'll invite him." Gabe picked the Steeler jacket off the back of Jenny's chair and held it out for her to slide her arms into. "C'mon, toots. I'll walk you home."

Two

GABE'S EYES FLUTTERED, uncertain whether they wanted to wake up or not. Sleep had come late the prior night and then the dream had come, the same dream yet again, leading to a fitful night. The alarm clock hadn't sounded yet, so he figured it was the dream that pushed him into this half state. He sighed and opened his eyes, at first cautiously, then fully. His tongue snaked around his lips, which had dried overnight, leaving them slightly cracked.

As his eyes blinked him fully awake, his face tightened. His eyes pinched at the corners and his mouth pulled in on itself. He slid his arm under the blanket and pushed his hand under his pajama waistband. As he felt between his legs, his eyes hardened and his mouth pinched even tighter. He pulled his hand out of his pants and brought it up before his face, spreading his fingers as he did so. The tacky liquid, strung between the fingers in a sloppy web, collapsed as he spread his fingers further apart.

Propping himself on an elbow, he took in his surroundings, as if getting his bearings for the looming day. Even though the rectory had been his home for the past nine months, his bedroom was still in the process of definition. When he moved in, the room was somewhere between monastic and spartan. The

empty walls were a stark, harsh white. The bed was the definition of simplicity: a single thin mattress with a military-brown
blanket and two thin pillows with white cases. While he made
the bed each morning before going down to breakfast, Dolores
would always remake it, tightening the corners into bounce-a-
dime tautness. Denise, the housekeeper on Dolores's days off,
left his bed alone but placed fresh flowers in a vase on his desk,
concentrating her efforts on the bathroom and delivering a fresh
smell that Dolores couldn't match.

Next to the bed was a small table with a standing lamp
behind it. Both looked like they'd been there for years. The table
usually held three books, evidence of Gabe's reading pattern.
He tried to keep three going at any one time: a serious novel, a
murder or spy mystery, and a work of nonfiction. He also kept a
list of books that he updated on occasion, books he knew he
ought to read but never would. *Madame Bovary* led the list, followed by *Canterbury Tales* and anything by Pynchon or Barth.
After three failed attempts, *Moby Dick* was a candidate for the
list, though Gabe was determined to give it one last try. Same
with *Don Quixote*.

On the other side of the table, sharing the lamp, were a
matching upholstered wingback chair and ottoman, each maintaining a kind of faded elegance. In their prime they must have
been an impressive showcase of their creator's embroidery skills,
each piece exhibiting a beautiful but worn flower arrangement,
with the patterns now barely visible.

Tucked into the corner on the other side of the room were
a basic wooden desk and a straight-back chair. The desktop was
strewn with Gabe's drafts of this Sunday's sermon, and a
stacked set of books fat with sticky notes—some of them Biblical
commentaries, others works by Merton and Aquinas—were on
the floor next to the chair.

Gabe had seen no need to change out or upgrade any of the furniture that had come with the room. The walls, though, were another matter. They had initially held a series of framed religious testimonies: a poster of the Sacred Heart of Jesus, a photo of Pope John Paul II, and a photo of Padre Pio, the Italian cleric who was famous for his stigmata and was under consideration for canonization. All of these had come down Gabe's first day in the room.

The walls had remained blank for a while as Gabe settled into his new parish and its surroundings. Then, during one of his neighborhood walk-arounds, he had been told by one of the stoop ladies that if he really wanted to get a feel for the neighborhood, he should go to the flea market every Wednesday and Saturday at the Valley View Drive-In. He had gone the first time as a lark, but over time, he had become a habitué.

After a few visits he had decided on two types of collectibles to adorn the bare walls of his bedroom. The first was commemorative plates, and the blank wall's first display was an Ike and Mamie inaugural plate. Next to it was a scalloped dessert plate commemorating Charles and Diana's wedding. They had been joined over time by four other plates, but there was still room on the wall, testimony to Gabe's rigor as a curator.

The facing wall contained four shelves, each one crammed with salt and pepper shakers, the second type of collectibles he'd settled on. Gabe had started the collection, but it had grown rapidly with contributions from his fellow priests and parishioners. Once, Dolores had tried to dust and clean the collection, but her attempts to rejoin the pairs had led to some strange unions, such as the RCA dog next to a pool table. By mutual agreement, Gabe was now responsible for maintaining that corner of his room.

Gabe reached behind him and grabbed a box of tissues with his dry hand. Placing the box on the bed next to him, he extracted a handful of tissues and dabbed at the fluid on his left hand, getting most of it. Then he rubbed both hands together with the disintegrating tissues, the shredded paper clinging to his fingers. Once he'd extracted the shredded paper clinging to his hand, he grabbed more tissue and jabbed impatiently, almost angrily, between his legs.

When he was sure he could stand up without dribbling, he got out of bed and stripped off his pajamas. He would come back after his shower and wipe the pajama bottoms down with a damp cloth, leaving nothing for Dolores to find and gossip about.

From the neck down, Gabe was a complete contradiction to the gentle-faced figure who met his parishioners after every Mass. His limbs had the lean, taut muscularity of a gymnast, while his torso had ab muscles reminiscent of prisoners who did thousands of sit-ups a day. His body fat was that of a boxer who had just made weight.

His face set in tight, unforgiving lines, Gabe walked into the bathroom, his legs spread slightly. Reaching into the shower, he turned both handles until a light steam rose, ghosting its way up to the ceiling, and stepped in, enjoying the shower for a moment. Then he planted both feet and put his left arm out straight, bracing himself against the wall with his palm. Taking a deep breath, he leaned forward and twisted the "cold" faucet hard to the left. His knees buckled slightly as the scalding water hit him with a steady flow of liquid pain, but he steadied himself and stood there, fists clenched, as he counted silently to five. Then he turned the cold water back on and picked up the soap.

With a visiting priest saying Mass that morning, Gabe was free to walk around the neighborhood for an hour or so. He dressed for the job in a polo shirt, jeans, light windbreaker, and running shoes without socks. He would come back and change before he went to the church, conducted office hours, and heard confessions.

Gabe didn't restrict his walks to his own parish. Once a week he would ride his bike over to one of Pittsburgh's ninety neighborhoods to get a feel for them. In many ways it was like visiting a foreign country, given the insular and ethnic feel most neighborhoods had, intentionally or not.

He walked briskly down the rectory stairs and into the kitchen. In contrast to the rest of the two-story house, whose design and furnishings dated back to its construction in the thirties, the kitchen was all stainless steel and modern lines—a facelift on a body that had long gone to seed. The industrial eight-burner stove and double oven, a gift from a dedicated parishioner who was a contractor, were clearly overkill, given that the rectory had housed no more than three occupants for the past forty years and that the priests who did live there, including Gabe, never entertained there. But knowing that the contractor had connections to the Mafia, no one had objected to his largesse.

Monsignor Keane, a notoriously early riser even in retirement, was finishing up breakfast as Gabe entered the kitchen. The elderly priest was a small man with impeccable grooming and a still-erect posture. His face was equally correct, with everything in proportion. What remained of his white hair had formed an unintentional tonsure. Nodding at Gabe's dress, the monsignor said, "Got another softball game today, Father?" Gabe smiled and refused the bait, simply taking his seat and nodding to Stella, one of Dolores' altar society counterparts. A cup of steaming black coffee was in front of him before he could shift his chair under the table.

"The regular, Father?" Stella asked.

"Please." He turned back to Monsignor Keane. "And how are you going to spend this beautiful day, Monsignor?"

"Morning in the garden, tending to my flowers. Then one of Stella's delicious lunches. Afternoon I'm hearing confessions two to five." He grimaced and smiled at the same time. "It's one of the few parts of the job they still allow me to do."

It was true. Gabe had been assigned to the parish as an assistant pastor upon graduation from the seminary nine months earlier. As with most first assignments, the plan was for him to serve the equivalent of an apprenticeship under the monsignor for a year or two, then take over. But the monsignor had begun to show signs of forgetfulness, coupled with erratic behavior. Then he slipped coming down the stairs one morning. And though he fell only four steps, the physical and psychological jolt seemed to shake him at multiple levels. He began to shuffle and look down at his feet rather than at his parishioners. Finally, after one truly bizarre Sunday sermon—in front of the packed 10:30 Mass no less—in which he had railed about how the Virgin Mary would be appalled at how women acted in the twenty-first century, it was clear that early retirement was called for.

And suddenly the "assistant" was gone from Gabe's title.

CONFESSION

Gabe knelt down, made the sign of the cross, and started right in, forgoing how long it had been since his last confession. "I can't tell if these dreams are a test from God about my readiness to be a priest or if it's just my subconscious fucking with me." He smiled into the gray latticed screen. "I like swearing in the confessional. It's like the first time you swear in front of your parents, trying to be a grownup."

His voice and face got serious. "I'll tell you this, though. If it's God, I want to say to him, 'Hey, if you're so all-powerful, either shut these dreams down, starting tonight, or at least change things up a bit. Toss in a Michelle Pfeiffer or Halle Berry for a change.' But no, it's the same sex-heavy dream every night. The same faceless woman. And the same onanistic result. This keeps up, I'm going to have to start buying my Kleenex at Costco."

He smiled at the reminder. "I know, I know. I never use the masculine pronouns for God with my parishioners. But I can't see a female divinity torturing me like this, turning my mind into a porno theater every night.

"One last thing. Don't pretend you don't know who I am. Hell, I've been at this game for less than nine months, but I can recognize most of my parishioners within the first fifteen seconds after they enter the box. Not by their voice but by their sins."

Three

PROMOTING GABE TO A FULL PASTOR position in the parish hadn't been an automatic or unanimous decision. The review board had been impressed by his qualifications and recommendations, but because he was so young, they thought his learning curve would be an apprenticeship of two to three years when they brought him into the parish as assistant pastor. So had Gabe. And they had placed him with Jerry Keane because they thought the monsignor's strict ways would tamp down what some of the board regarded as Gabe's overly secular pursuits. So when the monsignor's physical and mental conditions declined so quickly, the board was faced with the decision on whether to bring in another experienced priest for the next two years as Gabe grew into the job or promote "the kid," as many parishioners were advocating.

Before his assignment to the parish, Gabe had sailed through the first placement interview. The board had been impressed by his accomplishments, his clear sense of calling and purpose, and the recommendations of the majority of his teachers.

He had entered the seminary already versed in the New Testament and proficient in Greek and Latin, both languages self-taught. Though his academic emphasis was on the New Testament, he had begun studying Hebrew with Shmuel, an acquaintance from the interfaith group he'd belonged to since high school. While the majority of his fellow seminarians concentrated on Catholic theology and policies, Gabe had concentrated on Biblical history and archaeology. He'd even participated in a dig in Jerusalem near the Temple Mount the summer of his third year.

By his fourth year of seminary, he'd taken all the seminary's New Testament and language courses, so the administration had arranged for him to study for a year at Drew University, a Methodist seminary in nearby New Jersey, taking advantage of their advanced New Testament and Biblical languages curricula. Upon his graduation, the seminary had petitioned the archdiocese for a local placement, with an additional request that he be allowed to teach one class per semester in New Testament history and archaeology.

The parish placement was no problem for the board. After all, as one of the interviewers noted, "This guy's the most natural P we've interviewed."

"He's also the only five-star we've ever had who wanted to be a P instead of an A," another chimed in, then added with a chuckle, "though I don't know whether to admire him for it or ask him to check his answer again." The others had nodded at the joke as well as the truth behind it.

At the start of every academic year, the board met to determine the fate of the seminarians in that year's graduating class. They concluded each interview by assigning a "P" or an "A" to the seminarian in question, the former initial standing for a parish assignment and the latter for an administrative assignment. That designation would determine the student's academic calendar for his final year.

Though it was loathe to admit it, the Church had seen a steady decline of P designees over the past decade. The majority of seminarians seemed either uninterested in or unprepared for a parish assignment. And even though it broadened the definition of what could garner a P, the numbers continued to wane. At the end of this year's review, one of the senior members had looked at his peers and said, "Twenty years ago, at least half of our applicants would have been Ps. Now we're broadening our standards for American seminarians and still needing to bring in Filipinos to make up the difference."

The reason for this growing shift toward the administrative seminarians in their ranks was simple: the sixties. Institutionally, from the Peace Corps to multiple programs with assignments in the US, men who would have otherwise been drawn to the priesthood as a vehicle for service now found that they could achieve their social and political ambitions without having to enter the priesthood, with all its requirements and restrictions.

Socially and religiously, the sixties had been a twin-edged sword for the Church and its recruits. On the one hand, Pope John XXIII and Vatican II, with their progressive approach to Catholicism and its role in the world, had brought new Catholics into the fold. But the sixties, with its open approach to everything from sexuality to drugs, had also enlarged the number of seminarians who had targeted the priesthood as a means to hide from—or at least not participate in—the very society they were supposed to serve.

But these new candidates were almost exclusively and unapologetically administratively oriented seminarians, and most of them threatened to leave the priesthood if they were given a pastoral assignment. They wanted the structure and distance that a job in the Church hierarchy brought with it. Theologically and culturally, they were conservatives, yearning for the days before

Vatican II, for Latin masses, meatless Fridays, and celebrating the Mass with their backs turned to the congregation. They said they were only returning the Church to its roots when their pastoral counterparts, who were generally more progressive, accused them of taking the Church backward.

Gabe's original placement interview had taken place almost a year earlier. "This is the statement that stayed with me in one of the recommendation letters," Father Lathrop had said, sliding his reading glasses down from his forehead. "'If there's such a thing as a savant when it comes to the priesthood, he's it. I only hope the secular world doesn't get its hooks too deep into him.'" He closed the file and motioned for the priest nearest the door to let Gabe in. "So let's meet this wunderkind."

Months later, the same group considered Gabe from a different perspective while he sat in the lobby. It was no longer a matter of potential but of accomplishment and whether his performance in the parish thus far justified taking the unprecedented step of making him the pastor of a large working-class parish.

"He says a good Mass," Father Powers had said in an unexpectedly kind voice, given his serious countenance. The white-haired priest with a tan that came from his affection for tennis was one of the most powerful voices at the table. "His sermons, from what I gather, are excellent—thought-provoking without being controversial. It feels like he's been in the job longer than he has."

"The parishioners rave about him," said Father Anders, a stooped figure with Einstein-like hair. "About how much a part of the neighborhood he's become with his daily walks and frequent visits to local businesses, including restaurants and bars. And those with parents in the nursing homes appreciate the time he spends evenings there saying Mass, hearing confessions, or just visiting."

"Don't forget the impact he's having with the youth of his parish," Father Powers added. "His age has been nothing but a positive in that manner."

"So why haven't we already awarded the parish to him, if he walks on water?" Father Carlsen asked. His genial countenance made him the visual opposite of Father Powers, but in stark contrast to his appearance, his voice was harsh. The others eyed him carefully, since he was the priest closest to the archbishop in the group. When no one spoke up, he continued. "I'll tell you why. Because he's the most secular candidate any of us has ever placed. More secular than I'm comfortable with."

"So he's lived more fully in the secular world than most of our candidates," Father Powers said. "In my mind, that only enhances his standing. Let's face it, gentlemen. Most of the men who come before us are, to put it kindly, 'socially limited.' They come to us in part because they are uncomfortable with how they fit into the world, and they see the priesthood as a way to both live a life of service to God and insulate themselves from the pressures of daily life." He nodded at the file. "This guy seems to be comfortable in his own skin and in the world at large. I find that refreshing."

Father Jordan spoke up for the first time. "It's that 'world at large' I think some of us are concerned about." He was a large man, but his cassock fit his build perfectly and he was impeccably groomed. He seemed to be the only priest at the table who exuded the same confident presence as Father Powers. He opened his file. "I remember writing this at the end of our interview with Father Russell: 'In five years, will he be more comfortable inside the Church or outside it?'"

"And that concern was based on what, exactly?" Father Powers asked.

"Two things, as I recall. The first was his politics. We spent most of our time debating liberation theology with him, and as a result, we didn't delve as deeply into his secular pursuits as we should have."

"And by 'secular pursuits' you mean?"

"I did a little research before today's meetings. And it seems Father Russell has stayed in touch with his secular friends—has even had them over to the rectory on occasion. And a source tells me they smoke marijuana on the back porch. Whether Father Russell partakes or not, I don't know."

The group smiled as one when Father Jordan mentioned his source. Father Clemens spoke up. "By 'source' you mean Dolores, don't you? She's been funneling gossip to this group for the past twenty years. And to our discredit, we've lapped it up."

Father Jordan continued. "Dolores also tells me that Father Russell has the nuns over for dinner once a month and individual sisters more frequently than that. And that he seems to be particularly close to one of the nuns, a Jenny Bachino." He looked around the table. "Nothing suspicious there, I know. But you add this into our concerns about his politics and . . ."

"I know that not everyone at this table shares Father Russell's politics," Father Powers said, "but I thought those of us who disagreed with them agreed that there was certainly room for a Vatican II priest like him."

Father Carroll finally entered the conversation. "Yes, but let's be clear. He's on the far left of the political spectrum. Back in the day, we would have called him a Dorothy Day Catholic."

"Meaning?"

"Meaning his advocacy for the poor and his belief that the Church should insert itself into politics, in line with the core teachings of Jesus. This liberation theology bent is best kept down in Latin America. It certainly has no place in the US in the year 2000." He held up a hand as Father Powers started to speak. "Don't get me wrong, Jerry. There's room in the Church for priests like that, but keep them in our academic ranks, not in front of a church full of impressionable parishioners."

"I haven't heard anything about him proselytizing LT—or anything close to it—from the pulpit," Father Powers said. "Yes, he speaks to his parishioners about their obligations to the poor more than most priests, but that's his right. It certainly wouldn't justify our bringing in someone over him."

Father Powers surveyed the room before continuing. With the exception of Fathers Jordan and Carroll, the group seemed either in favor of awarding Gabe the promotion or at least leaning in that direction. "I want to be fair here. I may not share Alan's concerns about Father Russell's secular pursuits," he finally said, nodding toward Father Jordan, "but I think it's a fair topic when we bring him in. But just for my own curiosity, what's wrong with a priest being secular? In my day, that would have meant he could play stickball in the street with the kids and take them to the malt shop after Sunday school. And he could hold his own in sports talk in the bars with his male parishioners."

"And if it were still in the old days, you'd be right," Father Carroll said. "But today's secular offerings are more problematic. The temptations are larger and more attractive. What's that term the kids have? Sex, drugs, and . . ." He looked around the table for help.

"Rock and roll." A priest who had been silent to that point completed the phrase, seemingly pleased with his ability to contribute.

"Well, then, let's see what he has to say about his experiences with those components of today's culture."

"And whether his experiences are those of a witness or a participant," Father Jordan added.

The board tried to make the hearing look as informal as possible, with soft drinks, bottled water, and a tin of cookies in the middle of the table. But it had been clear they had an agenda and that Gabe's status was riding on his answers.

After some opening reassuring comments from Father Powers, the group had gotten down to business, with Father Jordan leading the way. "Father, you come from a different generation, one that, in my opinion, has moved more sharply away from many of the Church's core practices and philosophies than any generation I can think of. I'm speaking of sexual practices, of a tolerance for abortion, of challenging authority at every turn. Would you agree with that assessment?"

Gabe hadn't hurried his response, giving the opening question the consideration it merited. He also knew what was riding on his answers over the next two hours. "I can see how that would look from your perspective, Father. I think the source of this issue is that societies recognize and adapt to environments faster than institutions. The forties were a time of war, with institutions just holding the fort, so to speak, until peace arrived. The fifties were a time of recovery and prosperity, and an institution such as the Church was a reassuring part of that equation. And just when we're getting all comfortable and proud of ourselves, along came the sixties, with all its changes—from drugs to sex to music—and, as you put it, challenges to authority. Some institutions recognized that some of these changes were permanent— sexual liberation, for example—and adapted. The Church, in my opinion, did not. Which is why our numbers are dropping and our churches are closing."

Father Carroll leaned in. "The phrase I remember from that time was sex, drugs, and rock and roll. A very different trinity from the one that we worship, wouldn't you say?" When Gabe didn't respond, Carroll continued. "I'm curious about your experiences in those areas and how they affect your ministry. Are you familiar with the trinity of which I speak?"

"Definitely, Father."

"And may I ask, is this familiarity that of a participant or an observer?"

"A participant, definitely. I would have felt like a voyeur otherwise. A cheat. No, I was a willing participant. Though I'm not particularly proud of my level of participation."

"Can you expound on that, Gabe?" Father Powers asked.

"Sure. When I look back at my years before the seminary, as well as some of my activities during my seminary years, I feel a bit, I don't know, maybe not ashamed but certainly not proud. Not of what I did but what I didn't do." He looked around the table and saw a raft of puzzled faces, including that of Father Powers. "Growing up, everyone I hung out with plunged into the water headfirst. In everything. I, on the other hand, tiptoed in. As a result, I didn't have the same depth of experience—or learn the same lessons—as them. And I regret that, not just for my own experience but my ability to later understand and empathize with future parishioners."

"If you could give some examples, Gabe," Father Powers said, "that would help."

"Okay." He turned to Father Carroll. "I imagine that of your trinity, you're not that interested in my rock and roll tastes and experiences, so I'll just comment on the other two." He closed his eyes for a moment, steepling his hands in front of his mouth. The silence lasted past the point of comfort for some of the priests, but it was clear Gabe wasn't going to be rushed.

Finally, he lowered his hands and opened his eyes. "Before I answer your question, how specific—or explicit—do you want me to be? I don't want to offend anyone."

Father Powers smiled. "I appreciate your concern, Gabe, but be as explicit as you need to be to answer the questions. After all our years of hearing confessions, I'm sure we won't blush."

Gabe nodded. "Okay. Sexually speaking, in my group, I was always the laggard, whatever base you're talking about." Again, he saw the confusion on their faces. "You didn't have that phrase growing up? It's shorthand among teenage boys: What base did you get to? First base was kissing the girl; second base was touching her breast." He stopped and smiled slightly. "There was some confusion about whether touching the bra counted or if it had to be the bare breast. Third base was fingering the girl's vagina." Despite Father Powers' promise, he saw some of the men blush. "And a home run was sexual intercourse."

"And what's the highest base you ever got to?" Father Jordan interjected.

"Third. I had the opportunity to hit a home run on a few occasions, but I backed away each time. That's part of the regret I mentioned earlier."

"But you considered and rejected premarital sexual intercourse—a mortal sin," Father Jordan said. "That speaks well of you."

"If it spoke to my judgment and my honoring of Church law, Father, I would agree with you. But it spoke to my cowardice." This time he saw more interest than confusion, so he continued. "I was the Bill Clinton of my crowd, pretending that oral sex wasn't actual sex. As a good Catholic, I knew that premarital intercourse was a mortal sin, so I was determined to avoid it at all costs, even though I wound up looking like a hypocrite. Here I was, going to Mass every morning, serving as an altar boy whenever the regulars didn't show up. Then I'd spend the rest of the day running with a fairly fast crowd. And it was always a balancing act. How far could I go with sex and still be a Catholic—or more precisely, a priest?"

Gabe turned to Father Carroll. "To be specific, Father, I engaged in my share of kissing and groping in the back seats of cars or in my friends' houses when their parents weren't home. I gave and received oral sex, and I don't regret a single hand job or blow job I received."

To their credit, none of the priests—even his two main inquisitors—scowled or blanched at Gabe's directness. They had asked the questions and were determined to let him answer in whatever way he preferred.

"It was the ridiculous parsing I did that shames me to this day. How I'd try to convince myself—and God, if he was paying attention—that putting my tongue or finger in a girl's vagina was a venial sin but swapping that finger for my penis would turn that sin from venial to mortal. It's that kind of lopsided emotion that kept me a virgin to this date, not some profound moral stance. So yes, I'm probably more familiar with sex than my fellow seminarians, but that familiarity has just served to confuse me. Maybe that confusion makes me a better priest, since I have to assume many of my parishioners are confused as well. But that isn't why I did it."

Father Powers rapped the table with his knuckles. "I can speak only for myself, Gabe, but I think this is one of the more unique—and honest—conversations this table has participated in. Before we move on, I'd suggest we take a break." He looked around the table. "Without objection, let's take ten."

Drugs were the same as sex, Gabe explained to them after the break. "I experimented but didn't cross the line into more dangerous turf. Marijuana, almost daily for a while, until it lost its charm. And I found myself gaining weight from the munchies." He smiled and looked around the table at another sea of blank faces. "Amphetamines on occasion, but generally more for studying than recreation. Cocaine rarely. Too expensive, and all we did was sit around and talk over each other. But when my crowd graduated to drugs like ecstasy, LSD, and psilocybin, I stayed on the shore, saying that someone had to be the designated driver and the calming influence in extreme cases. But the real answer was that I was afraid of embarking on any journey I wasn't sure I could come back from. Especially with LSD."

A priest who had been silent up to that point spoke up. "I'm a bit confused here. You seem to be chiding yourself for a decision that seems both rational and correct to me."

"I'm just trying to answer your questions, Father, and give you a sense of my mindset at the time. Looking back, I have some regrets about my caution because most of my friends have a broader life perspective than I do as a result of their own experimentation. They learned things about themselves and the drugs that I wish I knew, both for myself and my parishioners."

The other priests looked at the priest who had raised the issue to see if he was satisfied. He nodded, more to himself than to them.

Father Jordan redirected the conversation. "What, specifically, drew you to the Catholic Church, Father? Given some of your essays and conversations with your spiritual advisor, specifically about women priests and papal infallibility, I would have thought you'd be more comfortable in the Episcopal tradition."

"I get that question a lot," Gabe said. "I especially got it from fellow seminarians during the year I spent in the Protestant seminary. And I had answers, but they were convoluted and filled with caveats. But I wasn't able to answer that question in a way that satisfied me until I took a marketing class during my year at Drew."

"You'll have to explain that one, Gabe," Father Powers said.

Gabe nodded. "The three core principles of marketing are audience, reach, and frequency. I analyzed Catholicism from that perspective. Audience: over one billion. Reach: a church in virtually every town throughout the world. And frequency: once a week—once a day in some places."

Gabe held up a hand. "I'm aware of the flaws in my reasoning. Islam has us beat by a mile in audience size. And they have us in frequency because they pray five times a day. And the Mormons might have us on reach. Those guys are everywhere. But I don't speak Arabic and I don't believe that Jesus visited Danbury, Connecticut, after his resurrection. So that left Catholicism."

Father Jordan frowned. "It sounds, Father, like you *settled* for Catholicism rather than embraced it. If that assumption is correct, how can you be a strong and able representative of the Church to your parishioners?"

"Because I believe, not just for myself but for my parishioners, that the Church is the best path to salvation. While I may not believe that my way is the only path to salvation, as most evangelists do, I do believe that when the Church lives up to its stated principles, it has the most potential to improve this world, both globally and at a personal level."

Father Creighton spoke for the first time. "What do you mean by live up to its stated principles, Father?" He was hunched over by bowed shoulders, so he seemed to be looking up at Gabe with eyes that hovered right below his eyebrows. "That sounds a bit arrogant to me."

"I don't mean it to, Father," Gabe replied. "But the Church I joined is the post-Vatican II Church with some very strong, progressive stances. It's the sign of a strong institution that can adapt to fit the times."

"And yet, much of the Church and its teachings get their value from their timeless nature," Father Creighton rejoined.

Gabe nodded. "And yet, if the Church hadn't evolved over the years, I think we would all agree that it would be extinct today. And that need for evolution has never been more urgent. As the good father pointed out, my generation has moved further from the standards and beliefs of previous generations than any in recent history. The children who came of age in the sixties are now adults, but their belief systems from that time have remained intact, for the most part, and they've imparted those values to their children. They're the people I'll be trying to reach as a priest and as a representative of Catholicism. And if the Church doesn't maintain its relevance to this new generation of believers, it runs the risk of falling into irrelevance."

"And if you were charged with this crusade of relevance, how would you proceed," Father Jordan asked, his voice dripping with sarcasm. "And be specific, Father."

Gabe returned to his silent posture with steepled hands. This time the priests waited patiently. "You spoke earlier of the timeless nature of the Church, and I agree with that. For me, the most timeless component of our faith is the example of Jesus. How he embraced the poor, the outcasts. How he questioned the earthly authorities when they contradicted his Father's will. The idea of service to others is not only what draws me to a life within the Church. It is also the example the Church sets for the rest of the world."

"And do you believe the Church is setting that example?" Father Jordan asked, the sarcasm now muted.

"I do, but it feels like the further one gets away from the institution of the Church, the easier it is to practice the teachings of Jesus. The Church, with all its wealth and political power, could rebalance this world dramatically if it focused more on its believers and less on itself. The poor need an advocate, Fathers. And the Church is the most obvious candidate."

"It sounds to me like you're talking about liberation theology," Father Carroll said.

"Call it what you will, Father, but I believe our obligation as a Church is to the least of our society, and to practice, both as individuals and as an institution, the example of Jesus. And Jesus was not an institutionalist. He was all about questioning the status quo."

"Forgive me, Father," Father Jordan said, "but at this moment, you sound more naïve than I believe you to be. The Church has survived for two thousand years by being a political as well as religious institution. In championing the poor as you advocate, we would find ourselves on the wrong side of the governments we need to coexist with."

"That kind of pragmatism can go too far," Gabe replied. "Think of Pius's alliance with the Nazis." He looked around the table. "Listen, Fathers, I can see that I've offended some of you. And for that I apologize. But you asked me why I became a priest and I told you: service to others. And if that philosophy puts me at odds with my own Church, then I need to reassess my calling."

"I don't think anyone is going that far, Gabe," Father Powers said. "But the reality is that you've joined and are the face of the Church, which is by nature conservative, religiously and politically. You may not like it—I sure as hell don't at times—but that's the Church you joined."

"I know that, Father. But the Church has shown its ability to change in recent years, for both good and bad, in my opinion. I'm hoping it will change again with the next pope, and for the better. That's the Church I want to be a part of and to represent."

"You mentioned the Church changing both for the good and bad," Father Powers continued. "I'm assuming the good was Vatican II?" Gabe nodded. "And the bad?"

"I believe John's successors have tried to undo the advances of Vatican II to bring us back to a religiosity that may play well in conservative areas like Eastern Europe but won't play in the US and elsewhere."

"Then are we to believe that you have a low opinion of Paul VI?" Father Jordan asked.

"I do. I believe he was not only conservative but mean-spirited. He set us back just when we were ready to leap forward."

"And John Paul II? He's been an inspiration to the oppressed, a real man of the people."

Gabe smiled. "My mother isn't a Church scholar, but she's a good judge of people. She said that Paul was a mean-faced little ferret and ruled like one. But John Paul, she feels, is more dangerous because he's so warm and loving while, at the same time, pulling the Church back to the Dark Ages."

"And do you agree with your mother's assessment?"

"Maybe not in such harsh terms, but yes."

"And as a priest, would you share your concerns and reservations with your congregation?"

"No. Not from the pulpit. Never. But if a parishioner came to me with those same concerns, I would share my perspective, if for no other reason than to show them that you can be a loyal Catholic while disagreeing with the Church at times."

Gabe looked around the table. The welcoming mood was gone, but apart from Fathers Jordan and Carroll, there seemed to be an openness to the discussion. "Let me pose a question to you gentlemen: How many of you believe that John Paul II will be alive at this time next year?" Not a single hand went up. "Me neither."

"And you pose this question because?" Father Carroll asked.

"Because the next pope will, in my opinion, determine the fate of the Church. If he is reform-minded and contemporary with an open mind regarding women, gays, and married priests, the Church will draw in a new generation of believers. But if he

continues the tradition of Paul and John Paul, our congrega-
tions will become smaller, older, and ultimately irrelevant. I
wouldn't want to be a part of a Church like that."

"Meaning what?"

"Meaning that if the Church continues its drift to the right,
I'd probably make my mother happy and become a university
professor." He looked around the table. "But that decision is at
least one pope and a number of years off. Until then, with the
blessings of this group, I hope to keep applying the lessons of
Jesus to the parishioners I serve."

Four

"'EVEN THOUGH HE'S BEEN in the parish a scant nine months, Father Russell has, by most accounts, had a measurable impact. His youth Masses with sermons delivered by teenagers have made Sundays cool again according to one of the attendees. According to the Pittsburgh diocese, 'Russell is the youngest priest to have a parish in the eastern US, and his youth helps him relate to his young charges.'"

Michelle looked up from the newspaper. "Why aren't you blushing?"

"Because you're the fourth person to read it to me today," Gabe said wearily. "Are you done?"

She looked back down. "Almost. Here's my favorite part." She adopted a teenage girl's voice. "'At times he feels like a priest,' that same young parishioner said. 'At other times he's just like one of us. Or a cool big brother, at least.' Russell also teaches a course in New Testament history at the local seminary, where he was once a student." She put down the newspaper and grinned at him. "You're a hit."

They were seated in the seminary's faculty dining room. Mornings and evenings it served as a cafeteria, with the residents helping themselves buffet-style. But during the middle of the day, the tables were set with crisp white tablecloths and fine silverware because the room was reserved for faculty and the retired priests who lived in a wing of the seminary. The waiters were seminarians dressed formally in hassocks. It was part of their rotation of jobs within the seminary, which included maintaining the grounds, janitorial work, dishing out food at breakfast and dinner, and working in the library. The room was large and high-ceilinged, the height drawing up and dispersing the conversations, making every conversation feel intimate.

"Can we get back to our lunch?" Gabe asked. "And my novel?"

"Don't you want to hear about why the archbishop thought you were ready for your own parish at such a tender age?"

"For the fourth time? I think I'll pass. I'm in the seminary bathroom this morning. I come out of the stall and one of the other professors says, 'How does it feel to be wise beyond your years?' He was only partly joking."

"Quit pouting, Gabe," Michelle said, delighting in his discomfort. "It's a good article. It'll drive up attendance all the way around. That's worth the little amount of grief you'll get from your fellow priests. And me."

"Don't forget my students. Most of them had copies this morning."

"Speaking of which, any new jokes?"

Gabe brightened. "Yeah. A priest is checking into a hotel, and he asks the clerk whether . . . ."

"I like where this is going," Michelle said, patting the manila folder on the table in front of her. "There's more flesh and blood to the characters. They're more conflicted. I'm as interested in them as I am in the plot. That's the sign of good writing."

Michelle Carlisle was the writing teacher at the seminary, a position she had held for the past six years. One of only three female faculty, she was in her mid-thirties and the object of schoolboy crushes of any seminarian with a heterosexual bone in his body. She was clearly capable of looking glamorous, but in deference to her teaching setting and audience, she underplayed her looks. Her face was strong-boned and tight-skinned, her cheekbones high and sculpted, her eyes dark brown verging on black. Apart from lipstick, her makeup was minimal, and she usually wore her hair in a ponytail. Her attire alternated between dresses or skirts and designer jeans.

Michelle's two-semester writing course was mandatory for all students. Over the course of the year, students developed their writing skills in three areas of writing: analytic, creative, and persuasive. For the first section, she had her students analyze current events on their own and then worked with them to relate those events to the religious teachings they were studying. In the creative section, she encouraged them to range as far afield as they could, with no restrictions on form or voice. That was the toughest section for both her students and her since creativity seemed to be in short supply within the seminary ranks. In the persuasive section, she taught them how to incorporate the lessons from the first two sections to create compelling and topical sermons.

Gabe had taken Michelle's class during his third year at the seminary and found it both enjoyable and useful in preparing the sermons he had to give to mock masses as part of his preparation for a pastoral placement. Inspired by the course, he had started writing short stories, which Michelle was happy to read and edit. Some of his stories were strong enough to warrant sending to university presses, she thought, and she urged him to do so. He had, and two had been published.

In his fourth year, he'd tried his hand at a novel. Michelle had been kind but honest in her appraisal. His core idea and its development were compelling. There was certainly something there. But his writing, at least his initial draft, didn't do the themes justice: The characters were too stock and too shallow, the voice was inconsistent, and the ending didn't quite deliver what the buildup had promised. Gabe had taken the criticism to heart and gone back to work, but only after asking Michelle for a list of novels and writing manuals he should read before starting work on a new draft.

She had obliged and in turn was impressed eight months later by the first three new chapters he had delivered for her review. This version, she told him, showed real progress, preserving the strengths of its predecessor while correcting many of the weaknesses. If he kept this up through the rest of the novel, Michelle told him, she could see it being published someday. And yes, she'd be happy to read and critique the rest of the book.

The result was the weekly Monday lunches. If Gabe had new writing for Michelle to review, he got it to her before her departure from the seminary on Friday afternoon. If he didn't, they discussed authors and books that had influenced them both and the lessons they might provide for Gabe in his writing.

At first, the lunches had focused only on writing, but as Gabe's novel progressed and needed less criticism, the conversation topics slid into their personal lives. Gabe had learned a bit of Michelle's past—or "backstory," the term she used in helping him develop his characters. She had been born and raised in a small farming town in Michigan, not the Upper Peninsula, she stressed, which featured a hardiness of environment and citizenry all its own, but still, an upbringing that few girls experienced. An only child, she had been raised without regard to gender, being expected to help her father with chores around the farm that required strength and endurance. At fourteen, Michelle took on the household duties as well when her mother died.

With her father not quite ready for her to move away, Michelle had attended the local college, where she majored in English. For her master's degree, she assembled the best of her writing and was accepted into the prestigious creative writing program at the University of Iowa. There, exposed to some of the best teachers in the country, as well as some of the most promising up-and-coming writers, she reached the hard decision—one her advisor concurred with—that her editorial skills were stronger than her writing skills and that she was better served concentrating on a career in either publishing or teaching.

She had met her husband John in Pittsburgh at the end of her first year teaching at the seminary. Just back from a two-year stint in the Army, he had put his business degree to use running the accounting department in his father's factory, with the implicit understanding that he was being groomed to take over the family business. After five years of apprenticeship, an increasingly impatient John had begun to take over operations, but his father wasn't ready to hand over the reins. Despite the conflict it would cause in his tight-knit family, John began to think about starting his own business, an initiative Michelle had encouraged.

From the Monday conversations, Gabe had picked up that Michelle's marriage was comfortable but stalled. Gabe found that he was the one who brought up John in their conversations, asking how the business was going, where they were headed on vacation, and how their weekend had been. Michelle answered every query but in tones that didn't encourage follow-up. After a while, Gabe learned not to raise the topic.

"Your voice is really coming along," Michelle said. "It's a lot stronger and more consistent this time around."

"That's a nice way of saying it was all over the place in the earlier drafts," he replied sheepishly. When Michelle didn't say anything, he smiled. "Thanks for not disagreeing with me. I reread the first draft twice before starting this version, and it was hard to read some chapters without wincing. Talk about the power of suggestion. You could tell with each chapter who I was reading at the time. The first chapter sounded like Steinbeck, the next Kazantzakis, the next Cormac McCarthy. It was 'story by Gabe Russell, narration by Sybil.'"

One of Michelle's students glided over and refilled their water without being asked. Gabe finished his halibut and put his silverware on the plate. "Okay, I've got a favor to ask. A big one."

"Ask away."

"Let me start with the numbers. Eighty to ninety percent of the parishioners who visit me during office hours are women. Confession numbers are a little lower, but not much."

"Got it," she said cautiously. "And?"

"And I'm not a woman. In fact, I'm finding I'm clueless about half the human race. I need to better understand women in general, and my female parishioners in particular, if I'm going to be of any use to them as a pastor or spiritual advisor."

"I think you're being a little hard on yourself, Gabe. Just the fact that you're aware of your limitations and are trying to address them puts you way ahead of the rest of the pack, at least from where I sit."

He acknowledged the praise with a slight bow of his head. "Maybe, but you need to understand how the Church—specifically the seminary system—prepares priests like me for our role within the Church and our place within the community. When

it comes to religious issues, we're well-schooled about the sacra-
ments, the miracle of the Mass, that kind of stuff—what some
would call the sacred side of the priesthood. Which would be
fine if my job description stopped at spiritual advisor. But when
it comes to the human side of my job, not the sacred part—and
I'm talking about the expectations that I'll be a counselor, a therapist, a community advocate, things like that—the seminary and
Church do nothing, and I mean nothing, on those fronts."

"I've looked at the curriculum here, and you're right. It's
almost all theology and Church history. But I still don't get what
you're asking from me."

"I need you to be my coach when it comes to women. To be
my 'woman-whisperer,' so to speak."

Michelle cocked her head and leaned back. Her eyes
searched his face, waiting for a smile or smirk. But his face
remained serious. "So you want me to be the Beatrice to your
Dante? Is that it?"

"Well, I was thinking about a more contemporary version,
like that woman who founded Cosmopolitan? What's her
name?"

"Helen Gurley Brown, you ass."

"Yeah, like that. But if you like Beatrice better, we'll go with
that."

"Explaining women to men? Talk about lifetime job security.
All right, I'm in. Where do you want to start?"

"Thanks. I really appreciate it. I've got a list of questions
back in my room. I'll bring them next time. For now, let me tell
you something I've noticed about virtually every woman who
comes to see me. They're really lacking in self-confidence. Some
of the older ones are obvious about it. They'll say things like
'But what do I know?' And virtually all of them are less certain
about things, including themselves, than the men I see."

Gabe moved his head far to the left and then to the right until a solid click emanated from his neck. "There. That's been there all day." He looked back over at Michelle. "Let me give you an example. I decided that for one week, I would open every meeting or session with a compliment. Usually that was a statement that they were looking good lately. The men—every one—responded, 'Thanks, Father. I've been working out a bit lately.' Or 'Thanks, I've been eating better.'"

"Whereas the women either deflected it or looked down in their laps and mumbled a thanks," Michelle said. "When they do that, they're thinking you're just trying to be nice because they can't believe it could be true."

"Now you see why you're my Beatrice. So why are these women so lacking in self-confidence?"

She didn't answer immediately. As Gabe had done earlier, she looked out the window, as if the answer were out there somewhere. Then she turned back to him. "The reason I'm taking so long to answer is that as I thought about your question, it occurred to me that there's a general response to your question and a local one."

"Start with the general, then let's see what the local boy thinks of your second answer."

"Okay. Growing up, and I'm talking the world over, it seems that women, more than men, start off with blinders on, like we're racehorses. And how open or restricted those blinders are or how open our field of vision is depends on any number of factors: our race, our family's financial condition, the community we live in. But along with race at the top is gender." She paused. "Am I making any sense?"

"Absolutely. Go on."

"Most women see only what's in front of them or what society allows them to see. Let me give you an example. This is something that meant nothing to me at the time but now sticks in my craw. In grade school, when they asked the boys what they wanted to be when they grew up, the list was pretty expansive, especially for rural Michigan. The boys in my class were going to be professional athletes, brain surgeons, astronauts. When it was the girls' turn, it wasn't completely stereotypic—you know, teacher, secretary, housewife—but there wasn't a brain surgeon or astronaut in the entire class. And when it came to asking where they saw themselves living as adults, the men had the same range, even though most saw themselves staying in Michigan. On the other hand, virtually every girl, your Beatrice included, had the same answer: It depends on where my husband gets a job. They had no ownership over their destiny." She looked at him and shrugged. "Blinders."

Gabe nodded, more to himself than to Michelle. "I like that image of blinders. It fits with what I'm seeing in my meetings with these folks."

"Now, before this turns into a pity party, things have gotten a lot better since the day I answered that question. A lot. The blinders may not be off for most American women, but the range of vision has widened significantly. You can credit the pill, the Women's Movement, court rulings—especially on abortion—whatever. But there's a sense of freedom and opportunity that wasn't there when I was a little girl."

"Now bring it a back home, to my beloved burg."

"Male or female, you're a lot more worldly than the average. What do you guys call yourselves?"

"You mean 'jagoffs'?"

She smiled. "Even I know that means 'jerk.' No, I can't remember the word, but I hear it around. John uses it sometimes to refer to himself. Starts with a 'Y.'"

"Yinzer. But as an outsider, you're not allowed to use it. It's like the 'N' word for blacks. We Pittsburghers, which is the proper term for us, can use it. You can't."

"Thanks for the teaching on local dialect. And the warning. Anyway, as an 'outsider,' to use your term, I've probably got a different perspective on things than a local like you."

"Except, since I was born in California, I'll never be regarded as a local. Maybe when I'm eighty. Maybe."

"Back to your question. The women here have blinders that are still pretty narrowly focused. They're probably still living in the house they grew up in, and they're expected to marry and stay within the neighborhood. They'll probably be right here for the rest of their lives, and that's not a bad thing in their eyes. And raising a family isn't a choice, it's an expectation. Or a sacred obligation. And finally, college is somewhere between a long shot and a pipe dream, if they think about it at all. And if they do, many of them will be seen as turning their backs on the neighborhood."

Gabe smiled at her. "For an outsider, you're pretty smart. And observant."

"Well, remember, I'm married to a Yinzer." The smile stayed on her face, but her eyes became more serious. "I've never asked you this, but the better I get to know you, the more I wonder: Of all the placements I'm assuming you could have had, why did you choose to stay here?"

"You're not the first person to ask me that. But the answer is pretty simple. My dad's got early-onset Alzheimer's, and I need to be here to help my mom. It's not bad now, but it's only going in one direction. We thought of going back to California, where he and Mom still have friends, but his doctors warn against uprooting him from everything he knows. So here we are."

"I'm sorry, Gabe. I didn't know."

"How could you? But don't think my decision was only about my Florence Nightingale duties. The teaching opportunity here also was a consideration." He looked around the dining room. "I'm happy with my decision."

Michelle had a two o'clock class, so Gabe walked her to her classroom. "You didn't tell me about your class. Any Hemingways in their midst? Or Pynchons, for that matter?"

"Not so far. They're trying, I'll give them that. But everything I'm reading is stiff. All surface, no depth."

"Well, you should know by now that we seminarians are an emotionally constipated group." He thought for a moment. "Same assignments you gave my class?"

"Same syllabus exactly."

They reached her classroom door. "Next assignment, try this," he said. "Tell them to write about what they think the hardest thing about being a priest is going to be. The most honest essay gets to skip the next assignment."

"You think that'll work?"

It's the only universal there is to this job. Every seminarian I ever met, now or then, is petrified he's going to screw up."

She waved the newspaper with the article about him. "Even the boy wonder?"

"Especially the boy wonder. Just this week I had a pregnant fourteen-year-old—pregnant by her uncle, no less—ask me about abortion versus adoption. And a gay husband who wants to leave his wife and kids and wants me to be the one who explains it to them."

"Not what you expected?"

"Exactly what I expected. And hoped for. I just thought I'd have more runway, that's all."

CONFESSION

"I've been trying a number of routines to stave off the dreams. The first was just to stay up later, work on the novel, and see if that changed my sleep patterns. It didn't. Then I added a glass of Scotch to the equation—and I don't even like hard liquor. But I liked the image of me as a hard-drinking writer, like Faulkner or Fitzgerald. Again, no luck. Finally, I took Dolores's advice and replaced the Scotch with a glass of warm milk with a splash of honey in it. Zero for three.

"I've added another thirty minutes to my Krav Maga work-outs, thinking that exhaustion might work. But I'm finding that these dreams are like weeds. However you try to kill them, they just grow back every night.

"I'm going to add fifteen minutes of meditation to the mix, starting tonight. If that doesn't work, I've saved the best for last: masturbation. Since the end result of the dream is a nocturnal emission, maybe I can short-circuit the process, kind of like robbing a fire of its fuel.

"I can still laugh about this, but not much longer. These dreams are starting to worry me. I don't know what they're trying to tell me, as both a man and a priest, but I know this: Whatever it is, it's not good."

Five

GABE STOOD IN FRONT of a small room packed with twenty seminarians, most of them in casual clothes and a few in Roman collars, as if trying to get a head start on being priests. The desks were old and haphazardly positioned around the room. Six students sat at a large table at the back of the room.

The whiteboard behind Gabe was full of Biblical verse notations. He gestured back at the board. "Start with those passages on forgiveness and develop your own sermon. And be original, guys. This is your message, not someone else's. Believe me, I'm going to know when it comes from you and when it comes from some book of sermons. More importantly, your parishioners will know as well. Mix the heavenly with the practical. When appropriate, use local examples or current events. This needs to speak to them and their world. No platitudes, no greeting card sentimentality or you'll be preaching to an empty church in no time. Write with two words in mind: unique and relevant. If you get stuck, office hours are Mondays and Wednesdays from two to three. Or you can find me in the gym three to five most afternoons."

He looked at the clock. "Okay, we've got ten minutes left. Before we get to the serious stuff, I heard one of you wants to play Stump the Chump." A hand went up. "Mr. Terry."

"Father Russell, can you tell me where baseball is mentioned in the Bible?" Mr. Terry looked around the classroom, a small smirk settling on his face.

"Please, Mr. Terry. Don't insult my intelligence. It's in Genesis—the very first words of the entire Bible, in fact. 'In the big inning—'" As the class groaned, Gabe gestured with both hands at Mr. Terry, as if to say he started it.

"How about tennis?" another student called out.

"You know the rules, Mr. Comstock. One verse per class. But since you've already blurted your question, the answer is Exodus 41: 'When Joseph served in Pharaoh's court.'" This time, the groans were louder.

"New Testament History and Exegesis" was an elective. It was the newest listing in the seminary catalogue, combining Gabe's years of individual study with his apprenticeship with Father Benoit, a biblical archaeologist on loan to the seminary from the École Biblique in Jerusalem. Impressed by Gabe's zeal and self-taught mastery of Biblical languages, Father Benoit had selected him as his teacher's aide for the second semester and then invited him to Jerusalem to work in the museum.

Gabe enjoyed teaching the New Testament class, finding it a welcome change and complement to his parish duties. His students were seminarians in their final year of study. Having been steeped in theology and Church doctrine, they welcomed the historical and archaeological perspectives that Gabe brought to the study of Scripture. Raised to believe that Scripture was timeless in its truth and directly from God, they found themselves challenged by their young professor to take a fresh look at the gospels and the teachings of Paul through the lens of the times in which they were written and the audiences they targeted.

While a class like Gabe's was standard fare in Protestant seminaries, where Biblical study by the congregation was fundamental, it was a rarity in Catholic seminaries. The difference came from the way each tradition approached Scripture. Protestants saw it as a cornerstone of their faith and often held weekly Biblical study groups, encouraging their charges to develop their own interpretations of what Jesus taught and Paul advocated. Catholics, on the other hand, saw Scripture as the basis of Church doctrine but nowhere as foundational as their Protestants peers viewed it. Beyond the New Testament readings incorporated into the Mass, a Catholic would rarely, if ever, encounter Scripture in their spiritual development, guided more toward the teachings of the Church Fathers. As a result, it was not surprising that Gabe's class was both incredibly popular among the student camp while viewed with a certain concern by the more traditional priests at the seminary.

The goal of the class, as Gabe explained in his opening lecture, was to approach Scripture, especially the New Testament, from two different directions. The first was to place the writings in their historical and cultural settings, with an emphasis on each gospel's targeted audience. This was particularly important in viewing the gospels. The second was to then see how that same Scripture had been interpreted and disseminated by the Church Fathers. And be prepared, Gabe had cautioned in his opening lecture, to find some incompatibilities between the two.

"Biblical exegesis," he explained in that opening lecture, "is most productive if you take a fresh look at the concepts of 'fact' and 'history.' Most of today's Christians, especially the evangelicals, view the gospels as historical accounts, as ancient journalism, when in fact, that was neither the job nor the intent of the early evangelists." He explained that the gospels were actually a form of propaganda—or better put, persuasion. Their primary job, as they saw it, was not to report but to convince. "As any propagandist knows, you tailor your narrative to your audience.

And with four different authors with four different agendas, you're bound to run into differences in both the recounting of events and their meaning."

Some of these were minor discrepancies, but some were critical. And understanding and resolving these issues before they were raised by an increasingly informed congregation, Gabe said, was a core part of the course.

"Take Matthew, for example, since he's our most popular evangelist. His job, as he saw it, was to convince first-century Palestinian Jews that Jesus was the Messiah, the fulfillment of Hebrew Scripture. So as a good lawyer—or propagandist— would do, he cites the Old Testament more than a hundred times as validation of his core points. And he's not even subtle about it. He takes the reader by the hand and explicitly says that this was fulfillment of prophecy." Gabe went to the board and wrote "Matthew➤Palestinian Jews➤Messiah➤ Old Testament."

He turned back to the class. "Luke, on the other hand, had little understanding of—or sympathy for—Matthew's audience. He was writing for an entirely different audience: the citizens of the Roman Empire. As a result, his Jesus was more a teacher in the mold of Socrates than messiah, a decidedly Jewish concept. Luke strips Jesus of many of his Semitic qualities. In fact, Jews fare poorly in Luke since their Messiah came to them and they were too dense to recognize it. And they had an active hand in his death." He went back to the board and wrote "Luke➤ Hellenists➤Teacher➤Hero Myth."

He turned back to the class. "Same figure, Jesus, and same time and events but recounted by two authors with two different audiences and two different agendas. And note that I said 'recounted,' not 'reported.' Matthew and Luke saw themselves as interpreters of the events they were recounting. Historical accuracy was not a major concern. And that same logic applies to Mark and John. So as you approach this course, keep in mind that we're dealing with four different writers and four different agendas, all commenting on one set of historical events."

He stepped back and pointed at the board. "For centuries, religious scholars and authorities have tried to explain and justify the differences among these four accounts. I'm not trying to spoil the movie here, but it can't be done. You can impose your own interpretation, of course, and your parishioners will accept it, since you're a priest. But our job, as I see it, is to educate our parishioners about these distinctions and the factors behind them, then let them decide for themselves what's true and what isn't."

"Excuse me, Father," a student said, raising his hand as he spoke up. He was short and intense, his upper body leaning over the desk as he talked. "But I've been taught—including at this seminary—that the complications you just raised are why the Church tells us our job is to interpret Scripture to our parishioners. That leaving them on their own to interpret the Bible is dangerous, in that the confusion you're talking about can cause them to fall away from the Church." He hesitated. That approach strikes me as a bit condescending, especially in this day and age."

"I agree with you, Mr. Mandell," Gabe replied. "But here's the deal—and believe me, you won't often hear me beginning a sentence with 'In fairness to the Church,' but in this case, you've got to remember that Catholicism started at a time when most of the faithful couldn't read or write. As a result, it was the job of the Church and its priests to read and comment on Biblical teachings.

"Protestantism, on the other hand, came of age fifteen hundred years later and had the benefit of both the Renaissance and the invention of the printing press. The Protestant leaders realized their audiences were more intelligent and independent than the faithful of the Middle Ages. So they founded their religion on the concept of empowering the faithful to study and make their own decisions, which left the Catholic Church with a tough decision. It could adopt this new approach to Scripture or it could double down on the idea of the priest as authority figure and interpreter of Christ's message. Guess which direction they chose?"

"Would the Church agree with that characterization?" Mr. Mandell asked. "Or is this one of those areas you cautioned about at in the first class where you and standard Church teachings diverge?"

Gabe smiled. "Touché, Mr. Mandell. And you're right. This is one of those areas of disagreement. But again, in fairness to the Church, old habits die hard. I think of it this way: For my parents' generation and every generation before them, doctors were like popes. They were infallible. If they gave a diagnosis, you didn't question it. If they prescribed a treatment, you did it. That's just the way it was. But as we got more educated, and as the sixties taught us to question authority, something has changed in the way most of us see doctors these days. They're fallible. They can make mistakes. They can be wrong in their diagnoses. As a result, we now want second opinions. In the future, we'll research both the doctor and the diagnosis online, something our parents wouldn't have done and couldn't have done, in any event."

Gabe walked over to the whiteboard, grabbed a marker, and wrote 'WWW' on the board. Then he turned back to the class. "Remember how I mentioned the impact the printing press had on religion, how it powered the Reformation? Well, these three letters are going to change our world—and that includes the world of faith—more than we can imagine. The World Wide Web is going to democratize knowledge by opening the doors to virtually every source of information in the world. It's going to make your parishioners experts—or worse, people who only *think* they're experts. As priests, you guys are going to have to defend every major belief or teaching, whether you espouse them or not. And since you're a representative of the Church, expect that, just like doctors, you and your beliefs will be researched and judged by your parishioners."

He tapped the board again. "It's a whole new ballgame, gentlemen. Bromides such as 'That's what the Church has always taught,' won't wash anymore. That's a big reason I teach this course. We're embarking on a new kind of Catholicism, what I would call a shared ministry. And when it comes to Scripture, that ministry will succeed or fail on how much you know and how you impart that knowledge."

On that first day of class, Gabe told his students what their final exam would be. Taking on the role of Biblical profilers, they were to use everything at their disposal—the gospels, the historical texts of that time, and analyses and interpretations of Jesus down through the centuries—to create their most accurate profile of Jesus.

"There are three major schools of thought about Jesus you should use as starting points," he explained, "but feel free to develop your own." He wrote a large '1' on the board. "The first is the one you're most familiar with, the one that started with Matthew and John and has been refined over the past two thousand years: Jesus is God come to Earth. He's divinity wrapped in human skin. Nothing is beyond his capacity, including rising from the dead." He wrote next to the number: "God become man."

"That's the image of Jesus that most of us grew up with. But during the twentieth century, historians tried to bring Jesus down to earth, to understand him as a product of his times. The Jesus they came up with was quite human—a man of humble beginnings who evolved into a brilliant teacher and political radical who attracted the attention of Rome and was crucified as a result. This is the Jesus of the gospel of Mark—the earliest gospel, by the way." He drew a "2" on the board, and next to it he wrote "Simple man➤great teacher➤crucified radical."

Then he wrote a "3." "This is where archaeology comes into play and why it's so important to the field of Biblical studies. As you know, there's no actual mention of Jesus in the historical records of his time, save for one line in the writings of Josephus. And we haven't dug up any chiseled stones that say 'Jesus slept here.'" He waited for the laughter to subside before continuing. "But archaeology rarely validates a specific person or event. It's more a mirror of the times."

He walked back to the board and drew a circle around "Simple man." "Some historians who took a hard look at Jesus during the twentieth century took the 'simple' to extremes. They argued that since Jesus came from Nazareth, a backwater village in Galilee, he most likely lacked the sophistication to develop the ideas that are attributed to him and that the gospel writers embellished him and his teachings significantly.

"But now, thanks to archaeology, we come to a third image of Jesus. This one stems from excavations at Sepphoris, a Roman-Hellenistic city only four miles north of Nazareth. It turns out that Sepphoris was far larger and more cosmopolitan than most of us originally thought. And since both Joseph and Jesus were identified as 'carpenters' in the gospel, it's logical that Jesus apprenticed with his dad. Which means he was exposed to Roman and Greek traditions and ideas."

He stepped back and gestured at the entire board. "So that's your final assignment, gentlemen. Give me your most informed profile of who Jesus was. And document how you came to that conclusion."

Gabe brought his attention back to the classroom. "Okay. Open forum time. What's on your fragile little minds today?"

A hand went up. The owner was small in stature with a large cowlick overhanging his earnest face. "How do we deal with parishioners who come out to us as gay? I know the Church's official stance, that it's intrinsically immoral and contrary to the natural law. But come on, Father. In today's world . . ."

"You're right, Mr. Phillips," Gabe said. "The Church is woefully behind the times on this one."

He paused for a long moment before continuing. "Listen, guys. I know some of you disagree with my beliefs, and I respect that. But some of you are also reporting what I'm teaching here to the administrators at this seminary. Some even to the archbishop's office. That part I don't respect."

He paused and looked around the room, noting that a few of the students couldn't meet his eyes. "Okay, now that I've gotten that off my chest, let me respond to Mr. Phillips. To be honest, I haven't tackled this topic in terms of the development of Church doctrine and its subsequent rulings on homosexuality. All I can tell you is what I do. First off, I need my gay parishioners to understand the distinction between their self-identity and their actions. They need to recognize they are one of God's creatures, and as such, they are deserving of uncritical love. And I really press them on this count, telling them they can't love another person fully until they love and accept themselves."

Another student spoke up. "But how about all the Biblical passages that their families throw at them, most of them from the Old Testament but some from the New Testament, all saying they're going to hell?"

"In that case, Mr. Hernandez, you fight Scripture with Scripture. If Jesus is the fulfillment of the Old Testament, that means his loving acceptance trumps Old Testament judgment and condemnation. Those Old Testament passages that evangelists love to cite are rendered obsolete by the coming of Jesus. Once you feel like your parishioners believe they're as deserving of love and forgiveness as the next guy, you can move on to their activities and whether they're sinful or not."

"Just so I'm sure, are we talking about sexual activity?" Mr. Hernandez asked.

"Usually, though for many it could be something as innocent as curling up with someone of the same sex. That kind of intimacy and the feelings it generates can be as eventful in their self-judgment as sexual intercourse."

"How do you counsel them about their sexual activities?"

"I tell them I don't distinguish between gay and straight sexuality, and neither should they. That if they're in a committed relationship, gay or straight, and have sex outside it, that's adultery. If they're sleeping with everyone who has a pulse, they're devaluing themselves. And if they're masturbating and think they're going to hell, I tell them that if that's the case, they're going to run into you there."

The class burst into laughter as the door opened and a startled Father McShane entered the room, his class standing behind him in the hall. Gabe looked back at the clock to find that they were five minutes into the next period.

Six

THE TWO PRIESTS walked together through the woods behind the seminary. The sun made its way through the heavy-limbed oaks on occasion, but they mostly walked in a gathering darkness. The path was clear of leaves for the most part. Gabe was dressed casually, in jeans, a long-sleeve T-shirt and running shoes. His companion was something out of central casting: tall and regal with a hard-boned, hawkish face and a full head of graying hair that was immaculately coifed. He wore a full cassock, the hem of which grazed the path as they walked. He kept his hands clasped behind his back and bent over slightly to hear Gabe better.

"You ever have a wet dream?" Gabe asked as they strode up a hill. Both men moved easily and athletically.

"Are you kidding?" his hiking companion said. "It's a rite of passage for every teenage boy. Like hair under your arms or your voice changing."

"Not me," Gabe replied. "I'm not kidding. Up until this month, I'd never had a wet dream. Not one. Growing up, I'd hear my friends talk about it, and I'd chuckle and give a knowing smile. But I had no idea what they were talking about. So when I finally had one a few weeks back, it freaked me out. Now they're a nightly occurrence. It makes me wonder what God's trying to tell me—or what I'm trying to tell myself."

"I hate to sound like a therapist, but has anything changed in your world recently? Anything significant, for lack of a better word?"

"Other than me being promoted to run the parish? You and I both know I wasn't ready for that promotion."

"But that's old news," his companion said. "And the archbishop and his team seemed to think you were ready. The reports I got when I moved back here indicate that the parish agrees with the archbishop. Most of them have really taken to you."

Paul Reynolds had preceded the monsignor at the parish, serving in that capacity for seven years. Charismatic and dedicated to his parishioners, he had been immensely popular. But as he explained to the archbishop at that time, he was an academic at heart, reading theology and Church teachings every night before bed instead of preparing for the next day's parish obligations. In short, he was cheating both his parish and himself. And so, to the surprise and disappointment of his parishioners, Paul resigned his position and went to Rome for a decade of theological study, much of it in the Vatican archives.

During his Roman sojourn, he had written numerous of articles and books about how the Church could modernize itself while staying true to its founding beliefs. His writings, as well as his television work as an authority on Catholic doctrine, made him an academic star. After multiple requests from a variety of universities and seminaries, the Church had finally agreed to send him back to the US for five years, each year spent at a different university or seminary. Paul's one request was that one of those years be a return to his old parish and seminary, where he had met and developed a friendship with the young priest who had assumed his place in the parish.

"This isn't a confession, just a conversation, so you can relax," Gabe said as they reached the end of the trail and turned back toward the seminary. "I'm just trying to figure out why, every night when I close my eyes, my mind turns into a porno theater."

"I'm jealous," Paul said. "Compared with yours, my dreams are pretty mundane. In my regular one, I'm late for Mass and there's a whole cathedral waiting. And then when I do get there, I'm in my underwear. It's the clerical version of the dream that everyone has about high school and the big test."

Gabe smiled. "Well, you're welcome to some of mine. To tell you the truth, for a sexual novice, I'm pretty impressed with some of the positions I'm able to achieve. I don't know if some of them are even physically possible. I may have to rent some movies to find out."

"Well, if you're going to do that, get the hell out of Pittsburgh. All you need is for someone like Dolores to catch you coming out of the Pink Pussycat."

They walked together in a comfortable silence. Then Paul looked over. "This woman in your dream, does she have a face?"

"Not yet. But each night her face gets a little clearer. I think I know whose face it'll wind up being. But for now, it's still a work in progress."

"And these dreams never happened during your time in the seminary, only after you were promoted?"

"Yeah," Gabe replied. "And that can't be a coincidence. It's like God's testing my resolve, seeing if I'm up to the task or if he should find someone else to do the job. Each day when I get up and wipe up the night's residue, I think to myself *Is this the day I fuck up, where I finally get exposed as a fraud?*"

He picked up a large oak leaf that had fallen on the path. It was beautifully veined and a healthy green that seemed out of place on the ground. Gabe kept it between his thumb and index finger as they walked. "You're going to say I'm being too tough on myself. Trust me, I'm not. I know I've done good work these past nine months. But I feel like a newly minted doctor who has only gotten easy cases his first nine months on the job. He's doing great, but in the back of his mind is a building panic, a fear that he's nowhere near ready for the life-and-death cases that are going to come his way."

Paul nodded. "If you think you're alone in that concern, let me help. Every priest I know, including me, goes through a period of self-doubt. It's usually early in their ministry, but like a midlife crisis, it can occur anytime. Or like a disease, it can reoccur."

They walked the rest of the way in silence. As they exited the woods, the seminary rising before them, a wall of gray interrupted only by slender windows, Gabe looked over at his companion. "You miss Rome?"

"It'll be there when I get back. In the meantime, once I finish up here, I've got three more university guest spots. That's three more cities where I can revel in what I miss most when I'm in Rome: beer and softball. Speaking of which, we need a centerfielder. Didn't you play flanker in high school?"

"I did, but team sports and I parted ways a while ago. Speaking of beers, though, a few of us newbies—priests and a nun—get together once a month as a kind of support group. It would be great if you could join us. Kind of show us the ropes as well as some of your scars. I'm not the only one who feels like he's working without a net."

Paul nodded. "Happy to. But that feeling you're talking about—working without a net? Get used to it. Because it never goes away. You just get better at faking it."

CONFESSION

"The dream continues to evolve. Or morph. I don't know the right word. When it first started, it was basically an orgy with faceless bodies involved in all types of sexual acts. And I was just an observer. Then the dream changed. The same orgy, but now I was a participant. And trust me, there was no act that I didn't engage in over the course of those first few nights. I was impressed by my stamina, if nothing else.

"The number of participants diminished over the next few nights until, finally, it was just me and a faceless woman. The sex has become less athletic and more intimate. I can see her body clearly, but her face is a blur. It gets a little clearer every night, which worries me, since I think I know where this is all heading."

He leaned his forehead against the screen and picked up the slight scent of the lavender cleaning agent the janitor favored. *"I keep trying new techniques, new routines to interrupt or stave off the dreams. Nothing works. These dreams are like a weed you kill every day only to see it grow back every night."*

Seven

MICHELLE AND GABE were finishing up lunch. By tradition, they didn't critique his novel while they were eating, catching up instead on the goings-on in their very different lives. She'd never been friends with a priest, and though a few of Gabe's friends were recently married, they didn't have the perspective on marriage Michelle had.

"What was the fallout from the article, Father Modesty?" Michelle asked, her eyebrows raised in innocence.

Gabe kept his eyes on his plate. "You were right. There were more folks at the regular masses, and the youth mass was packed." He pushed his plate to the side and nodded at the folder in front of her. "What'd you think?"

"You got a novel on your hands, kid. It's a light year from the first draft. Your voice is strong and consistent. Better yet, it's unique. That's what they're looking for these days."

"Well, if that's the case, a lot of that is due to you and these sessions."

Michelle motioned to the waiter to clear her plate. "I've got a confession, Father. For the past two years I've been freelancing as an editor for two New York publishing houses. They're always looking for fresh voices." She patted the folder. "I'd like to submit the first fifty pages to one of my publishers, if that's okay with you."

"I'm good with that. And flattered. What would it mean if they like it?"

"An advance for you. And a possible full-time job for me."

"Here or New York?"

"New York."

"Huh." He looked out the window. "What's John think about all this?"

"He doesn't know yet. John's a Pittsburgh boy, through and through. No point in raising the issue if there's no job."

"But don't you think he'd be . . ."

"John's still the guy I married." She saw him smile and shook her head. "I can see you thinking, 'Oh isn't that sweet,' but the emphasis is on 'still.' John and I have been married eight years, and he hasn't changed a lick in that time."

"And you have."

"And I have. So if your novel is as good as I think it is, he and I will have some talking to do. And you'll have a better editor than me to work with."

She opened the folder. "But until I'm replaced, I'll keep doing my job." She pointed to a page with circles on it. "Here the mother seems a bit stilted, both in her behavior and her dialogue. I've heard you talk about your mom and how strong her personality is. Put some of her into this character. Not a ton but some. It will keep her from being a caricature."

She paged through the manuscript and stopped at a second area. "And this page. I love your dialogue. It's gotten a lot more natural. But I lose track of who's talking right about here." She tapped the page. "It wouldn't hurt to get a few identifiers— names, gestures—in there to break it up and keep the reader focused on who's saying what."

She stacked the papers and handed them to him. "Otherwise, I really liked these last few pages. How's it feeling to you?"

"It's coming together. I thought about what you said a couple of sessions back, about not articulating the emotions so much and letting the reader deduce them. And I tried it for the next couple of chapters. If you agree that it works, I'll go back to the earlier pages and fix them. But only after I'm done with this draft."

Gabe nodded his thanks to the server as he swept the crumbs off the tablecloth with a flat-edged knife. "My big problem right now isn't the actual writing, it's finding the time to write. So my new rule is, regardless of what I'm doing—unless I'm out on an emergency call—I stop at eleven, pour a glass of wine, and write for at least an hour before calling it a day."

"Well, whatever you're doing, it's working. So keep it up. It's always good to have a fallback line of work in case this priest thing doesn't work out."

Eight

GABE WAS BAREFOOT and drenched in sweat. The small beads at the beginning had morphed into drops and finally streams that flew from his face and arms as he swung an arm at his target. His sleeveless sweatshirt, gray to begin with, was now almost black with sweat. The muscles in his arms quivered and swelled like little rivers as he swung one arm up in a blocking motion and drove his other hand—a three-finger knife, the thumb and pinkie pulled under—into the throat of the figure in front of him. He stood back for a moment to gauge the impact of his strike, the sweat rolling off his wrists and face, joining the small puddles on the mat beneath his feet.

The figure staggered for a moment, then righted itself. Frowning, Gabe stepped back in and drove a right, then a left, into the exposed throat. This time the figure toppled over. Gabe nodded and then righted the plastic dummy with the heavy base and shifted his attack to the abdomen. Dancing on his toes, he drifted around to the back of the dummy and attacked the kidneys. After five minutes of concerted attacks, he walked over to the bench, took a large bottle of water out of his gym bag, drank long and slow, and sat down.

The gym was on the fourth floor of the seminary, with its view of the surrounding forest and Pittsburgh in the distance its only redeeming features. None of the retired priests used the facility, save for the large steam room, and the vast majority of the seminarians, either because of workload or a lack of interest, hadn't even set foot in the facility. Which meant that Gabe and a handful of professors and students had the place to themselves. Which was good, Gabe noted to Sister Jenny as he gave her a tour of the facility, since the equipment was tired at best, including such throwbacks to the fifties as Indian clubs and medicine balls.

Gabe had been practicing Krav Maga for six years. His current routine was to work out four days a week for forty-five minutes of punishing exercises that left both him and his workout dummy the worse for wear. While Krav Maga had a belt system like most martial arts, both Gabe and his tutor eschewed them, though his training partners, on the few times that he had trained with someone other than Benni the dummy, told him he was a mid-level black belt.

He had come to Krav Maga by necessity and chance. In the first week of his freshman year, he had been doing speed workouts on the school track when he caught the eye of the football coach who was running the team through heavy sweating two-a-days. The coach had sidled over to Gabe during his cooldown period and asked him if he had ever played football.

"Some," Gabe answered. "In middle school."

"What position?"

"Flanker."

"So you can catch?"

"I guess." He cocked his head. "Why are you asking, Coach?"

"Because my team's got everything I need to go far this year except speed on the outside. And you're the fastest kid I've seen at this school. He nodded over at the practice field. "Any interest in trying out?"

"No, but I appreciate your asking."

"Can I ask why?"

"Because I hate getting hit. In the games, okay. But I always hated practices with all the hitting. It just felt like practiced pain. Not for me."

When the coach nodded, Gabe started to pick up his training bag, which contained water and warm-down sweatpants. But the coach put a hand on the bag until Gabe looked up, asked him to wait there a few minutes, and sent the quarterback over to Gabe with a ball. The two boys talked, and then Gabe looked over at the coach for a moment and nodded his head. The quarterback stepped back ten yards and lofted a few soft passes. When Gabe handled them with no problem, the boy stepped back with each pass, putting more speed on his throws. Gabe caught most of them with ease.

The coach had seen enough. He walked over and nodded to the quarterback, who tossed him the ball and returned to the team. "What if I promised that you didn't have to get hit in practice, just learn the plays and show up on game day? Even if you don't catch a pass all year, you'd be helping us because with all your speed, you'd stretch the field and keep at least one defender occupied."

Gabe had asked for a day to think it over. During that time, several the players had approached him, encouraging him to join the team. Most had been seniors who would normally not be caught dead speaking to a freshman. The attention worked. Later that day, Gabe told the coach he was in.

Being on the team had immediately elevated Gabe's status at school. Being one of only two freshmen on the varsity team carried extra weight. And then the season started. In the early games, the other teams were surprised by Gabe's speed. The quarterback knew it was hard to overthrow him. Together, he and Gabe teamed up for nine touchdowns his freshman year and fourteen his sophomore year.

But the summer prior to his junior year he had made the decision to quit the team and concentrate on his studies, which included concentrated study of the New Testament and later, teaching himself Greek and Latin. His decision sat poorly with both the coach and the team, who made Gabe the target of their slights and then their bullying.

As part of his new interest in religious scholarship, Gabe had joined an interfaith dialogue group that had been formed and was chaired by a troika of rabbi, minister, and priest. It met weekly, and Gabe was the youngest of the group. When he started showing up at meetings limping or bruised from his run-ins with the football team, the rabbi, Shmuel Pressman, had pulled him aside and asked what was up. Gabe explained about the retribution and added that it didn't show any signs of letting up. The rabbi had nodded and gone back to the group discussion.

The next week, he handed Gabe a piece of paper with a telephone number on it. "This is Benni, one of my congregants. He's Israeli. His job in the IDF, the Israeli Defense Forces, was to train soldiers on how to defend themselves—or better, to take down their assailants—in any situation."

Gabe and Benni spent their first two years together working on Gabe's body and mastering each move, one at a time. At the end of the first year, Gabe's assignment was to pay a visit to his football tormentors, one by one. Since it was October, Gabe had asked if the assignment could wait until after the football season was over, which Benni had agreed to. The first week of January, three seniors, including the captain, hobbled their way to school, two with broken noses. After that, Gabe was left alone.

In the third year, Benni taught Gabe how to put his moves together into action, with Benni placing Gabe in increasingly difficult situations in terms of settings and number of attackers. The practice had taken an eighteen-month hiatus while Gabe studied at another seminary. But he had continued his practice on his own and had returned, to Benni's surprise, with stronger skills than when he had left. That left Benni free to shift from physical skills to Gabe's mindset.

"Technically, you're there," he'd said in his heavily accented English. "The skills, you got. The strength of your blows: above average. But Krav Maga is with the head. The body's job is just to be ready with the mind designs. So now we work on your mind."

Benni pointed at the dummy, a flesh-colored torso with a finely chiseled human head. It looked like the top half of an Oscar statuette. "That thing is good for the practice, but that's all. It's like one of those clowns you give your kid that pops back up every time you hit it. I don't know too many attackers who stand perfectly still and wait for you to hit them." He waved his hand, dismissing the dummy from the conversation. "Now we move from your body to your mind, because your mind is the pilot. The body is just wings. The question is, can you fly this plane, especially in bad weather?"

"If you're wondering whether I could put these counters and assaults to work in a real-life situation, I can assure you—"

"You can assure me squat," Benni said sharply. "You worry me, Gabriel. You know why? Because you're a good guy. You have the heart that bleeds. You believe in crap like mercy and second chances. In what I'm preparing you for, there's no room for hesitation or pity. You need to be quick and merciless. Which is where your mind comes in."

Benni pushed his face closer to Gabe's. "A friend of mine, he a cop back in Israel. Got this routine with new recruits to weed out the street cops from the desk ones. Takes just one day. By the end of that day, my friend knows who's who—and more importantly, so do they."

He took a sip of water. "First stop is . . ." He searched for the English word. "Slaughterhouse. Regular routine, they drive the cows into chutes, quick kill with a bolt shot into their temples, then their throats are slit. Since they're going to die anyway, the owners give my friend permission to let his trainees pull several of cows from the execution line and shoot them at close range. If you can't shoot a cow, you sure as hell won't be able to shoot a human being. Or you'll hesitate, and you're a dead man."

"Okay, but how does—"

"Next stop is the morgue, just so they get used to the idea of people who were alive but are now dead. Just like that. Final stop is slide show, where they see photos of gunshot victims of varying types. First photo is a small caliber suicide, peaceful face with a hole in the temple. Next is one where the cop shot at close range. They see an incomplete face: eye gone, most of a cheek gone, a chin and mouth not there anymore."

He looked Gabe directly in the eye. "A weapon is only as good as you use it. My friend's lesson to the new cops: Too many cops were dead because at the critical moment, they couldn't imagine themselves pulling the trigger and having the face in front of them explode like a melon."

Gabe nodded. "So you're wondering if I'm a street cop or a desk cop."

"I wonder if a priest, or a wannabe priest, can be a street cop. Same with a rabbi. Your life is about others first. That makes you suspect in my eyes. In my world, you can't think of the other person except as a target. You got to think of yourself first."

"I understand what you're saying, Benni, and all I can say with total assurance is this: I'm sick of being a victim, a human punching bag. I'm done with that. So let's get on with it."

Gaining what Benni referred to as the Krav Maga mindset took another year of training. Over that period they worked on situational response—which skills to employ in specific situations. Gabe practiced for unarmed assailants, both singular and multiple, for an armed assailant in close proximity, and for both indoor and outdoor attacks. At the end of that year, Benni pushed Gabe out of the nest, urging him to continue his mental and physical practice on his own.

At Gabe's graduation from his training with Benni, which took place over a pitcher of beer at a nearby tavern, Benni had both toasted and cautioned him. "You have the muscle skills and mindset. From here on, you don't do one without the other. Your arms and legs, they're musical instruments." He tapped his temple. "But your mind, he's the conductor. Keep it as sharp as your body. Whenever you practice now, you think real world. You think of an attack and your response. You don't react. Reaction is muscles. You assess the attack, and your mind's job, as the conductor, is to bring all your instruments—no warmups, no overtures—into a full blast. And remember: Never hesitate. Hesitation equals death."

Across the workout room, a man in a karate gi was moving through his forms. He looked to be in his late thirties, though the fluidity of his movements were those of a younger man. A brown belt cinched at his waist, he floated across the mat, his feet touching down lightly before springing into another set of moves. He never seemed to settle or gather, his movements graceful and precise.

After finishing his forms, he walked over to where Gabe was sitting with a towel around his neck. Like Gabe, he was rich with sweat. Keeping a respectful distance, he nodded at the battered dummy. "I've watched you brutalize that poor thing for the past few months. Still can't figure out what martial art you're practicing."

"It's called Krav Maga. It's the Israeli army's version of hand-to-hand combat."

"That explains why I never saw you practicing any retreat moves, huh? Everything was forward-moving."

"There's nothing defensive about Krav Maga," Gabe said. "It's aggressive from the jump. No rules. Anything goes."

"I know a number of martial arts, but this is a new one on me. Mind answering a few questions about it? Just a few?" The man extended his hand. "Andy Morgan. I teach sociology here."

Gabe eyed his questioner with caution. One of the things he liked the most about Krav Maga was that he could practice it alone, without a partner or class, and for the most part, in silence. No jock camaraderie, no cheering each other on. But this man was a practitioner, not a jock. Gabe appreciated that the man had approached him, something most men, Gabe included, wouldn't do.

"Gabe Russell. Biblical Studies. The first rule of Krav Maga is don't defend, attack. Don't wait to be sure of the nature or severity of the threat. Always strike the first blow when possible."

"And if you're wrong about the threat?"

"Then you're wrong, but you're alive. Second, disable or disarm first, then finish. Too many people go for a finishing blow too soon, resulting in disaster or death."

"Can you give me an example?"

"Sure. When you think about areas of vulnerability on someone attacking you, what comes to mind?" He raised his voice sharply. "Quick! You're being attacked!"

Flustered, Morgan looked over at the dummy. "Eyes. Groin."

"Which is exactly what your attacker is also thinking. So he's protecting those two areas. Which leaves the throat and knee exposed."

"And if they come at you from behind?"

"Same two spots, but use your elbow and heel. And if your attacker is too close to strike at them, you'd be surprised how painful an instep strike can be."

"You're right. None of those would have come to mind. But today I saw you concentrating a lot of your action around the face."

Gabe nodded. "The nose is a great target. Pop it once and their eyes water so much they can't see to hit you. Hit it dead-on, you break it and it bleeds like crazy. Blood is a great deterrent in attacks. Finally . . ."

Gabe stopped, picked up his gym bag, and started to leave.

"Finally," Andy Morgan prompted.

Gabe stopped for a minute and measured his words. "Finally, if you break the nose and they keep coming or they're armed, once the nasal bone is loose, you can use the base of your hand and drive it up into the brain. Death is instantaneous."

"Damn," Morgan said. "I've heard about that, but never practiced it."

Gabe nodded and picked up his bag. "Nice talking to you." And he left.

Nine

"SO, DANNY, HAVE THEY set a date for when you get your parish?" Jim asked.

The four priests and Jenny, now joined by Paul Reynolds, were sitting on folding chairs circling the desk in Gabe's classroom. Given the sensitive topic they were there to discuss, as well as the possible need of a whiteboard, they had moved their location from the local tavern to the classroom. There was a cooler full of ice and beer on the floor next to the desk, and everyone was on their first beer.

"Next month," Danny replied.

"I'm jealous," Michael said. "I've been trying to get out of the diocese offices and into a parish for the better part of two years now. The administrators there can't believe I want to leave. Everyone in the office except me petitioned for their placements."

"You should never have told them you were good with computers," Jenny said. "It's like when I was growing up. My mom told me to never tell anyone I could type ninety words a minute or I'd be a secretary all my life."

Michael turned to Danny. "You scared?"

"Shitless." Addressing Gabe, Danny asked, "Weren't you at first?"

"I was on a straight Imodium diet the first three months." He nodded at the chuckles, but his face was serious. "But it gets better. Doesn't it, Jim?"

"On that front, yeah. But eight years on, I'm still overwhelmed at least once a day, wondering what the hell I'm doing in this job and if I'm fit for it."

"I'm down to twice a day for self-doubt," Gabe said. "Not on the Imodium but on episodes of self-doubt." He looked at Danny. "Look, you're going to fuck up. Just try to make them minor fuck-ups."

"And know we're here for you, Dan," Jim said. "Unless you really fuck up. Then you're on your own." The rest of the group nodded in agreement.

"My guess," Gabe said, "is that the older priests have the same moments. They just have fewer of them and won't admit the ones they *do* have to rookies like us."

The entire group swung their eyes toward the veteran in the group. Paul, startled by the silence, looked up from the notes he was writing and nodded. "That churning-stomach thing that you guys are talking about, yeah, that goes away after a couple of years. But the moments of self-doubt, Gabe's right when he says we're just better at hiding them. From each other as well as from our parishioners."

Paul looked over at Michael. "Gabe tells me you're an essential member of the archbishop's team. My condolences."

"Do you know the archbishop?" Michael asked.

Paul nodded. "From when I was running what is now Gabe's parish. Frank was an officious prick back then, but he was only a monsignor. I hear that the promotion hasn't changed him much."

"Sounds like you knew him pretty well."

"Well enough to hate him. My parish didn't fall under his authority, but that didn't stop him from constantly opining on how 'loose' I was, in both my theology and in how I ran my parish. He was like one of those generals who rises through the ranks without ever seeing battle."

"Have you seen each other since you got back?" Jenny asked.

"Just to nod at each other across the room at university functions. It would kill me to have to call him 'Excellency' if we ran into each other. And I'd bite my lips off before I kissed the bastard's ring."

"So the two of you are close," Gabe said.

"Who says wisdom is the province of the old?" Paul smiled and nodded with his chin toward Michael's laptop. "If it doesn't bore you guys too much, can Mike bring me up to speed on what you've discovered so far?"

Michael tapped the screen. "Don't worry, you're coming into this movie just past opening credits. We're just getting started with our assignments." He turned his screen so Paul could see it. "This whole thing started with all the talk floating around about Ferguson. You know who we're talking about?"

"Not personally, but Gabe filled me in."

"Ferguson got us all wondering how bad this pedophilia thing is and how much of it might splash back on us. I told everyone I'd do some research for our next meeting. Which is tonight."

"Great. Then I'll shut up unless there's an area where I can contribute."

Michael placed his laptop on the table so the others could see. "If you're wondering whether Ferguson is a one-off or a symptom of something larger, let me share this gem from last week's Knights of the Cross dinner. I was at the archbishop's table with six other priests. The topic of Ferguson didn't come up, but in some ways, he was like the turd in the punchbowl. Everyone was aware of him but no one wanted to comment."

"Nice imagery, Mike," Jenny said.

"Anyway, later in the evening I found myself at the bar with one of the archbishop's guys, and he tells me, out of nowhere: 'Here's the sad truth, Mike. Ever since the sixties and the sexual revolution, the number of new priests has shrunk and the number of departures has risen. So if diddling a few kids is going to keep our priests in the fold and the Church functioning, it's the price we're willing to pay. I'm not saying I like it or support it, but that's the reality we're living in.'"

The room was silent as they digested the anecdote. Finally, Jenny spoke up. "What he's saying is that my kids are collateral damage, fuel to keep the Church functioning." She shook her head. "Bastards." No one said anything. "Sorry, Mike. Go ahead."

Jim intervened before Michael could continue. "Before you go any further, I need to say something." His eyes glided from face to face, never settling or meeting their eyes. "I've been thinking about this ever since we last met, and I've come to a decision." He let out a long sigh. "I appreciate what you guys are doing—especially you, Mike—but I'm going to have to recuse myself on this one. I've seen our archbishop in action, and as Mike and now Paul can attest, he's a vengeful SOB."

His eyes finally settled on Gabe. "Maybe I'm just being a coward, but I feel my parish really needs me. Good things are just starting to happen on some of the programs I've put in place, and I'm not going to be doing them any good if I'm in Nome, Alaska."

The table went silent. Michael looked at his laptop. Jenny looked down at her napkin and straightened it needlessly. Danny broke the silence. "I'm out too. I'm this close to finally getting a parish assignment. That's what I joined the Church to do. Not to be a part-time Columbo."

The group looked to Gabe, but Gabe's eyes were on Paul. "What's your take?" he said.

Paul nodded. "Jim and Danny are right. Power is everything to our esteemed archbishop, and he'll go after anyone who threatens that." He looked around the table. "You all should think about that before you go any further in this investigation."

Jenny spoke up first. "It's an easy call for me. I'm in. These are kids we're talking about, kids no different from the ones I've been teaching the past eight years. And yet it's like they're not even human beings to these bastards. So count me in."

As if choreographed, all eyes swung to Gabe. He nodded at Jim and Danny. "Before I say anything, I want to tell you two that I absolutely understand and respect your decision. No hard feelings at all. You've got to do what's best for yourself and your parishioners. In my case, I'm going to stay involved for the same reason: It's what's best for myself and my parishioners. Just at the local level, I need to know if there are any threats to them. From anyone.

"But it runs deeper than that. Our jobs require our parishioners' trust in the Church and in us as its representative. And in the case of pedophilia, if they find they can't trust the Church, then they have to at least be able to trust me. Which means I have to be on the right side of this issue." He nodded at Michael's laptop. "And I have to be able to prove I am. So I'm in."

"And by 'right side' you mean?" Paul asked.

"If the pedophilia scandal breaks and people find how deep and systemic it runs, without being too dramatic here, we're going to be like Germany after the Holocaust. People are going to want to know what we knew and what we did about it. And by people I mean not only the press but our parishioners. You don't need to be Nostradamus to predict that Mike's newfangled machines are going to let everyone see who knew what and when. And what they did about it. We can't pretend that we don't know what's going on any more than the Germans could. The Germans knew. And now so do we. When they write our history, I want to be part of the resistance, not one of the occupiers." He looked around the table, then blushed slightly. "Sorry for the self-righteous diatribe, but count me in."

Michael took a moment for the emotions around the table to settle. Then he opened his notebook. "Let me show you what I've discovered so far. Then we can decide who does what." He looked at Jim and Danny. "You guys are welcome to stay, but—"

"No, you're right," Jim said. "We're either in or out." He stood up. Danny hesitated for a moment, then nodded and got to his feet. The two priests left without saying another word.

Michael watched them leave and then turned back to the group. "A couple of things before I show you what I've got. First, the Church documents everything. It only allows access to a select few, but it documents *everything*. If it happened, it's been recorded." He tapped his computer. "Maybe in here. Maybe on paper. Second, when it comes to computers, these guys are idiots. It took me two minutes to get into Ferguson's email account and see all his connections. None of the guys he communicated with—and almost all of them were priests—had a clue how to obscure their communications. They used simplistic passwords or no passwords at all and didn't encrypt their conversations."

"Any chance they can trace this back to you?" Gabe asked.

"Not currently. The IT guys—the information technology guys, the ones who run the computers, printers and such—they're just one step from the priests in my office in terms of computer fluency. They're ex-seminarians who weren't deemed ready for either a parish or full administrative placement. They've got one job and one job only: to keep the computers up and running." He rapped his knuckle against the screen lightly. "But that's today. If the powers that be have any reason to suspect me tomorrow, they can elevate it to pros who could find me in less than an hour."

"Which means," Jenny said, "we can't give them any cause for suspicion. At least for now. Once we've got the bastards, we can be as public as we want."

"Okay, Mike," Gabe said. "What've you got?"

Michael knuckled the screen with a force that surprised everyone, himself included. "I started by following Ferguson's emails and who they went to. He sent one about his most recent 'encounter,' as he termed it, to six people. Five priests and a layperson."

"So one bad apple becomes seven," Gabe said. "Hardly an orchard. Isn't that how the Church would present it?"

"Someone took their analogy pill today," Michael said, smiling. "First the Holocaust, now apples and orchards. But since you asked," he said dramatically, tapping a key. "Here's your orchard."

The screen exploded from six data points into a spiderweb of connections. "It's a bulletin board. It's how these bastards communicate."

"I'm not as computer savvy as you guys," Paul said. "Can you clarify for me?"

"That's what made the discovery of this possible, Paul," Michael explained. "These guys are no more familiar with computers than you are." He nodded at the screen. "They're leaving evidence of their activities all over the place, like rat droppings."

"Another memorable visual," Jenny said. "Looks like Gabe isn't the only one who took his analogy pills this morning. So were you able to trace it back to the head rat?"

Michael grinned at her. "Meow, Jenny. The answer is a solid no. When it comes to computers and communications, this guy is as brilliant as his followers are clueless. I can trace the interactions between the participants, no problem." He pressed a key and a complex network of connections popped to life. "But your head rat uses multiple masking services, so his location and computer address change constantly and aren't traceable. He's slick. For example, look at this."

Michael spun the laptop back around and keyed in some strokes. He hit "Enter" and the spiderweb of connections turned into a simple screen with a ladder of messages on it.

"At the beginning of all this, this guy tried to get the other priests to use basic security tools that could block their identities and make their messages untraceable. He hand-fed them commands and destinations that would protect them from people like me. But most of his network have Paul's level of computer skills, so they kept screwing up even the most basic stuff. When that happened, they'd get frustrated and bypass the system, communicating directly with each other. Rat Boy realized he had to come up with a new approach that even a computer moron could use without setting off alarms. What he came up with was brilliant in its simplicity: a hosted private discussion group, like a bulletin board."

"I'm assuming you're not talking about the kind that hangs on my classroom wall," Jenny said.

"Similar, but electronic. Any of you guys ever used Schoolmates.com?" The table shook its head collectively. "It's how high school and college classes stay in touch with each other after graduation. They share news, plan reunions, and so on.

Our leader went to Schoolmates and created an imaginary class from an imaginary seminary. Then he invited Ferguson and his pals to join. Once they joined the private group, they could communicate to the other members in a forum that no one would ever think to visit, much less investigate."

"Communicate what kinds of things?" Jenny asked.

"Things that made me want to throw up when I saw them. Mostly files—video files—of their parties. Or private 'encounters.'"

Paul looked at the screen. "Jesus. Look at the numbers. So much for the bad apples argument. How pervasive is this thing?"

"There are thirty-six members of this particular discussion group," Michael said. "That's our starting number. But some of these guys mention having their own bulletin boards. Which means what we're looking at here might just be the top of a pyramid, a collection of leaders, each with his own bulletin board and set of followers."

Paul looked at the screen and the connecting lines. "I was in before I saw this thing, but now, what do you need me to do, Michael?"

Michael tapped a key and a spreadsheet with three columns came up. He highlighted the first one, which contained only five names. "Let me show you this and you'll see where I'm hoping everyone fits in. I'm starting with priests convicted of pedophilia. Hence the small list. All five were disciplined by the Church. None did any prison time."

The three others peered at the spreadsheet. "I don't recognize any of these names," Jenny said. She turned to Gabe. "You?" He shrugged, as did Paul. "You would have thought we'd have heard about it, either from the news or from gossip."

Michael nodded. "In all three cases, part of the plea bargaining included no public admission. And the archdiocese kept each case under lock and key. Hell, I work there and I'd never heard of any of them."

"If the Church is so good at protecting its pedophiles, why do you think these five were caught and convicted?" Jenny asked.

Paul answered her question. "Two things would be my guess. The first is that these guys were probably so stupid or so obvious that the Church had to ask. But they also gave the Church something to point at to show how serious they were about it."

Michael tapped the second column, which was twice the size of the first. "These are priests who are accused and under investigation. I'm spending most of my time here, seeing what the cops know and what the Church is doing about them."

He then pointed at the third column. "This is where I could use some help. This column is priests who have been transferred at least three times in the past five years."

"Smart," Gabe said. "I wouldn't have thought of that."

Michael nodded. "Here's what I'd like us to do. I'll keep pursuing the names in the first two columns, widening the search beyond the diocese. I'll give Jenny and Gabe access to the Church's mainframe, and they can see where this third column leads." He saw the panicked looks on both their faces. "Don't worry. I've put together a quick guide that tells you what keys do what and where to look. Anything comes up that you don't understand, give me a shout."

He returned his attention to the screen. "Very few priests are transferred that often. My guess is that a few of them were transferred for legitimate reasons—maybe a family crisis or something like that. But the rest, I think that's where we're going to find the real pedophiles."

"Where do I come in?" Paul asked.

"I'd say roughly half of my searches are fully computerized, meaning their complete history is on the computer. I think Jenny and Gabe will find the same thing in their investigation. The other half is the files in transition from paper to computer. If we're following a hot trail and it suddenly cuts off, it would be great if we could pass it to you and you pick up the trail on paper."

"This is right up my alley. I've spent the last decade piecing together documents and connecting dots across centuries, so tying together recent records should be a lot easier. And if it isn't, that'll tell us how serious the Church is about covering this stuff up."

Ten

GABE LOOKED OUT at Jenny's second grade class. Twenty-two eager faces stared back at him. Gabe had explained their upcoming First Communion, including walking them through the distribution of the bread and grape juice to allay the fears that Jenny said had been building all week. For many, this was their first direct interaction with a priest, and it showed in their faces. Some were awed, some fascinated, some frightened. At Jenny's request, he wore what she termed his "clerical casual" outfit for the day: Roman collar, jeans, and a sweatshirt with the school's logo and Latin motto on it. Jenny wore her standard outfit: layperson's clothes, the only identifier of her religious status a stiff modernized coif that swept her short hair back.

"Okay, that wraps it up as far as your First Communion goes. Any other questions?" A hand went up. "Yes, Ms. Alberts."

The little girl stood up. She was wearing the standard parochial school uniform: white blouse on top of a skirt with overlapping blue and black patterns. Jenny told Gabe the school looked like one large field hockey team. "Father Gabe, Bobby Sherwin says that we're cannibals because we eat Jesus's body and blood on Sundays."

Gabe looked over at Sister Jenny, who just raised her eyebrow and smiled. It was clear this topic had come up before.

Now it was his turn in the ring. He took a seat on a stool next to Jenny's desk and faced the class.

"Actually, that one confused me when I was your age," Gabe began. "But here's how I thought about it then, and it's still how I think about it at every Mass I say." He put his elbows on his drawn-up knees and leaned forward slightly. Many of the children mimicked his posture.

"When Jesus knew he had to leave this earth, he wanted his apostles—and people like us—to know that he would always be with us. And there's no closer way to be with a person than to be inside that person. And how does something get inside you?"

A voice piped up from the back row. "You swallow it?"

"Exactly. And when you eat something good, you get that nice, full feeling. And I think that was what Jesus had in mind when he came up with Communion. He wanted to give us all that warm feeling. That's it. Nothing to be scared about. No matter what Bobby Sherwin says."

This was the part of his job that Gabe liked the most, translating the core ideas and practices of the Church into terms and actions that his charges could understand and incorporate into their lives. He remembered his own early days with Catholicism and how harsh and unyielding the teachings—and often, the teacher—seemed. Those teachers, both nuns and laypeople, reminded him of the hall monitors in his middle and high schools, the kind of people who loved to find the smallest infraction and then levy the harshest punishment.

✟ ✟ ✟

Now that Gabe had his own parish to run and religious training to oversee and impart, he experienced for the first time the scope and impact of conservative parochial education. When he had first come to the parish, he thought he'd be competing with the public schools for students. Instead, he found a waiting list for the lower and middle schools. It was, according to Monsignor Keane, a testimony to the timeless value of a Catholic education. Sister Jenny, on the other hand, saw it as parents trying to protect their children as long as possible from the attractions of secularism.

Whatever the reason, Gabe was also surprised by how many parents from his working-class parish could afford to send their kids to these schools, especially since most families had more than one child in the system. That was until the monsignor explained that the Church had classified his parish as a "backbone" community, meaning its numbers had stayed steady, even grown slightly, as numbers around parishes in the rest of Pennsylvania and elsewhere continued to shrink. Seeing these backbone communities as the religious equivalent of fire breaks, the US Council of Bishops underwrote much of the cost, allowing the backbone communities to keep tuition remarkably low. As a result, Gabe found that over 70 percent of his parishioners had attended St. Mary's for grades K-6, and half of them had gone to Bellarmine for junior and senior high school.

St. Mary's, like virtually every Catholic elementary school on the East Coast, had long based its religious teachings on the Baltimore Catechism. The use of "the Baltimore" shouldn't have surprised Gabe. Despite his worldly airs, Paul Reynolds was a Church traditionalist at heart, so he'd been comfortable running a Baltimore school. Monsignor Keane, Reynolds' successor, was a Baltimore devotee through and through.

A holdover from the days of call-and-answer rote learning, the Baltimore consisted of a series of questions and simplistic answers students were required to learn and recite back to their teachers. In seminary, Gabe and his fellow students would jokingly pose Baltimore questions to each other, seeing which of them could come up with the word-for-word answers most quickly. One seminarian would stop another in the hall and ask, "Why did God make you?" And the answer would come back, almost reflexively. "God made me to know him, love him, and serve him in this world and to be happy with him in the next."

The Baltimore was also where Gabe's parishioners learned about the difference between mortal and venial sins—grievous versus slight offenses—as well as the existence of and distinctions among heaven, hell, and purgatory. While Baltimore Catholics made up the bulk and core of Gabe's parishioners over thirty, he was determined their children, who were now in his charge, would not become as rigid or as afraid of God as their parents.

In his first week after assuming clerical responsibilities from the monsignor, Gabe met with the nuns who ran the school and had them list the top five changes they'd like to see. By a long shot, eliminating the Baltimore and any teachings of a punitive God had been item one. Item two was modernizing their dress, eliminating the habit in favor of the minimal uniform Jenny was wearing today. Gabe had agreed to item two on the spot and told the sisters he would work with them to develop a new style of dress that would satisfy both them and the archbishop.

Classroom décor had been an item that required some finessing. For both financial and religious reasons, classrooms were spartan in nature. Children sat in rows of metal desks with polished laminated wooden surfaces, and there was not a single word written on or carved into the desks. The walls were festooned with religious posters and photos of the pope and archbishop. Gabe told teachers to consolidate all the Church photos and posters on one wall and open up the rest of it to the students. The result was a blend of religious iconography, cartoon characters, and photos of the current hot boy bands.

When he talked to the religion classes, both at St. Mary's and Bellarmine, Gabe was glad to discover that somehow, the kids' concepts of God and the afterlife were far more loving and accepting than that of their parents—and of the Baltimore. Heaven, for most of them, was a reunion with dead friends, relatives, and pets. Or it was an omniscient experience from which they were able to look down on all the world's goings-on, from their friends' bedrooms to the White House.

Hell was a touchier subject. Most parents, it seemed, had long invoked the concept of hell and eternal punishment as part of their parenting. Gabe approached this issue from the side, rather than taking it head-on. He spoke to the students of a merciful God, one whose nature was incongruous with eternal damnation. If required, he could cite multiple Biblical passages that supported his interpretation, but he believed the kids would conclude on their own that the absence of this loving God and the wonders of heaven was punishment enough.

Purgatory, most of his older parishioners believed, was a fiery place where your venial sins were purged from you. "Like you were placed on a barbecue," Danny said one day over beers, "and God takes you off at just the right time—toasted, not charred." There was no Biblical basis for purgatory, but since the kids never brought it up, Gabe left it alone.

"Now remember, your First Communion is also a time for celebrating another first. Who remembers the other one? Mr. Iles?

The boy leapt to his feet. "Confession, Father."

"That's correct. And you don't need to stand up when you talk to me. After all, Sister Jenny doesn't," he said, shooting her a quick grin. "Yes, confession. And who can tell me what confession is? Yes, Ms. Cummings?"

"It's when you talk to God in a little box."

Gabe looked back over at Jenny, who had turned away to hide her smile. "That's right. Confession is where you can talk to God. About anything. Something that might be bothering you. Something you're sorry about. And here's the deal: Whatever you tell God, it's a secret. From your parents, from Sister Jenny. From everyone. It's between just you and God."

A voice came from the back row. "But you're there, aren't you?"

"Yeah, but just to help in case you get stuck. And when you're done, I give you a few prayers to say to let God know you're sorry. And then he forgives you."

It was clear that some of the kids were following him, some not. "You know what a do-over is? Like in kickball?" He saw a sea of nodding heads. "Well, confession is God giving you a big do-over, as long as you're sorry for what you did. I mean, how cool is that?"

Gabe stood up, and despite his admonition to Mr. Iles, the class stood as well. He smiled at them and motioned with his arm over at Jenny. "And with that, I'll leave you in the capable hands of Sister Jenny."

She told the class to get out their notebooks and write about what they wanted to cover in their first confession, then walked Gabe to the door. "Proud of how you handled the body and blood of Christ question, aren't you?" she said teasingly.

"I was about to go into the difference between transubstantiation and consubstantiation, but I ran out of time. Speaking of which, Margaret DelVecchio and a few of her pals from the Altar of Mary Society stopped by to tell me about a deal they had with Monsignor Keane that they want me to honor."

"Do tell."

"As you know, they're strong believers in transubstantiation."

"You gotta admit, it's a helluva parlor trick—transforming bread and wine into the actual body and blood of our Lord."

"Margaret said to me, since I'm literally creating Christ's body, she and her friends are extremely uncomfortable picking up the bread because they don't know what part of Jesus' body they might be touching. You with me?"

"I'm already there. I just want to know what term they used for our Lord's genitalia."

"They went with 'man parts.' They asked if I'd go old school and place it directly on their tongues."

"And will you?"

"It's the least I can do to protect their delicate sensitivities."

"And that's why they say you're wise beyond your years." She smiled as he winced. "We still on for movie night?"

"Absolutely. You got the purse, so you smuggle in the beers. I'll get the popcorn. No butter, right?"

Eleven

"WELL, THAT'S SIX BUCKS and two hours I'll never get back," Jenny said. "You pick next time. Just no Pauly Shore or Jon Lovitz."

"That was one time. And I was sorry ten minutes into it. At least the popcorn was good. And the beer."

They were in a tavern two blocks from the cinema. Jenny was sipping a scotch, neat. Gabe was working on a tall mug of beer, its sides sweating. "By the way," Jenny said, nodding at Gabe's beer, "you don't need to cough to cover the sound of popping your beer in the movie. We're grownups now, in case you haven't noticed."

"Old habits die hard." He took another sip. "How's everything in room eight? The kids ready for their big day?"

"As ready as they're going to be. I think you talked a few of them off the ledge today. The true test will be how many show on Sunday."

"I enjoyed it. First Communion is one of my favorite days. They'll never be as pure in their faith as they are right now. I envy them that."

"Speaking of kids, this pedo thing is staying with me in a bad way. Not just Ferguson, but what we're discovering. These days when I encounter a priest I haven't met before, I wonder if he's one of them. And I look at the kids in the school, some of them *my* kids, and I think about some fat middle-aged fuck doing the things to them that Mike was talking about. And I don't just want to throw up, I want to get a gun."

She eyed Gabe over the lip of her glass. "Can I ask you a question?" When Gabe nodded, she continued. "How personal is this thing to you?"

"You mean, was I ever abused by a priest growing up?"

"Or any other adult."

"No. Not even close. You've met my parents. I had a *Leave It To Beaver* childhood. And all the priests I served were good guys. Never even a sniff of any of them being bent."

He took a long sip of beer and looked around the bar. It was after ten and the remaining patrons were all regulars, deep into their alcohol of choice. Then his eyes settled back on Jenny. "But you're right. It is personal for a couple of reasons. I don't think I've ever told you, but in high school, I got community service credit for working afternoons at a shelter for abused children. The evidence of the abuse these kids suffered wasn't just physical. That faded for the most part once they were under our protection. But the psychological scars showed no sign of lessening. You could tell that some of these kids—most of them, I'd bet—were damaged for life." His eyes left her face and settled on his beer. He put both hands around the mug, his knuckles whitening.

"Some of those kids," he continued in a husky voice, "you couldn't touch at all. They'd cringe or start shivering if you approached them. But the opposite reaction was also present. My most vivid memory is of a ten-year-old girl who used to approach me like she was twenty-five. She was so mature and so flirtatious, it was scary. And sickening."

"Must have been tough," Jenny replied and then paused. "You said a couple of reasons."

"You know that I played football back in high school? I didn't go out for the team, but they needed someone fast who could stretch the field and catch the ball. So they pressured me to play, put me at flanker, and we wound up winning City my sophomore year, which is a huge deal in Pittsburgh."

Jenny chuckled. "Even a field hockey gal like me knows about City."

"But when I got serious about the priesthood—reading Scripture and teaching myself Greek and Hebrew—I didn't have time for both. So I quit the team."

"Which I'm sure went over well."

He nodded. "When I didn't show for that first practice, Coach sent a group of them to talk to me. When I told them that my mind was made up and I was staying with my decision, they started in on me. Whether it was at the coach's direction or on their own, I don't know."

"What do you mean, started in?"

"Beatings, mostly. Four or five of them would wait for me after school. They made sure not to break any bones in case I changed my mind and rejoined the team. But damn, it was painful. And it was every day."

"Jesus. Every day?"

"Well, I got weekends off. But during the week, I felt helpless, and that feeling grew throughout the day as I wondered where they were going to catch me and what kind of pain I was in for. That feeling, but a lot worse, must be what these kids feel every day. Wondering each day if the priest is going to call them to his office. Or the sacristy. Or the rectory. And who among his friends he might have brought along with him to join in the fun. And some of these kids are so much younger than I was. So yeah, it's personal."

They finished their drinks, and Gabe walked Jenny back to the apartment she shared with another nun. The building needed new paint and some attention to the shutters, but it was what the two women had wanted, both in size and location. Situated in what real estate agents termed a "transitional neighborhood," it had its share of petty crime but had escaped the interest of the gangs so far. Jenny and Gabe ascended the twelve stairs to her doorway, and she gave Gabe a hug and a kiss on the cheek before going in.

Enjoying the balmy evening, Gabe strolled back to the rectory. It was almost two miles away, but he wanted to walk off the beer and have a clear head when he got back. The night was clear and the wind short of bracing, which were just what he needed. Many of the surrounding buildings were dark and some were abandoned, but the streetlights all worked and the sidewalks were clear, except for the occasional clump of leaves or cigarette butt.

He ambled rather than his usual brisk stride, nodding at those walking toward him, mostly couples or groups of teens chattering at each other. The relaxed pace allowed him to work out a critical scene from his novel that awaited him back at the rectory. He and Michelle were in agreement. He was forcing the action rather than letting it develop. The pace was hurried when it should have been deliberate, letting the scene take its time in both development and presentation. As he walked, Gabe came to the realization that the writing was rushed because he was in a hurry to get to the next chapter, which was fully formed in his head. With that in mind, he began to replay the scene in his head.

A few yards ahead of him, two men had stopped on the sidewalk to light a cigarette, one of them cupping his hands around the lighter's flame. As Gabe moved off the sidewalk to go around them, both men dropped the relaxed posture and slid over, blocking his path. The taller of the two produced a knife, which he waved menacingly at waist level, out of anyone's sight but Gabe's. The other man placed a hand on Gabe's shoulder, giving the impression to any passerby that this was just three friends talking.

"Here's how it plays, Jack," the shorter one said. He had a ragged haircut, an incomplete goatee, and rugged breath. "You'll reach into your back pocket and take out your wallet. Then . . ."

He stopped as Gabe extracted his hands slowly from his jacket pocket and raised them, not all the way into the air but with his palms next to his ears.

"Hey, hey, motherfucker," the taller one said, raising his knife to chest level. "Put your hands down. We're just three pals who—"

Without lowering his hands, Gabe shot his right arm out, driving the knuckles of the curled-under fingers of his left hand into the speaker's throat. As the man's hands flew up to his throat, his knife took a piece out of his own cheek, drawing blood. His partner's eyes were still on the blood when Gabe drove the palm of his other hand up into his chin.

As both men staggered and straightened their legs for balance, Gabe cocked his leg, turned to the side, and drove his foot into the left knee of the attacker with the knife. Then he repeated the move with the partner. Two audible cracks sounding almost like gunshots split the air and the two men collapsed. Gabe closed quickly to stop them from crying out, but whether from shock or disbelief at the sudden change in situation, the two men simply groaned and rolled on the sidewalk, clutching their shattered knees.

Crouching down between the two men, Gabe rested a calming hand on each of their shoulders and surveyed the street. The only people were on the other side, walking away from them, paying them no mind. "You're right, guys," he said in a low voice. "We're just three pals sitting here, shooting the shit. So here's my contribution to our conversation. And I'd like to make it without interruption or cries for help. Otherwise . . ." He pressed down with each of his thumbs into the tissue where the shoulders rose up into the neck. Each man winced, their heads turning toward the pain. Gabe released the tension but kept his thumbs over the tender spots.

He bent down even further, his voice almost a whisper. "You're going to be in the hospital for a bit. I'd use that time to make some big decisions." His voice took on an edge. "Such as the one I've got to make right now." The men looked at him with desperate eyes. "I'm weighing the value of your two lives against the grief and suffering I can see you inflicting on these good people in the years to come." He removed his hand from a shoulder and waved generally at their surroundings. Then he replaced it and pinched again for emphasis. "Now, I could kill you both right now and save the neighborhood from all that pain and loss. Or I could put you in wheelchairs for the rest of your life, which would put a dent in your mugging careers. Nod if you understand me."

Confused by the soft voice, the men didn't initially answer. But when Gabe pressed down slightly with his thumbs, both men nodded. "Now take out your wallets and hand them to me." As they did, he released his grip on their necks, reached into his pocket, and took out a pen and a small notebook. Once he'd copied down their names and addresses, he tossed the wallets on the ground in front of them.

"As you recuperate and consider your career options, remember this: I know what you two fuckheads look like. And where you live, which, by the way, is my neighborhood. That makes it personal." He lowered his face. "My brother is a cop. I'm going to have him run your names every few months or so. And if I see those names come up related to any criminal activity, I'll come back and finish the job. Are we clear?"

This time the men nodded immediately, but by then, Gabe had stood up and turned from them to resume his leisurely walk. Ten yards away, he stopped and retraced his steps. The two men scuttled on their hands like crabs, dragging their useless legs. Gabe stood over them and held up a finger. "And if anyone asks, especially the cops, I'm a bald, heavyset guy in his forties."

CONFESSION

"I put two people in the hospital yesterday. I'm not proud of it, but not ashamed, either. Faced with the same decision, the same two guys, I'd do it again. They're the type that not only hurt people, they damage them. And they don't give a shit. So my question there was how far to go to ensure they don't inflict this kind of damage again.

"Once you've been assaulted—mugged, raped, whatever— you're not the same. You're uncomfortable out in the streets, in your own home, in your sleep, in your own skin, even. That's the kind of damage these guys do.

"I remember my mom saying she thought rape should be a capital crime. Her argument was that rapists damage their victims so drastically—changing the way they live their lives and see themselves—that it should be a capital crime. I get what she's talking about."

He leaned forward and dropped his voice. "But what surprised and alarmed me a bit was how good it felt, both while I was doing it and afterward. It felt . . . clean. Especially considering how muddy my life is these days. When I heard those knees snap yesterday, that felt clean. I don't think I turned these guys' lives around, but I think I put the same fear in their minds that they inflict on their victims. And that's a good thing."

Twelve

MICHELLE RAISED HER WINE GLASS and swirled the rich red liquid, admiring the legs as they dragged their way down the side of the glass. "I've got no idea what I'm supposed to be looking for when I do this," she said, "but damn, do I look sophisticated."

It was evening, and they were in Reyna's, a four-star restaurant on the second floor of the Fairmont. The restaurant was a study in understated elegance with highly polished cherrywood tables as rich in color as any of the reds on their wine list. A series of overhead baffles swallowed the noise from the kitchen and the sound of people talking in the dining room, allowing for private, even intimate, conversations.

The invitation had caught Gabe by surprise. At the end of their Monday lunch, Michelle had said she wanted to take him to dinner on Friday to thank him for unlocking the talents of that semester's class. The assignment about the seminarians' most pressing concerns regarding their upcoming ordination and assignments had resulted in several excellent, searching essays. More importantly, their introspection had carried over into the next round of essays, to the point that it had the makings of one of her most rewarding classes. And she attributed a lot of that to Gabe.

Though he had agreed to the dinner on the spot, in the ensuing days, he had rethought his response and considered cancelling. To be sure, he enjoyed Michelle's company almost as much as he enjoyed Jenny's, but there was an underlying tension with Michelle that both attracted and worried him. As he had mentioned to Paul, he was keeping himself open during this period when he was trying to figure out if the Church was moving forward or backward. But in the quiet of his room at the rectory, when he was most honest with himself, he felt he was stepping into a river that looked placid but whose current was deceptively strong and capable of carrying him in directions that might be out of his control. His confusion and hesitancy reminded him of his high school days and what he called his cowardice in the areas of sex and drugs. This was another opportunity, and while it didn't call for an immediate decision, it felt like the moment of decision was just over the horizon. And this time, he had no idea whether he should jump in the water or stay safely on shore.

"Let me guess. Most of the essays had to do with women. Not in a sexual way but in an I've-got-no-idea-who-these-people-are way."

"Almost all of them," Michelle confirmed. "How to counsel them about things like birth control, abortion, sexual issues—things like that. Basically, women scare the hell out of them."

"They should. When it comes to women, every priest I know feels out of his depth, no matter how long they've been serving. I'm glad some of your students are recognizing this before they discover it for real." He smiled at her. "But remember, you're *my* Beatrice, not theirs."

"Not very Christian of you. Or sporting."

"Yeah, well, it's a jungle out there."

Later that evening, Michelle said, with slight hesitation, "Ever since you suggested that essay topic, I've wondered what your answer would be now that you're in the arena." She tipped her wine glass toward him. "So, tell me. Nine months in, what's the hardest part of being a priest?"

"I'd rather hear what you think of the chapters I gave you on Monday."

"And I'd rather be sitting here with Denzel Washington. Answer the question."

He took a sip of wine and savored it, taking his time. "This job has two parts. The first is ministering to the sick, the dying, and people in crisis. I like that part, and I'm good at it."

"That's what I hear. What's the second part?"

"Being God's representative on Earth."

Michelle looked at him skeptically. "Seriously."

"I'm being serious. The Latin phrase the Church uses to describe the role of the priest is '*In persona Christi.*' It means 'in the person of Christ.' The Church teaches and parishioners like mine believe that I'm Christ's representative on Earth and that he speaks through me. Not infallibly—only the pope can do that—but with unique insights into God's will."

"And all this time I thought I was just having lunch with a priest."

"Well, that's understandable. You're a heathen. Seriously, though, you don't know what it's like, counseling these hard-core Catholics. They're sitting across from me expecting some slice of the divine to come into the room. Me, I woke up this morning, looked in the mirror, and saw a twenty-six-year-old who's often in over his head. But it's clear they're willing to ignore their eyes and see someone who can interpret the will of God to them."

"Hell, that's a load for anyone, much less someone just starting out," Michelle said. "No offense intended, Gabe, but I'd want to see a therapist for my personal problems. And as mature as you might be for your age, you're lacking in real-world experiences."

"No offense taken. I feel the same way. But you weren't raised Catholic. For the faithful, it doesn't matter how old I am. In their minds, if I'm a priest—in this case, *their* priest—God is talking to them directly through me."

"How do you handle those expectations?" She held up a cautioning hand. "I'm assuming you don't feel God is talking directly through you. Or do you?"

"Hardly. If they're determined to hear directly from God in our meeting, I tell them it doesn't work that way and that I'm God's interpreter. Then I point out that interpreters sometimes get it wrong. They should hear what I have to say but make up their own minds. Usually I remind them of my age and say there's value in seeing a professional. But it usually doesn't register. I'm their last stop." He stopped and smiled. "What grade would my little rant have earned me?"

"A solid B. It wanders a little bit, but the content was compelling."

"I would have given me a C+." He paused, then smiled apologetically. "I'm about to change the subject, which I have no right to do since you're picking up the check. But I've got another favor to ask."

"I've never been asked a favor by God. Or his representative here on Earth. Ask away."

"I need you to expand your role as my Beatrice. Last time, I asked you to help me explain women and their poor self-images. You helped me out, more than you probably know. But the more I meet with my parishioners—and remember, the vast majority I see in my office and the confessional are women—the more I feel I'm babbling, throwing ideas together to make it seem like I know what I'm saying. But at the core, I'm clueless about what it's like to be them, which makes me feel like a fraud."

Michelle shook her head slightly. "You've got to cut yourself some slack here, Gabe. Even at your age, you know more about women than most men I know. And what you don't know, you're smart enough to ask. So give yourself a little credit." She settled back in her chair. "What do you want to know?"

"Let's start with the basics. Tell me the top three things we men don't understand about you womenfolk." He saw the look on her face. "I'm serious."

Michelle motioned to the waiter and asked for a pen and paper, then she pointed toward the restaurant entryway. "Go take a walk. Hit the bathroom, explore the lobby, whatever. Come back in ten minutes."

When he came back, a piece of paper sat in front of Michelle. A number of items had been crossed out and others had been elevated with an arrow to the top of the page. She looked up and smiled. "The trouble was knocking it down to the top three."

"We're that clueless?"

"Yeah, you are. And most men, as we've already discussed, don't know how clueless they are. Which brings me to something I was thinking about as I put this list together." She looked across at him and waited until he nodded for her to continue. "If you want to *really* do something for the women in your parish, do this. When a couple comes in, ask the woman the same question you just asked me. 'What do men need to know about what it's like to be a woman in today's world.'" She held up a finger. "And tell their husbands they can't interrupt."

"I like that. I don't think the couples coming to me are used to assignments like that."

She kept the finger strong between them. "But I need you to hear *this*. If you open the door to that conversation, you've got to protect the woman afterward. You've got to tell the men that if there are any repercussions from these sessions, physical or otherwise, it's a serious sin. And I'm dead serious about that."

"I can see that. Okay, good counsel. Now hit me with your list."

She didn't need to look at the paper. "Number one, talk *to* us, not *at* us. And quit talking *down* to us, for God's sake. We're not twelve." She tapped the piece of paper. "Number two, when we talk, just *listen*. Don't try to solve things on the spot. Guys think they need to be the expert or Mr. Fix It on everything. We don't need an instant solution. If there was one, we wouldn't be talking to you about the problem. So just shut up and listen."

She hesitated. "Number three isn't going to go down well in a traditional parish like yours. But it's this: They're *our* bodies, not yours. Whether it has to do with sex or abortion, the only rights you have in this area are what we give you." She took a sip of water and smiled sweetly at him. "Aren't you glad you asked?"

"Actually, yeah. This is exactly what I was looking for." He raised his glass. "Between the free dinner and the valuable advice, I feel like I'm robbing the bank here." He clinked his glass against hers. "Writing coach, then marriage advisor, now woman whisperer."

She looked at him steadily over the rim of the water glass. "Maybe the relationship could do with a little complication."

Over coffee and dessert, Gabe looked at Michelle over the rim of his cup. "How are things at home? And if it's none of my business, say so."

Michelle sat back and considered the question. Gabe stewed in the silence, wondering if he'd just spoiled what had been a very enjoyable evening. But when she leaned forward, her face was earnest, with no trace of anger. "What the hell. It's your turn to be *my* Beatrice." She paused, as if getting her bearing.

"Okay, Father. I'm not confessing, just giving you the lay of the land. I don't know if you've encountered this issue in your counseling yet, but John and I have a major difference when it comes to children. He wants them and I don't. At least right now."

"You're right. I haven't heard that one yet. In my parish, it's more a matter of how soon can we start and how many should we have."

"Then John would fit right in." She sighed, long and hard. "I want to be fair to John in this conversation. He's been clear about wanting children from the day we met. I'm the one changing the rules here. And that's not fair to John. I know that. But I need to be fair to myself as well. And as I look into the future, I realize I'm not ready to be a mother—and maybe never will be." Her lips pursed and her eyebrows raised as she awaited his response.

"Has this been an issue throughout the marriage or only recently?"

"John wanted children from the get-go, but I was determined to establish myself professionally first, and he agreed, albeit reluctantly, to a five-year window."

"Which you're past by, what is it, three years?"

She nodded. "And now the term 'biological clock' comes up in our conversations. Not nightly, but it's there, ticking loudly away."

Gabe motioned to the server for a refill of his coffee. When the server departed, he said, "I don't think I'm telling you anything you don't already know, but what I've learned over the past year is how essential the idea of being a father is to most men. And I mean essential. Most of the men I talk to would consider themselves incomplete—failures, even—without children. It completes their definition of family and of themselves. Even the deadbeat dads and the ones who discipline their kids with a coat hanger mist over when they talk to me about their kids."

"When John talks about the ticking biological clock and the need to get going right now, I tell him we can always adopt. But he'll have none of that."

"I'm not surprised. I don't know if we have any adopted kids in any of my schools. If there are, they keep it to themselves. It just isn't the Pittsburgh way. Everything here—the neighborhoods, the churches, the restaurants—is a reflection of your heritage. And an adopted kid will always be an outsider. I know how backward that sounds, but it's the way it is."

"Is that how you feel?" Michelle asked. "After all, you were raised here."

"You've got to remember, my parents are native Californians. They're existentialists, and they raised me to believe that the things that happen to us post-birth—the people we meet, the things we encounter—shape us far more than heritage or genetics. But the bulk of my parishioners believe the opposite. They want to look at their kids and see themselves, not just in looks but in customs and values. I'm assuming John is in that camp."

"Big time."

"Do you think it's a deal-breaker or is it something that can be resolved—or at least better addressed—with a marriage counselor?"

"If it isn't a deal-breaker, it's close. Same with the possibility of moving to New York, which I haven't raised yet. But you add the two of them together . . ." Her voice trailed off and she looked away, her eyes shining.

✝ ✝ ✝

After dinner, Gabe walked Michelle to her car, refusing her offer of a ride back to the rectory. It had been an interesting evening, and at times, a confusing one. He wanted to process it while it was fresh in his mind, and the rectory didn't seem the place to do that.

As he walked briskly along the busy sidewalk, stepping into the street briefly when things got too crowded, he played back some items from the evening. To start, there was the invitation itself—dinner instead of lunch. And was there anything to the choice of a hotel rather than a stand-alone restaurant? Finally, there was her cryptic statement about how the relationship could do with a bit of complication.

And then there was the hug at her car. Their physical contact to date had been minimal, so the hug had been new ground. And while Gabe was normally a demonstrative man, especially with his parishioners, the hug with Michelle had been longer and warmer than he had expected. There was no kiss, but the moment seemed to almost call for one, and it was Gabe who had ended the hug.

Reaching the rectory after a thirty-minute brisk walk, he poured himself a glass of wine and went upstairs to write. But he stared at an empty page for over an hour before giving up and going to bed.

Thirteen

PAUL DOVE, extending his body above the concrete court, and his gloved hand, fingers splayed, clawed only air. The blue ball skittered past him, coming to rest on the dirt surrounding the court. He and Gabe, both in sweatpants and T-shirts, were engaged in their weekly game of three-wall, a form of handball played outside on the concrete walls and courts used by tennis players to hit against.

Once the game was over, the two men retreated to the back side of the concrete wall, where they sat, knees up and shirts off, warming their back against the wall. Gabe reached into a small cooler and brought out two sports beverages. Handing one to Paul, he asked, "Did you get my email about speaking to my class about Vatican II?"

"I did," Paul replied, twisting the bottle open and taking a long swallow. "You know that's not my area of expertise, right? I'm sure there are other priests, like some of my dorm-mates, who could do a better job."

"Yeah, but you're the Church historian. You can put it in the context of Church history and policy. And you were about the age of my students when it took place. I think they'd like to hear what it was like. Hell, *I'd* like to hear what it was like."

Paul leaned back and lifted his face to the sun, letting it dry the last of the sweat from the game. "It was our version of the sixties," he said, his face still upraised, eyes closed. "Saying Mass in English, facing the congregation, the end of meatless Fridays—these were ideas that just made sense. It felt like anything was possible: married priests, women priests, acceptance of gays."

"What do you remember most about that time?" Gabe asked.

"This warm, confident feeling that I'd joined the right team. That's what I remember most." He looked over. "It was a heady time."

Gabe let Paul's thoughts settle in his mind. He took off his gloves and tossed them in his gym bag. "And then John died," he said, almost under his breath.

"And Paul came in, and I'm ashamed that he and I share the same name. The rest is history. He had no interest in modernizing the Church, and neither does John Paul. John Paul likes it fine the way it is."

"I'm sure John Paul wishes he could undo everything Vatican II set in motion," Gabe said. "My guess? When no one's around, he probably waxes nostalgic about the Inquisition."

Paul looked over. "Having second thoughts about the team you joined? It would only be natural. You're one of the more secular priests I know."

Gabe ignored the question. "What direction do you think the next pope is going to take the Church in? Especially in the area of social justice."

"We're back to liberation theology, aren't we?" When Gabe nodded, Paul continued. "C'mon, Gabe. You know the score on that count. Even if we get a reformer pope, they're going to keep it contained to Latin America, like a lab experiment. It's too radical for anywhere else, especially the US."

"What the hell happened to the idea that the teachings of Jesus should be the pillars of the Church?" The frustration was clear in Gabe's voice, as was the bitterness.

"Don't play the naïf with me, Gabe. Even if it wanted to, the Church could never get governments to rebalance the scales in favor of the poor. The first thing you learn when you get to Rome is that the number one guiding principle of the Church is power. Expand it where you can, but never do anything to lose it. If you hear about the poor in the halls of the Vatican, often it's in terms of the quote from Matthew that the poor will always be with us. The unstated sentiment seems to be that the poor deserve their lot in life. That's the Church you think is going to advocate liberation theology worldwide?"

Gabe sighed. "I know you're right, but the hypocrisy is just so galling." He looked out over the fence and into the trees surrounding the sports complex. "You know what I hope for? I know I'm Mary Poppins here, but I'm hoping that in my lifetime, we elect a pope with Franciscan values who shines a light on our cardinals and bishops living in palaces while praising the virtues of the simple man. I want that pope to quit raising money from the poor to build ornate churches."

He looked over at Paul and smiled bitterly. "You want pie in the sky? How about all those priceless paintings and statues in the bowels of the Vatican doing nothing. Slap a price on them and sell them to museums or private collectors—whoever will pay the most—and use that money to create programs for the poor that other governments could emulate?"

Paul reached into the cooler, extracted an icy beer and raised his eyebrows at Gabe, who nodded. Paul gave him that beer and reached back into the cooler for its partner. "You've got a lot of Don Quixote in you, kid. You know that, right?"

"I just want the Church to quit living in the past and see that its best hope—forget gaining power, I'm talking about survival—is to become relevant."

"And if it doesn't?"

Gabe thought for a long moment. "You know Albert Schweitzer?"

"The jungle doctor? Sure. What's he got to do with this?"

"Before he became a doctor, Schweitzer was one of the top Biblical scholars in the world. I still use his books in my class and in my research. He had this deal with God that he would pursue his own selfish goals until he was thirty. Then he would devote the rest of his life to service of others. True to his word, at thirty, he quit academia, went to med school, and moved to Africa to start his clinics."

"And that figures into our discussion how?"

"Once the new pope is installed, I'm starting my own clock. If in five years we're not on the road back to Vatican II or something as meaningful or progressive as that, I'll have to reconsider my calling."

Paul's face lost its half-smile. "Do you know how arrogant you sound? Or childish? That if the Church doesn't change enough to suit you, you'll take your marbles and go home?"

"I know how it sounds, Paul, and I'd never say it to anyone but you. But this is *my* life, and I'm not going to spend it, to use your analogy, tilting at windmills. If the new pope wants to preserve the status quo—or keep retreating—I'll just turn in my collar. The Church and I will part as friends. No harm, no foul."

Paul took a long pull at his beer, his neck muscles rippling. Then he looked over. "I'll say this for you, Gabe. Talking shop with you is never boring."

Fourteen

THE WOMAN RANG THE DOORBELL and stepped back, smoothing her clothing with both hands. Looking down, she saw that the gesture had produced little effect and shrugged. She was in her standard work garb: dark-blue jeans with no crease, a slightly wrinkled beige blouse, and a blazer that had been stylish years ago but was now just barely functional. In her late thirties, she wore her wiry-curly hair a little longer than shoulder length, tied back in a loose knot. Her skin was between bronze and cocoa, indicating a mixed ancestry. Her eyebrows were untended, her nose blunt and hard. Everything about her was solid and functional.

As she waited, she took in the house in a studied, professional glance. It was a solid two-story affair, rich in ivy and brick. The paint was fresh and the grounds—what she could see of them in the dark—were well-tended. Instinctively, she surveyed the house in terms of its points of entry for any burglar to access. There were a few she'd point out to the owners at a later date, if appropriate, but not tonight.

The door opened slightly and an elderly woman peered out. There was nothing welcoming about her. Experience more than age had pinched her face. Her gray hair was worn in a timeless bun, and her dress was an equally timeless black.

"Is Father Russell in?" the visitor asked.

"This is his residence," the older woman said in a condescending voice. "You can see him during his working hours. Morning Mass is at seven, confessions are—"

The inquiring woman flashed her badge. "Detective Carla Jessup. I'm not one of his flock. I'm here on business. Is he in?"

The woman reached for Carla's badge and put on the glasses that hung on a string around her neck. She took her time, scouring the badge before returning it to Carla. "Let me check." She shut the door, leaving Carla on the porch.

A minute later, the door reopened and Gabe appeared in jeans and a long-sleeve T-shirt with the name of a half-marathon on it. He ignored the proffered badge and motioned her in. "I see you've met Dolores. If it had been Juanita, you'd already be sipping coffee."

"Tell Dolores she can work the receiving desk at the precinct anytime she wants. Do you have a few minutes to talk, Father?"

"Sure. Would you like to come inside or would you rather go for a walk?"

"Inside, please. I've been on my feet all day. Also, I've never been inside a priest's house before."

"We call it a rectory. You're not Catholic, are you?"

"Lapsed. Early and permanent. Rectory, huh?"

"It's like that Steve Martin line: 'Those French—they have a different word for everything.' That's the Church. It's not a house, it's a rectory. It's not a ruling, it's a canon. It's not a book, it's a missal."

He led her into the formal living room, where a fire offered a welcoming warmth. There were two wingback chairs in front of the fireplace, one of which had a glass of wine next to it and papers scattered around its legs. Gabe motioned her to the other chair.

"I'm working on Sunday's sermon. And I'm stuck, so thanks for the unanticipated visit. Can I get you a glass of wine?"

"Sure. I'm only sort of on duty."

Gabe cupped a hand around his mouth. "Dolores? Would you be a dear and bring the detective a glass of the zinfandel? The good stuff." He looked over at Carla. "I'd get it myself, but this is her penance for leaving you outside."

They warmed up with small talk about the weather and the Pirates until a sullen Dolores brought a half-full glass of wine and placed it on the table next to Carla.

"Now, what brings you to the . . ." He smiled at her. "Rectory?"

Carla took a sip of wine and nodded her appreciation. "I transferred here last month. Whenever I get a new assignment, one of my first priorities is to get to know the bars and churches. And this precinct is over eighty percent Catholic. So here I am."

"That eighty percent number is deceiving, Detective Jessup."

"Call me Carla."

"Then call me Gabe. We Catholics are like the Jews. There are the observant ones and there are those who only see the synagogue on High Holy Days. My parishioners range from those who attend Mass daily to those who see the inside of a church at Easter and Christmas. I'd say it's split in half between the two groups."

"Yeah, but I hear that you're as much a beat cop as a priest, that you do a lot of walking around and listening to folks, Catholic or not. I'm curious about your take on this precinct . . . parish."

Gabe grinned. "You cops. You have a different word for everything."

Carla smiled as she looked down at her notes. "As the new kid, I'm open to any insights you can give me. Anything I should be on the lookout for, legal or otherwise?"

"How well do you know Pittsburgh, Carla?"

"Born and raised. My precinct used to be the twenty-second, two over from here. I was stationed there for twelve years."

"Well, then, I'm flattered that you chose our precinct for your new assignment."

"Don't be. I was transferred here. Over my objections." She looked at Gabe over the edge of her raised glass, weighing her next move. Then she sighed. "Look, this is going to come out at some point, so here it is. I was heading up the investigation into Father Ferguson. You're familiar with the good father?"

"Only by name. And the gossip, of course."

"I wasn't happy when the Church took over the investigation. Vocally unhappy, in fact. Hence the transfer."

She looked around the room, deciding where to take the conversation. "Look, Father. Gabe. I don't know if priests are like cops, but when there are pending investigations into one of our own, we close ranks, presenting a solid front. But behind the blue wall, we talk up a storm and analyze the merits of the accusations. All in-house, of course, but we talk." Her eyes firm, she stared at Gabe for a long moment. He looked back, seemingly comfortable with the topic and tension. "I'm not asking you to snitch, but if you hear anything about Ferguson that I should know . . ."

"I doubt that I'll hear anything. But if I do, aren't you off the investigation?"

"Officially, yes. But before they pulled the investigation from me, I'd assembled quite a bit of evidence against the good father. Which is currently sitting in boxes up in my attic. If I come to believe that the Church is serious about the investigation and not trying to bury it, I'll share my boxes. If it isn't, I'll hold onto them, on the off chance that the good father sins again. Do you know who the lead investigator for the Church is?"

"No idea, Detective."

"Carla."

"Carla. As I'm sure you learned during your preliminary investigation, the Church keeps its investigations secret. And its secrets even more secret."

"Then tell me this: If I were to deliver my evidence to the archbishop, would it be welcomed?"

Gabe thought for a moment, then said, "If you're asking for my advice, I'd say to keep your evidence safe, and don't tell anyone where it's stored."

"Thanks for the honest answer. I haven't gotten many of them when it comes to this investigation."

She took a last sip of wine and savored it. "Can I ask you one last thing?"

"As long as it isn't about my age, sure."

She smiled. "Then I'll be going." But she made no move to leave. "I'm curious. Is your youth a hindrance to you in this job? If I were still a Catholic and went to Mass, I'd expect the priest to be Irish with a drinker's nose, not some guy who looks like he just started shaving."

Gabe returned the smile. "Yeah, those days are in the past, for the most part. You're just as likely to get an import these days, someone from the Philippines or Latin America. If we relied solely on homegrown priests, half our churches would be shuttered."

"Huh. Didn't know that. Are there many like you out there, you know, who look like they're getting their priest merit badge?"

His smile broadened. "Not really. I think I'm the only priest under thirty with my own parish. The archbishop's office just found that out, and now their PR department is going to make a big deal about it."

"Well, since we're both relatively new to this parish-slash-precinct, I'll make a deal with you. You hear anything I should know about anything that feels off, criminal or not, let me know. And I'll do the same for you."

"Meaning if you hear the new kid, the one getting his merit badge, is screwing up, you'll let me know?"

"Count on it." She stood up. "Thanks for the wine. And the chat. Anytime you want to compare notes about our shared district, drinks are on me. We'll go to one of the local bars and give Dolores a heart attack."

Fifteen

"FATHER, I HEARD SOMEWHERE that you spent a year in a Protestant seminary. Is that true?"

As a number of hands came up, Gabe realized the question was of interest to most of his students. "It was more like three semesters, Mr. Merrick, but yeah, it's true," he replied. "I had taken all the Biblical courses this seminary had to offer in my first three years. My peers were all concentrating on theology, but I was focused on Biblical languages and history. My academic advisor knew the dean of the seminary at Drew University, a Methodist school. He agreed to let me study there in return for my teaching a seminar on Catholicism. It was a good deal all around. Why do you ask?"

"My cousin's majoring in sociology at Pitt. Her thesis is on contrasting the roles of ministry within different religions. She says the differences between ministry in Christianity, Judaism, and Islam are fairly clear. But she's having trouble articulating the differences *within* Christianity between the Catholic and Protestant traditions. Do you have any nuggets I can pass on to her?"

"In fact, I do. This topic came up in the course I just mentioned." He looked around the class. "You guys interested in this or should I take this up offline with Mr. Merrick? Hands. Who wants to see my brief but riveting presentation on priests versus ministers?" Virtually every hand went up.

"Okay. I'll digress, but only briefly. We need to get through the first half of John today. But to kick things off, what's the most critical component of your final year of preparation to become a Jesuit priest?" Hands went up.

"Mr. Fallows."

"The Spiritual Exercises of Ignatius?"

"Which I believe you're undertaking when this course is done, correct?"

"Correct. Starting in April."

"Can you summarize for those who are still a year or two away from the exercises what they are and why they're so critical to your development as a priest?"

Mr. Fallows took his time answering. "They're a four-week retreat we undertake with the help of a spiritual advisor. The first week is on the nature of sin and God's mercy. The next three all focus on lessons from Jesus's life and how to incorporate them into our life and ministry. The second week examines the life of Jesus up to his final journey to Jerusalem, the third focuses on the passion, and the final week examines his resurrection and ascension."

Gabe nodded. "Beautifully done, Mr. Fallows. And how does your spiritual advisor—I believe it's Father Marengo, right?—define the significance of the exercises?"

"As he's explained it, the goal is to deepen our relationship with God, to understand better how to use the role that Jesus plays in our ministry, and to help us interpret the will of God to our parishioners."

Gabe smiled. "You're on a roll, Mr. Fallows." He turned back to the class. "Anyone want to take a guess at what your Methodist compatriots are doing their final year?" The class was silent, their faces rapt. "If I just showed you their academic schedules, you'd think they were sociologists or psychologists in training. You'd see classes in marriage counseling, how to establish and run a youth center, and how to set up and run weekly Bible reviews."

He walked over to the whiteboard. "In my last month at Drew, I participated in a panel on the very topic that Mr. Merrick's cousin is writing her thesis about: the differences in the roles and responsibilities of the ministers in the Catholic and Protestant traditions. As I tried to make sense of it myself, I came up with this visual."

He uncapped the red marker and drew a large hourglass on the board. "This is the role of the priest in Catholicism, as I see it." He tapped the top of the hourglass. "This is God and the Church." He tapped its bottom counterpart. "And this is the Catholic faithful, one billion strong."

Then he drew a circle around the narrow channel connecting the two. "And this is the priest. His job is to be the go-between, the translator between the two. To interpret the beliefs, teachings, and rulings of the Church. And to represent the needs of the faithful to God and the Church. It's a helluva balancing act, representing one to the other."

He turned back to the board, this time drawing two long blue rectangles, one atop the other with six inches between them. "This is how I view mainstream Protestantism. Same two components: God up here, the faithful below." He then drew a stick figure beneath the lower rectangle, its arms touching the blue box. "First off, notice the physical position of the minister in Protestantism. He's not squarely in the middle of anything. He's under the faithful he serves. His role—or hers, since Protestants are a bit more enlightened that we Catholics when it comes to women and the clergy—is not to interpret God to his congregation but to push them closer to God so they can have their own one-on-one relationship with him."

He turned back to the class. "Most of the participants were surprised when I explained the Catholic model. Some of them found it arrogant that we priests could presume to assume the mantle of God—or Christ."

Mr. Mendes spoke up. "Father, how do you explain that two traditions founded on the same person and teachings could come up with such different approaches?"

"I've thought about that question a lot, Mr. Mendes. I think it all comes down to how and when each of them was founded." He saw the confusion in their faces. "Let me give you a more current example. See if this makes sense. Take just this century. Your grandparents were probably raised during the Depression. That event colors everything for them—what jobs they have taken, how they think about money, what they're afraid of. Now jump forward forty years to the generation that came of age during the sixties. What the hell do they have in common with the Depression generation?"

Seeing the confusion dissipate, he continued. "It's the same with religion. The Catholic Church started two thousand years ago when the emperor was considered a God and the masses couldn't read or write. Socially and religiously, they were told what to think and how to act. There was no independence of thought or action.

"Martin Luther came along, and he was living in something equivalent to our sixties. The printing press was making its presence felt, the Renaissance was in full bloom, and people wanted to think for themselves. He and his followers read the tea leaves and changed the role of the minister to one of facilitator: helping the faithful make their own decisions. It was a stroke of genius, and Catholicism is still trying to catch up."

"So what lessons did you take away from your Protestant experience?" Mr. Mendes asked.

"Two things: First, our model of ministry can easily slip into arrogance. I—and you guys—need to watch for that because arrogance and authority don't play well in today's society. Second, we need to invite the faithful to the party. Your parishioners will be more educated than any generation in history, and they're about to be even smarter as this World Wide Web takes hold. Answers like 'Because the Church says so' won't work with them. They respect Rome, but they're going to want you guys to think for yourselves and encourage them to do the same."

He looked up at the clock. "All right, let's get back to the Gospel of John, who has a very different version of Jesus and his teachings than his Synoptic brothers."

CONFESSION

"Things are heating up. Mike is being recruited by the guys in the cottage. They invited him over to watch Monday Night Football, which is their version of a gateway drug. He's begged off, but he says he can only do that a couple more times before they give up on him.

"I like to think I'm a pretty empathetic guy, but these guys have got me on tilt. Take their recruiting techniques. I understand about successive approximation and all that. But still, there comes that moment when, if I put myself in their place, I'm inviting a priest I barely know to join me in having sex with kids. I can't envision how I could pull off a moment like that.

"Same thing with the kids. I know the playbook— just a different version of successive approximation. But again, there's that Rubicon moment when I move from whatever bullshit theology I've been espousing to the kid to a request—or demand—for sex. And I'll probably have to be explicit. I was reading one of the online postings, and the priest was advising a fellow pedo to just take his cock out and tell the recruit to suck the sin out of him. No way I can visualize that. No fucking way."

Sixteen

DRESSED IN HER SCHOOL UNIFORM, her face earnest and fearful, the little girl knelt on the padded kneeler. Despite Jenny's preparation and Gabe's pep talk to her class the previous week, the girl found the darkness of the confessional claustrophobic and disorienting. The screen and the anonymity it promised froze her confession in her throat. As he had with many of the girl's second grade predecessors that afternoon, Gabe needed to identify himself from the darkness and joke around with her a little bit before she relaxed and began her confession.

"Bless me, Father, for I have sinned. It has been . . . well, you know this is my first confession. My sins are, I pushed my little brother down when he made fun of my hair. And I picked my nose in class." She stopped. "Is that a sin?"

"Which one? Knocking your brother down or picking your nose."

"Picking my nose. I know knocking Bobby down was a sin."

"Picking your nose, especially in class, is gross. But it's not a sin."

"Okay. And I tried to cheat off Paula Pearson's test, but she caught me and put her hand over it. Does that count?"

"You bet. Just because you didn't see the answer doesn't make you innocent. It just makes you a lousy cheater. What else?"

"That's it."

Gabe sat on the other side of the screen and waited. "That's it, huh? Nothing more?" He waited, but the girl was dug in. "Okay," Gabe said, giving up. "Then let's hear your first ever Act of Contrition. And don't worry. If you get stuck, I'll help you."

"Oh, my God, I'm really sorry for having offended you . . . thee. And I detest all my sins because of . . ."

"Your just punishment."

"But most of all because they offend you, oh God, who art . . ."

"All good and deserving."

"And you deserve all my love. I firmly resolve, with the help of your grace, to sin no more and . . ."

"Avoid the."

"Near occasions of sin. Amen."

"That was very good, Rachel. Your penance is three Hail Marys, two for the cheating and one for pushing Bobby."

"Only one for Bobby?"

"Yeah, it sounds like he kinda had it coming."

Rachel was the last of the class to make her confession. As she exited the confessional, Sister Jenny motioned to the class sitting in the pews adjacent to the confessional to stand. Gabe exited his side of the confessional to a collective "Thank you, Father Gabe." Then the class filed out.

Gabe waved as the class left and reached back into the confessional, retrieving a large plastic bottle of water. Hearing twenty-two first confessions had been more arduous than he'd anticipated. Unlike his adult confessions, where he did most of the listening, these first confessions had required a lot of coaching and encouragement. His throat was dry and ached slightly. He wished he'd conducted the first confessions in a separate session rather than at the start of his regular hours. Now there was a line of waiting parishioners—all of them women—looking at him expectantly. He nodded to them and returned to the task at hand.

It was a traditional confessional, a small box whose thin air was heavy with pain and secrets. On Gabe's side was a folding chair upon which he had placed a cushion, though some priests saw it as part of their own sacrifice to go cushion-less. On the confessing side there was nothing except the barely padded kneeler and a handle in the wall to help the older parishioners lower and rise. Months ago, Gabe had petitioned for a chair on the confessing side, but it had been vetoed by the archdiocese without explanation.

He had barely settled back into his seat when the door on the confessing side opened. Over the past nine months, Gabe had learned that the manner in which the door opened was a harbinger for the confession to come. A brisk, confident open usually indicated a brief, almost aggressive, confession—not so much an unburdening of a trauma as a completion of an item on a to-do list. A weak or hesitant opening meant Gabe had to work at carefully extracting what his visitor had come to confess but was too shy or nervous to articulate.

This time the door opened confidently. Gabe recognized the perfume before he heard the click of the door. His visitor launched right in. "Bless me, Father, for I have sinned. It has been two weeks since my last confession."

"It's good to see you again, Angela."

"Isn't this supposed to be . . . synonymous, Father? Aren't you supposed to call me 'my child'?

"It would be if you weren't in here every two weeks, my child. Or if you gave Monsignor Keane a chance to hear your confession every once in a while."

She dismissed the monsignor with a puff of air. "I like talking to you, Father. You actually listen. The other priests, it's like they're just waiting to get to the punishment part."

Gabe smiled into the darkness. It wasn't the first time he'd heard that, not only about Monsignor Keane, but also about some of the priests in the nearby parishes. One of his parishioners told him that some of the women from nearby parishes had begun coming to his parish for their confessions, and she had said it in a low voice tinged with resentment, as if she were describing "those people" moving into the neighborhood.

"We call it penance, Angela. But I know what you mean. I've had some of those priests in my own life. Okay, let's get to it. If you stay in here too long, people will start to think you're an actual sinner rather than the saint you and I both know you are."

Angela giggled, then righted herself. "Okay. I lied. Jeez, a bunch of times. More like fibs, really. And I had a few too many three times since we last talked. I kept count. And I thought bad thoughts about my mother-in-law. And I . . ." She paused, thinking hard.

"That's it?"

"I guess so. Isn't that enough?"

"I guess it'll have to be. Okay, my child. For your penance, say one Our Father."

"That's it?"

"No. For the rest of your penance, you are not to return to this confessional for at least three weeks. Or until you commit a mortal sin. Whichever comes first."

"Thank you, Father," she said in a slightly girlish voice.

As Angela departed, a hand gripped the top of the door, preventing it from closing. Gabe saw the outline of a woman framed in the doorway before it closed. The shadowy woman moved slowly and hesitantly toward the kneeler. She lowered herself awkwardly and gave out a small yip when one knee missed the kneeler and hit the floor.

Then she settled in and began in a clenched, timid tone. "Bless me, Father, for I have sinned. It has been three months since my last confession."

Gabe recognized the voice, despite its tone. "Your voice is different today, R . . ." He caught himself before saying her name. "Is there something wrong with your jaw? Did you just have dental work?"

"I had an accident this week, Father. I slipped on our walkway and broke my jaw."

"I'm very sorry to hear that. Are you in much pain?"

"No more than I deserve."

"That's an odd statement. Is there—"

Ramona plowed ahead as if she hadn't heard him. "My sins are, I am a poor excuse of a wife. I have only one job, and that's to keep the house and provide for my husband. And I can't even seem to get that right."

"I doubt very much that you're a poor excuse for a wife, as you put it. We'll get to that in a minute. Can you give me some examples of why you have such a harsh opinion of yourself?"

"After all these years, I should know what my husband wants," she said, her voice having the feel of broken glass. But as she continued, her tone steadied and the words became rote. "I should anticipate his needs and provide for them. In the kitchen, in the bedroom, with what I wear. But I just do the bare minimum. And he deserves better than that."

"I'm hearing your voice, my child, but I'm not sure those are your words. They sound like something an angry husband would say. I want to hear what you think, not what he does."

"No, they're my words, Father. I can't seem to do anything right. And after all this time, if I can't do it, it must be because I don't want to. And that makes it a sin, doesn't it?"

"This isn't a question of sin, my child. It's one of communication, and it's a longer conversation than this confessional can accommodate. It would be better if you—or better, you and your husband—came in and talked to me. Or saw a marriage counselor."

Ramona issued a slight chuckle through the wired teeth. "I can assure you that neither of those things are going to happen, Father. No, this is on me."

"Then *you* come see me, Ramona. At the very least, we can work on ways to make you a little safer at home. Because this is proving to be a very dangerous neighborhood. All those falls on dangerous driveways and stairs. And the odd thing about it is that it's always women who do the falling. We need to see what we can do about that. Do you understand me, Ramona?"

"I do, Father. But marriage is twenty-four hours a day, 365 days a year. You can't be de-icing my sidewalk every day, so to speak. Do *you* understand *me*, Father?"

Gabe sought a rejoinder but had none. He sighed, louder than he'd intended. "I do. Okay, then, here's your penance. When you leave here, before you go home, sit down in the pew and tell yourself ten times how great you are and how lucky all the people in your life are to have you. Especially Eddie. And when you get home, I want you to sit somewhere quiet and say it again. Ten times. Okay?"

An hour later, he heard the door close as his last parishioner exited the confessional. Checking his watch, he saw he had time for a light Krav Maga workout before catching the Pirates game at one of the bars where they knew him, but not as a priest.

Except the door didn't close completely. The wheezing sound stopped short of the click and then began again as the door opened. Gabe sighed and sat back down.

A hard, rushed male voice started in as the man was still kneeling down. "Bless me, Father, for I have sinned. It's been, I'd say, six months since my last confession." It was a voice Gabe thought he knew, but not from the confessional. He put it aside for the time being knowing it would come to him.

"Six months. Have you been busy all that time or just sinless?"

The man frowned at the screen. "A little of each, I guess. Anyway, my sins are, I cheated in cards a couple of times, overcharged a few customers at the garage, and was a little too rough on my wife."

"Let's talk about the cards and the garage for a minute. I mean, there's cheating and there's cheating, right? There's cheating an old lady out of her life savings. But the kind of cheating you're talking about, I put that in the caveat emptor category. Ever heard of it?"

"Is it a new prayer?"

"It means people should know better. The guys in your poker game know you, probably even know you're cheating. Right?"

The voice lost its wariness. "Right."

"And anyone who brings a car into a garage should do their homework ahead of time and know what things cost. Otherwise, they're suckers, and you can charge them whatever you want."

"That's how I see it."

"That's bullshit, pal. Both cases. And you know it. These aren't 'oops' sins, the kind where you screw up and are sorry right away. You plan these sins in advance. Maybe that's okay with your pals, but your customers trust you."

"Listen, Father. Just because—"

Gabe jumped in. "Hey, if I'm wrong here, tell me and I'll apologize." There was a long pause with nothing coming from the other side of the screen. "Then knock the cheating off. I'm serious. Okay, now tell me what you mean by when you say you were a little rough with your wife."

"Well, we got in an argument. You know how these things go. And she tried to slap me. I pushed back and she fell. And I feel really bad about that."

"Well, remorse is important, especially if it's real and not just something to get God off your back. But here's the deal: For confession to really work, for you to be truly forgiven, it has to be based on truth. So I need to know if this is the first time you've put hands on your wife."

There was a shifting sound as the man started to leave, then thought better of it and settled back on his knees. But his voice took on steel and anger. "This isn't how it works with the monsignor."

"Then I'd suggest you wait and do your confession with him. He'll be here on Friday."

"It can't wait. I'm heading on a week-long road trip with my cousin tomorrow, and I want a clean soul in case we get in an accident or something."

"A clean soul? Like the milk bottle the nuns used to teach?"

"I know my catechism. My soul's gonna be pure white when I leave here today. Maybe it'll get a little dirty with small sins, but it's only moral sins that can—"

"It's mortal sins, but go on."

"It's mortal sins that can turn it black. And if I get hit by a truck while it's pure white—like on my way home tonight—then I go straight to heaven. No purgatory even."

"Well, if that's what you were taught, then I'll honor the terms. But I still need to know a bit more about pushing your wife. It sounds like a onetime thing, since you feel so bad about it."

There was some hesitation before he spoke again. "Well, not actually. But it's the first time it was big enough to be a sin."

"Meaning what?"

"Meaning she had to go to the hospital."

Realizing now that he was talking to Eddie, Ramona's husband, Gabe leaned forward, now on high alert. Eddie was not a churchgoer, but Gabe had met him out on his stoop a few times during his neighborhood walk-arounds. He and his brothers were talking trash to passersby and had toned the language down only slightly when they saw Gabe.

"And what did you learn from this incident?"

"To go a little easier next time, even if she gets out of line."

Gabe remembered the tremor in Ramona's voice, not three hours earlier. The helpless tone as she considered her options and came up empty.

"Let me ask you this. Do these incidents happen often or only after you've had a few?"

There was a slight relief in Eddie's tone. "Mostly when I've had a few."

"Okay. I think I'm getting it. Let's look at it this way: Do you remember your Act of Contrition?"

"My what?"

"The prayer at the end of confession, right before you get your penance."

"Oh, that. Yeah, but the monsignor usually helps me a bit."

"For today, let's jump to the end. Do you remember the part that starts 'I firmly resolve with the help of thy grace?'"

Eddie jumped in eagerly. "I remember that part. To sin no more and to . . ."

"Avoid the near occasions of sin. Gabe paused to let the words sink in. "Those are two separate things. The first is to sin no more. Can you promise me there'll be no more laying of hands on your wife? Or any other woman, for that matter?"

"I'll try, Father. But you don't know what it's like to be married. They know how to push your buttons."

"And that merits a trip to the hospital?" Gabe waited for a response, but Eddie was dug in. "Okay," Gabe said finally. "Now here's the second part: the near occasions of sin. It means to stay the hell away from things that might lead you to sin. You get where I'm going?"

"Sort of."

"Let me give you an example. Say a guy comes in and tells me he likes to molest kids after being on one of those online porn sites. If he's serious about quitting his behavior, what should he do?"

"Get rid of his computer. I'll tell you, Father, if I ever caught one of those pervs near my kids or their school—"

"*Your* near occasion of sin is booze. You just told me the only times you hit your wife are when you've got a load on. So if you're truly sorry and determined never to hit her again, you'll quit drinking."

"Listen, Father—"

"But I wasn't born yesterday. I know how important it is to have a few with the boys after a long day."

"You got that right."

"So here's the deal. If you want to leave on your trip with a pure white milk bottle, then you have to promise me that when you've had a few too many, you will stay over with one of your pals. You don't go home. Can you promise me that?"

"I'll try. But you have to—"

"You have to do more than try. You have to promise me, right here in front of God, that if you tie one on, you will stay with your pals."

This time Eddie made it to his feet. "Hey, I know my rights. If I'm sorry, you have to forgive me. Let's get the monsignor over here right now and work this out."

"I'd love nothing better, but I've got to get to the hospital for evening Mass. Let's make this deal: I'll give you your penance, since you seem so remorseful. It's twenty Our Fathers and twenty Hail Marys, by the way. And let's part friends."

"Meaning what?"

"Meaning take your business to another parish from now on. Or another priest."

Seventeen

THE TWO MEN sharing the hospital room were orthopedic twins, each sitting up slightly in his bed, his left leg straight, elevated, and encased in plaster. It being the first time for either in a hospital, they appreciated much about their new surroundings, including the food, especially the pudding cups. The perk that most impressed them, though, was their ability to self-medicate with a simple depression of their thumb, causing morphine to creep into their veins.

The door opened and Carla peeked her head in. Seeing that the two men were alone, she eased herself into the room, a look of sympathy plastered on her face. She extracted her notebook and consulted it before speaking. "Mister Gentry and Mister Flanders, I'm sorry to be meeting under these circumstances." She unhooked the badge secured on the front of her belt and flipped it open as she raised it for their examination. Before they could focus on it, she flipped it shut and clipped it back on her belt.

"I'm Detective Carla Jessup. I was here on another case, and a nurse told me about you two and your unfortunate accident. She said you guys were being chased by a gang and had to jump off a wall to escape. And since this incident took place in my precinct, here I am."

She opened her notebook and looked at it for a moment. "Let me make sure I've got this straight. You both landed on the same leg." She nodded at their suspended legs. "And both of you shattered your knees." She gave them a sympathetic look. "Ouch. I mean, what are the odds of that happening? You should submit this to *Ripley's Believe It or Not*—get something out of it, at least."

The two men stayed silent. Carla let it build until the one on the left filled the void. "Well, shit happens."

"Boy, does it ever. You know, I'm glad you said that because I love that phrase. It explains so much. But here's the deal, guys. When shit happens in my precinct, especially mysterious shit, I get curious. I need to see what I can do about it, especially when it involves both a gang and a hazardous setting. For example, maybe I need to get a fence or signs put up around that dangerous wall you guys jumped from." She gestured at her notebook. "Can you guys tell me where this wall is located so I can check it out, or has the trauma of your fall dulled your memories?"

She pulled up the only chair in the room and placed it at the foot of the two beds. Then she waited. After two minutes of silence, the other one, the one with the bad haircut and goatee, spoke up. "No offense, Sarge, but don't you have better things to do with your time?"

"Sarge. I wish." She leaned closer and lowered her voice in conspiracy. "Guys, can I share a secret with you? I know how to use a computer. Marvelous things. You hit a few keys and they spit facts back at you. When the nurse told me your story, I keyed in your names." She held up two pages filled with type. "You guys are two of my more active citizens. Mostly petty stuff, to be sure. A conviction here or there, but mostly cases that never made it to court because of witnesses changing their minds. With some persuasion on your part, I'm sure." She put the pages down. "In short, the usual street punk crap. But no real violence. Until now. What happened? You finally pick on someone who knew how to fight back?"

She corrected herself. "I should say some *ones*. It had to be more than one person to do this kind of damage to a couple of street-wise guys like you two."

The two men exchanged glances. Then Flanders, the one on the left spoke up. "It was just one guy, but he came up on us from behind."

"Big guy, heavyset in his forties," Gentry added, looking over at his friend, who nodded. "And bald."

"I was just about to ask for a description, so thanks for that. He came at you from behind, you say?" Both men nodded. Carla adopted a puzzled look. "Then how'd you get such a clear look at him? And how come all the damage came from in front?" She raised a hand. "Just trying to get my bearings here, guys."

"He had some kind of Romulan move, where he touched our necks and paralyzed us," Flanders said, Gentry nodding in support. "Then he came around front and did this to us," he added, nodding at his leg.

"That sounds unfair, paralyzing you like that. Otherwise, I'm sure either one of you could have torn him apart in a fair fight. Am I right?"

The two men looked at each other, uncertain of her tone. She was either new to her job or fucking with them. They couldn't tell which, but having spent enough time around police officers, both knew the best course of action was silence. They kept their mouths shut and their faces empty.

Carla stood up and flipped her notebook shut. "Okay, boys, I'm off. You've both been a big help. It shouldn't take me long to find your assailant. I don't know that many forty-year old heavyset bald guys who know Romulan moves."

Eighteen

THE TWO PRIESTS entered the high school track through the open gate, their pace strong, their strides even. The running singlets clung to their bodies, the sweat forming a large half-moon, starting at the top of their shirts and working down to their navels. They had started at the seminary, running the first few miles through the forest that backed up to the chapel. The path was well-trodden but narrow, forcing the two men to run single file. The trees were heavy with leaves, as if readying themselves to drop once autumn gave them the signal.

By mutual agreement, Paul was in charge of designing the routes for their runs. He generally chose a different route for each outing, saying he was determined to see as much of Pittsburgh as possible before he left. Given that most runs were unique, he carried a three by five card with the route in his left hand. After the tenth such run, Gabe had chided him, saying that he seemed determined to cross every one of the city's 446 bridges, an allegation that drew only a small shrug in response. But that day, Paul had reverted to their favorite route, through the Allegheny Cemetery. With its hills, proximity to the river, and eclectic wildlife, it was a welcome change from their urban runs.

The track they entered was well cared for, with the surrounding buildings showing new coats of paint. Both the girls' and boys' track teams were out on the field, with activity concentrating around the high-jump and pole vault pits.

"What's your pedometer say?" Paul asked Gabe as they jogged around the track, cooling down.

"A little over six miles. Just short of a 10K."

"Some speed work to finish up?" Paul nodded at the track ahead of them. Before Gabe could answer, Paul took off, his speed impressive for his age. Gabe caught up to him halfway around the track and the two continued apace, Paul pulling ahead slightly at the finish. They slowed to a walk, then ambled over to the bleachers and sat down.

"Bastard," Paul said, regaining his breath. "I saw you slow down at the end, letting me win."

"Just trying to lessen my time in purgatory."

They sat together in companionable silence, both of them resting their forearms on their knees, letting the sweat drip down from their chins. Without looking up, Paul said, "How are the dreams coming? I'm asking out of prurient interest, not as your mentor."

"I thought you hated that word."

"I do, but if it gets you to open up about naked women and orgies, I'll use it."

"In that case, I'm going to find out what the Pink Pussycat charges and charge you the same rate," Gabe replied. "As for the dream, it's getting more explicit. My partner now has a face. It's Michelle, the teacher I was telling you about. I'm not surprised. She's attractive, and I've had a bit of a crush on her for years now. As have most seminarians."

"Any danger of your acting on that crush? Living out the dream?"

"The truth? I don't know. If the occasion arose, I don't know what I'd do. I hate to sound like Father Zen here, but my most honest answer is, I'd probably act within the moment." He looked over at Paul. "You ever fall off the wagon, sexually speaking?"

"No. I came close a couple of times back in my thirties. But once I got past them, it's been smooth sailing."

After a few minutes they stood up and stretched their hamstrings on the bleacher railing. "Something on your mind?" Paul asked, looking over. "This isn't our usual day to run."

"I've got a question I think I know the answer to, but I'll ask it anyway." He leaned into his stretch, watching the sweat drop from his chin into a small pool at his feet. "How sacred is what we hear in the confessional?"

"That's an easy one. And you're right. You already know the answer. It's absolute."

"But aren't we in the same position as lawyers and therapists? If we believe the person is a threat to themselves or others, don't we have an obligation to report them to the appropriate authorities?"

Paul looked over with understanding eyes. "I'm sympathetic, Gabe. But this is a topic I've spent some time studying, tracing it back through our history. And the Church is adamant about the sacred nature of the confessional. Hell, we've had saints who were martyred rather than disclosing such secrets."

"Huh. I didn't know that. I thought I knew most of the saints."

"Well, I'm exaggerating a bit to make my point. But the answer doesn't change. What we hear in the confessional is absolute in terms of privacy." He looked over. "Sorry, pal."

"What if someone confesses to me that they're going to kill someone? What do I do then?"

"Theologically, you're screwed. I know how that sounds, but it's Church policy. If what you're talking about is real, rather than one of those what-if questions for your class, your only resource is to use the confession to talk the person out of whatever they've disclosed they're about to do. Or thinking about doing."

"Then can I at least put the fear of God in them by saying that once the sin has been committed, if real damage is done, I'm free to go the police about it?"

"You can try that and hope that your parishioner doesn't out you to the archbishop and his henchmen, in which case you're in deep trouble." He looked over and winked. "Having a good time?"

Gabe smiled in spite of himself. "The more comfortable I get in the confessional, the more comfortable my parishioners are in sharing things. Which is a knife that cuts both ways. It's only a matter of time before I wind up with the hypothetical I just posed you. And when that happens, I don't know what I'll do."

"Oh, I think you do," Paul said. "You just won't like it. Or yourself."

Nineteen

GABE FINISHED HIS LECTURE on the infancy narratives in the gospels and turned to the class. "Any Stump the Chump questions for today?" No hands went up. "Okay, then I'll give you a freebie to amaze and amuse your friends. Since our topic today had to do with amazing births, which person in the Bible, outside of Adam, had no parents?" He gave them a moment before turning and writing on the board "Joshua, son of Nun." He let their groans settle and then asked, "So what's on your minds?"

Jeremy Haskell raised his hand. He was one of the older men in the class, having received his calling after a stint in the military. He still had the military buzz cut and upright posture of his previous calling. "Today's lecture reminded me of something I've wondered about for a while. Why does the Church put so much more emphasis on Mary and virginity than Protestants do?"

"You're right, Mr. Haskell, that one's a puzzler. Think about how many Catholic churches are named for Mary. Now find me a single Protestant church with Mary in its name. And that's in the US. Go to Latin America and you'll find that Mary is almost as popular a figure as her son. I can't explain either discrepancy, either between us and the Protestants or between us and Latin

American Catholics. But for the virginity part of your question . . ." He paused. "I've got a mini-lecture I was going to do during week eighteen, but we'll get to it now."

He unscrewed the cap of his plastic water bottle and took a large sip of water. Looking out at his students' faces, he could tell this was a topic of interest. "Many of you have asked why I spent—and still spend—so much time learning Greek and Hebrew. Well, you're about to find out, because the concept of virginity and its Biblical basis has as much to do with language as with theology."

He wrote a single Hebrew word on the board, then wrote "Isaiah 7:14" next to it. "The Church bases its teachings about virginity on the narratives we just analyzed, about Mary's conception and her virginity. But it goes back further, seven hundred years back, in fact, to our friend Isaiah."

He surveyed the class for a moment. "Okay, pop quiz. Remember how, on the first day of class, I said the gospels were not historical documents, but rather . . ." He motioned for them to finish the sentence.

"Propaganda," one voice rang out.

"Brochures," another said.

"Now let's return to Mr. Haskell's question about virginity and examine how the different evangelists approached this topic and that of Jesus's birth. Let's start with Mark, the earliest of the gospels. Surprisingly, he has nothing to say about Jesus's birth. Not a word. He begins his gospel with Jesus in his thirties and his meeting with John the Baptist. So the earliest gospel either had no knowledge of the stories surrounding Jesus's birth or didn't find them relevant to his narrative.

"Now let's look at John, who came along fifty years after Mark. He opened his gospel with: 'In the beginning was the Word. And the Word became flesh and dwelt among us.' You couldn't get any further from Mark if you tried. If Mark's Jesus was a man with unique insights and teachings, John's Jesus is God barely disguised by his human skin."

He could see that the entire class was caught up in his narrative. "Which brings us back to our friends from today's narrative, Matthew and Luke. Go back to my opening lecture. Who was Matthew writing for? Anyone?"

Mr. Hernandez answered that one. "The Jews."

"Correct. And what were the Jews of Jesus's time most fixated on?"

"The coming of the Messiah," answered Mr. Hernandez again.

"Mr. Hernandez is correct. The Messiah has always been a critical component of Hebrew Scripture, and the first century was a time of political and religious unrest, the kind of time crying out for the Messiah. Matthew's job, as he saw it, was to tell them that the Messiah had already come, but that everyone except the early Christians missed it. As proof, Matthew refers repeatedly to the Old Testament as proof of Jesus's messiahship. In fact, he uses the term 'this is to fulfill the Scriptures' twenty times."

He turned back and pointed with his marker at the board. "So let's look at Isaiah's verse through Matthew's filter. Mr. Haskell, since you opened this can of worms, read this verse to us."

Haskell looked in his Bible, found the verse, and read, "'The virgin shall be with child, and bear a son, and shall name him Immanuel.'"

"Thank you, Mr. Haskell." Gabe looked around the room. "If you're wondering why I asked you to bring a Bible to class today and didn't specify the version, there's a reason for it. Anyone got a different version from what Mr. Haskell just read?"

A hand went up. "Mr. Bonsall?"

Mr. Bonsall read, "'Therefore the Lord himself will give you a sign; the young woman, pregnant and about to bear a son, shall name him Emmanuel.'" He looked up at Gabe, puzzlement on his face.

"A bit different from Mr. Haskell's version, isn't it? And that, gentlemen, is why I study Scripture in its original languages. Because otherwise I have to trust translators, and I'd rather depend on myself than someone I've never met. Now back to Isaiah, because the translation of his writing has influenced Church teachings—and girls' behavior—for two thousand years."

He tapped on the Hebrew word. "This one word—*almah*—is where it all begins. *Almah* in Hebrew means 'a young woman.' And before you ask, yes, Hebrew does have a term for 'virgin.' Isaiah is saying that the Messiah will come from humble beginnings. He'll be a regular Joe, one of us. There's nothing miraculous in what Isaiah is predicting."

He took a sip of water and looked at the clock. "But when it came time to translate Isaiah into Greek, the translator had a choice." He wrote a word in Greek under the Hebrew word. "*Parthenos* means 'a physically intact virgin.' The translator could have gone with *gynae*, which is Greek for 'woman'—and the source of the word 'gynecology.' He tapped the Hebrew word. "That would have been the most accurate translation of *almah*. But he went with *parthenos* instead, which was then translated into Latin as '*virgo intacta*'—no translation necessary."

He stepped back from the board and looked at the words, letting the silence build. "Now we get to the post-evangelist period when the Church was trying to establish itself. The early Church Fathers weren't fools. They knew the Church's future lay with Rome and Greece, not Israel. And since the Greeks and Romans liked miracles and heroes and stories of Gods interacting with humans, it was natural that the evangelists would interject some into the stories around Jesus's parentage, in the same way that Athena came from Zeus."

Mr. Phillips spoke up for the first time. "That explains the idea of the Immaculate Conception, but not the fixation on virginity for future generations."

"True, Mr. Phillips. It's hard to tell how much stock the evangelists put in virginity as a model for future behavior rather than as a miracle story. But we don't have that problem with the early Church Fathers. They took *virgo intacta* and doubled down, declaring Mary to be not just *virgo intacta* but a perpetual virgin as well."

"Which means Joseph was more of a saint than we give him credit for," Mr. Haskell opined. The class laughed softly.

Gabe nodded. "Touché, Mr. Haskell. A friend of mine—a nun, if you can believe it—said that Joseph should have been canonized just for having the longest case of blue balls in either Testament."

A single nervous laugh turned slowly into a roar of laughter.

He looked at the clock and picked up his notes. "Okay, let's bring it back home, gents. For next class I want your thoughts on how you'd handle a seventeen-year-old girl who's told you she's worried that she's going to hell because she went 'all the way' with her boyfriend. Use all the tools you've developed, from this class and others. But above all, use your common sense. Put yourself in her shoes, the pressures she's facing from friends, parents, perhaps from the boyfriend, and from the Church."

Twenty

THEY SAT FACING EACH OTHER in two comfortable chairs in the lobby of the Westin hotel, a small fire in a fireplace a few feet away. Two glasses of zinfandel sat in front of them. "I'm glad this worked out with our schedules," Michelle said. "I felt bad about having to cancel our Monday lunch, especially since you're on a roll with your writing."

Gabe nodded at the folder on the table in front of them. "What'd you think?"

Michelle grimaced slightly. "Since I'm your biggest fan, as well as your current editor, I need to pour some cold water on this week's output."

"Let me guess. The sex scene?"

"Uh-huh. Listen, few writers write well about sex, so you've got company." She smiled sympathetically. "I can't speak for all women, Gabe, but I can't remember the last time my breasts heaved or I took a 'tumescence' in my 'eager, trembling hands.'"

"You're saying I should quit reading Georgette Heyer?"

She smiled slightly. "And lay off the Harold Robbins and Jacqueline Susann, while you're at it." She slid a piece of paper across the table. "Here are five authors who write a good sex scene. Read them and take another shot. If it still rings hollow or trite, do like they do in the movies. Have them head toward the bedroom, then pick up the action post-coitus, when they're cuddling."

He took the sheet and looked at it. "Thanks. Yeah, I was kinda out of my depth there." He folded the paper and put it in his backpack. "I'll have something better for you next week. And I promise to lower the turgid factor."

They spent the next few minutes catching each other up on how their respective classes were doing, Gabe sharing the latest jokes from his seminarians and Michelle sharing the better essays from hers. Finally, Gabe leaned forward slightly. "I feel a little bad about abusing your generosity, since you're picking up today's check, but it looks like I'm going to need a bit of your Beatrice advice." He smiled. "Maybe I should put you on retainer."

Michelle cocked her head. "I'm happy to help. And flattered. But shouldn't you be expanding your sources beyond just me? I don't feel that comfortable speaking for fifty percent of the planet."

"You've got to recognize how limited my resources are, woman-wise," Gabe said. "Jenny's never been married and barely even dated before her calling. My mom was born with an independent streak and has a rock-solid marriage, so she's no help. You're the one who's most acquainted with real life."

"Aren't some of your high school friends married by now?"

"Yeah, but they're still in the googly eyes phase. I'm counseling people who are way past that. People who are struggling to stay together." He smiled disarmingly at her. "Like it or not, you're it. You're my Beatrice. And before you object any further, your advice has worked so well that one of my female parishioners told me I'm getting a reputation for being 'one of the girls.'" He raised his eyebrow at her.

"That's high praise. We women don't toss that phrase around lightly." She squinched her mouth, mulling over the request. "Okay. I'll help where I can. What's going on?"

"My new fans, the women who come to confession or see me during office hours, are now bringing their husbands in for marriage counseling, telling them to listen to Father. I mean, what kind of wisdom or experience do they think a twenty-six-year-old virgin can offer in the areas of marriage and sex?" Michelle's eyebrows arched at the word 'virgin,' but Gabe was looking out the window. "But there they are, sitting in front of me."

"Do the men want to be there?"

"Nine times out of ten, no. They sit with folded arms in front of their chests, and their voices have an edge to them. Won't look at their wives; barely look at me. I try to break the ice by asking about their kids. I've learned to stay away from asking about how their kids are doing with school since that can be a contentious topic. So I ask Mary Margaret to find out if the kids are involved in any sports, and we break the ice that way. And if the husband warms to the topic, I steer it toward whatever Pittsburgh team is in season. Pirates, Penguins, Steelers."

"So how can I help?"

"The only marriage I'm familiar with is my parents', but like I said, unless they've fooled me my entire life, theirs is almost a model marriage—stable and loving. Which I'm finding puts them in the minority these days."

"Not necessarily. Remember, you're only seeing parishioners who are in some form of distress. You're not seeing a random sample of your parishioners. Anyway, back to my question. How can I help?"

"I'll give you an example. This couple is sitting there in front of me, the friction between them almost electric. At least one of them, usually the husband, doesn't want to be there. These two are on separate islands that are drifting farther apart. While I can start the session by acknowledging the distance, I'd rather try to take them back to a time where they were a unit and loved spending time together." He paused and took a healthy sip of wine. "What do you think?"

The resulting silence was long but comfortable. Gabe watched Michelle considering his question, the lines around her mouth and eyes deepening as she concentrated. Finally she shifted her gaze from the tablecloth to Gabe. "Do you know that Who song, 'Bargain?'" She didn't wait for an answer. "There's a line in it. 'One and one don't make two, one and one make one.' I love that line. When a marriage clicks, you're *one*. In everything. It's a great feeling. It's the two of you thinking and acting as one, as corny as that sounds. That's what you want your parishioners to remember. You want to help them try to regain when things get rough. And they *will* get rough."

Gabe smiled at her answer and started to thank her, but she raised a hand. "But there are also times when you're not one, when one and one don't make one, so to speak. There's you, there's him, and there's it—all the things that are wrong between the two of you. It's kind of one and one making three, and if you don't catch it in the early stages, it's a weed that can choke a marriage to death."

Gabe looked up in surprise at the emotion and urgency within her response. It felt like she had just crossed a line without intending to. He could see that the same thought was dawning on her, and now that she heard herself out loud, she was embarrassed by having revealed more than she'd intended.

"Am I to assume you and John are currently in the one and one equals three phase?"

"Boy, you're astute. I can see why you're considered one of the girls. But yeah, it's been a long time since one and one equaled one with John and me."

"Can you put your finger on what's wrong?"

She looked out the window, her eyes filling, though she didn't seem to notice. "I like my life these days. It was already good, but now it feels like it's starting to open up in a new way. But John's life, at least from what I can tell, is shrinking. His father isn't turning over the business to him the way they agreed. It's frustrating. And painful. When I try to talk to John about it, he goes quiet. But it's an angry quiet. And if I try to press the subject, he gets up and leaves the room." She grimaced. "But it's *how* he gets up that worries me. He stands over me, almost threatening me."

Gabe leaned forward. "Has he ever—"

"Hit me? No." She stopped herself. "Well, just once. He was sorry immediately. I could see that." Her eyes took on an imploring quality. "He's a good guy, Gabe. Just not these days."

"What are you guys going to do?"

"I suggested going to see a marriage counselor. That led to another stalk-out. So he's sleeping in the guest room for now. And I'm going to see a therapist on Friday."

She left her wine glass half full, picked up her briefcase, and nodded at the folder. "Clean up the sex scene. Or eighty-six it."

Twenty-One

☩

THE GROUP—Gabe, Jenny, Michael, and Paul, joined that night for the first time by Carla—was gathered around the kitchen table in the rectory. Dolores had prepared a meal and reluctantly departed, Gabe having given her the night off. He had walked her to the door to ensure she didn't stay around and listen in.

Paul smiled as Gabe walked back into the kitchen. "Wise man. Dolores has many fine qualities, but discretion isn't one of them."

Carla nodded in the direction of Dolores's departure. "That woman scares me. And I don't scare easily."

By unspoken but common agreement, dinner conversation had stayed away from the investigation. Part of it was Dolores's presence and part of it that the group, with its expanding membership, was feeling its way into its new group dynamic with a cop now part of the equation.

With the dinner dishes cleared and the after-dinner port poured, Carla took out a file she had rescued from her attic and went through it in some detail with the group. Any doubt about Father Ferguson's innocence or alternate explanations of his behavior vanished under her onslaught.

"And that's the point where I had to stop," she said, tapping her pen on a diagram.

"It's a helluva lot more than I've been able to glean from the church records," Michael said, looking both impressed and shaken.

"There's no way to leak any of this and get Ferguson's case reopened?" Jenny asked.

Both Michael and Carla shook their heads at the same time. "I hate to sound callous," Carla said, "but we need to let Ferguson go. He's yesterday's news. The captain has agreed to let the Church handle it, so any action against him would be regarded as malicious prosecution."

"And if the case was reopened," Michael continued, "the Church might wonder where the cops were getting this new evidence. If they called in their IT pros, they'd probably be able to discover our investigation. Even if they didn't, they'd notify the archbishop about the holes in his system that we've been able to exploit. Detective Jessup is right."

"Carla."

"Carla is right. As shitty as it feels, we need to let Ferguson go. Besides, as we're discovering, there are a lot of Fergusons out there. And if we can show how systemic this thing is, the authorities can take over and discover the full extent of the network, which might give them another shot at Ferguson and other pedos who have been protected."

"What network are you talking about?" Carla asked.

Gabe nodded at Mike's computer. "Show her your visual."

Michael brought his screen to life and tapped on a few keys. A web of connections showed up on the screen. He tapped the center box. "This is Ferguson. By following his online activities and communications, I was able to discover that he wasn't acting alone. He was part of a network." He tapped a box and the screen morphed, showing a vast web of connections. "These are his tier one connections."

"Tier one meaning?"

"It means you're either part of—or the leader of—a separate network from Ferguson's. I think of it in military terms. From a hierarchy standpoint, tier one guys are like colonels, each with his own command. In some cases, the network is as small as three priests. The largest I've found so far has eighteen. They have a bulletin board they use as well as their one-to-one communications. It's well-organized. Sick but well-run."

"Can you go up and down or just down on your hierarchy?" Carla asked.

"Down only, for now. On the upside, I can tell that there's no other layer between the tier one guys and their commander, their general. But he knows how to cover his tracks in ways the rest of the network don't. My guess is that even his colonels don't know who he is."

"How tough is it to go down?"

"Not tough at all. Ferguson and his pals all walk around with their electronic zippers down. They either don't know shit about security or think their leader has them well-protected."

"What are they posting on the bulletin board?" Paul asked.

"You name it. Files, videos of their activities, names and addresses of their victims for anyone new to a parish or just visiting."

Carla's eyes were glued to the screen. "And these are priests we're talking about," she said, almost to herself.

"A few of them invite pedo parishioners to some of their events," Gabe said, looking at the screen, "but for the most part, it's a network built by priests for priests." His eyes turned to Carla. "Based on what you see, do we have enough to shut this down. Or publicize it, at least?"

"Criminally, there's no question," Carla said. "If I can validate what Mike has just shown me, there is evidence of criminal collusion. But politically, we're talking about two organizations that don't want to touch this thing. Your guys want to protect their own and my guys are afraid to upset your guys and their followers. It pains me to say it, but politically, your Church trumps my precinct. My captain is not a bad guy, but you don't get to be a captain without being able to read the political winds. And right now, the political winds are telling him to leave it alone."

"Is there anything we can do to change his mind?" Jenny asked.

"Let me give that some thought," Carla replied. "In the meantime, send me what you just showed me and a sampling of some of the emails." She took out a pen and notebook and scribbled on the page. "Send them to this email. It's my private account. I won't be able to work on it in the office. Our IT guys are better than yours seem to be. But let me rework what I've got at home in light of what I've learned tonight, and I'll get back to you."

"How long do you need?" Gabe asked.

"Give me two weeks. Then let's get back together."

Twenty-Two

CARLA HAD OFFERED JENNY A RIDE back to her apartment after the dinner at the rectory, but Jenny said she wanted to walk off the heavy meal. She stared across the table at Gabe until he got the hint and volunteered to escort her. They walked Michael, Paul, and Carla out to their cars, then they started down the street toward Jenny's apartment.

"One of my kids' parents gave me two tickets for Saturday's Pirates game," she said as they strolled, her arm draped casually though his. "Interested?"

"Yeah, unless it's the Mets."

"It's the Dodgers, you ass. Do you want to know who's pitching before you decide?"

Gabe smiled. "Sorry. It's just that the Mets suck so bad these days that those seem to be the only tickets I get offered anymore. Anyone but them, count me in."

They walked along in a comfortable silence, taking in the quiet of the evening. As they turned a corner, the wind picked up and was in their faces. Jenny hunched her shoulders and tucked her head slightly into Gabe's arm.

"How are the kids doing now that First Confession and First Communion are behind them?" Gabe asked.

"Great, though Sandra Victor is still mortified that she dropped the host."

"If she's still talking about it next week, have her drop by my office and I'll let her know that Jesus is like a cat. He always lands on his feet."

She looked over at him. "When the kids do come by, you're keeping your door open, aren't you?"

"Seriously? It's come to that?"

"Not about you, specifically. I'll tell you if I ever hear anything. But yeah, it's come to that. Or if it isn't already here, it's coming fast, so get ahead of the rumors." She looked over at him. "Sorry for being Debbie Downer, but the rumors and whispers are already out there, thanks to assholes like Ferguson." She took his arm. "So leave your door open, and make sure Mary Margaret sees you do it. She'll make a great character witness, should it come to that."

Gabe frowned but nodded his assent. "Speaking of kids, I've got a question for you. I've got a pretty good idea how these priests are recruiting their teenage victims. They've got religious retreats, the altar boys, and group outings. The opportunities are there. But how do you think they find the younger kids, like the ones you teach?"

"That's been bugging me ever since we started this thing," she said. "At first I came up blank. Then I realized I'd have to think like a pedo to really figure it out. So I started looking at my kids—in the classroom, out in the recess yard, wherever—with fresh eyes. And the group that stood out for me were those usually left out. You know, the kids chosen last for teams and the ones eased out of a group they used to belong to. And the bullied ones. Especially them, since they've already shown an inability to stand up for themselves."

She looked up at Gabe, whose eyes were fixed on the street ahead, though it was clear he was listening. He nodded at her to continue. "If I were a priest with access to children, I'd find an excuse to call them to my office, turn the conversation to what's going on in their lives, and be as sympathetic as I could be. That kind of sympathy is something most of these kids haven't experienced, at least recently. And that sympathy, coupled with the power of the collar—then I'd have them."

"Which makes it difficult, if not impossible, to catch them in the act."

"One more thing," Jenny said, her voice halting. "And I hate to say it after what we've just celebrated with my class, but I can see these priests using the confessional to do their recruiting."

"How so?"

"Let's say a teenage boy comes into the confessional, knowing it's a safe, private place to discuss possible homosexual leanings, however faint. Or he's confessing to watching porn, maybe even gay porn. That kid walks out of the confessional believing he's found a nonjudgmental adult who really listens to him. He doesn't know he's just placed a bull's-eye on his back. Maybe the priest lets the boy and the topic rest for a week or two, then he calls the kid to his office. They just talk: how normal it is to be curious about those kinds of thoughts and feelings; how a lot of people don't understand that there are different types of normal for different types of people; how normal all of this is. And we're off and running."

Jenny took her keys out as they climbed the stairs to her front door. When they reached it, she unlocked the door and turned back to Gabe. "You're one of the good ones, Gabe. Don't forget that. Everyone knows that, especially the kids. I just don't know if that puts you in the majority or minority these days." She kissed him on the cheek and went into the building.

As he walked away from Jenny's apartment house, Gabe felt both his body and mind tense up. Practicing what he'd learned in meditation, he took an inventory and noted the clenched fists, as well as the anger in his walk. His mind, which normally could hold and rotate numerous topics, was fixed on the conversation with Jenny and the playground scenes she had depicted. He took a seat on a street-facing bench and meditated for ten minutes or so, his long, slow breaths restoring him to something approximating equanimity.

The conversation with Jenny, especially her cautionary tone, reminded him of a recent gathering of priests during which Gabe had found himself assessing his compatriots from a new perspective. First unconsciously and then deliberately, he wondered which, if any, were pedophiles. Aware of this shift in mindset, he stepped back and examined the basis of his judgments. He found that the priests he was most suspicious of were all physically unprepossessing with weak chins, fleshy lips, or slumped postures.

He chastised himself for these facile judgments, knowing that they stemmed from his years as a gym rat and the emphasis—or value system—it had around fitness. He was practicing lazy judgment.

At the same time, he wondered, for the first time, how *he* might be viewed, using the same lens. How suspicious were some of his congregants, given his proximity, both in age and geographically, to their kids? And the pedos, were they looking at him as a potential recruit, wondering and discussing how best to approach him?

Replaying the conversation with Jenny, he realized the open-door policy was just one of his behaviors that needed changing. He was by nature a physical person. His parents were both huggers. Whether it was hugging his friends hello and good-bye or accepting hugs from his parishioners, he was not only comfortable with it but saw it as part of his core beliefs: Affection should be physical. His arms, chest, and cheek were all part of how he communicated with his parishioners. Especially the children, whether he saw them daily in the parish school or on Sundays. Many of them seemed to not just want but demand physical contact. All of this had to change. All because of assholes like Ferguson.

Up ahead of him, the door of one of the neighborhood's more popular bars opened, issuing a range of noises, from drunken voices to pinball machines to the faint sound of Patsy Cline singing "Crazy." The door started to close, then opened again as a figure staggered out into the night. There was something familiar to him, but Gabe couldn't place him initially.

A cry came from inside the bar. "Just one more, Eddie."

"Can't, boys. I promised the nag I'd be home in time to tuck the girls in." Eddie listened to something someone in the bar said and chuckled. "Yeah, she's not nagging so much these days through that wired jaw, is she?" He listened some more. "You said it, not me."

Gabe realized that whatever road trip Eddie had been on, he and his milk-bottle soul were back. Worried about Eddie's destination, Gabe lagged back, following the swerving figure without any fear of being spotted. As he tracked Eddie, Gabe muttered to himself, "Don't go home, idiot. Don't go home. Go somewhere and sleep it off."

But as Eddie turned the corner, it was clear his destination was his house. Gabe widened his view from Eddie to his immediate surroundings and saw he had two blocks to figure out the best course of action. He saw ahead in the next block a patch of darkness, a gap in the streetlights. Quickening his pace, he closed silently behind the weaving Eddie. As Eddie entered the shadowed area, Gabe came up from behind and stunned him with two cupped palms to the ears. Staggering, Eddie lurched forward, but Gabe closed quickly and caught him by the shoulders. As Eddie tried to regain his bearings, Gabe wrapped both forearms around his neck and squeezed, causing Eddie to lose consciousness and slouch into Gabe's arms. Gabe secured the unsteady figure and eased him down three stairs into a nearby basement stairwell. Then he gently tapped his face until Eddie stirred.

"Eddie, Eddie," Gabe said in a hoarse working man's voice. "You fucked up, man. Putting Ramona in the hospital like that. Now some of the wives, mine included, say they'll go to the police next time we put a hand on them. And some of us can't afford to have the cops nosing around our affairs. So I got sent to give you a message."

Eddie relaxed slightly. He was still trying to get his bearings, but the voice was soothing, reassuring. And the message was just that: a message. He wasn't comfortable with the two fingers parked along the side of his neck, but the other hand was patting him on the head reassuringly. He relaxed into the grip.

Gabe's tone hardened. "Now I know you're a mechanic, so I'm gonna spare your fingers. Your choice: I either break some of your ribs or take out a knee. Just one knee, snap the tendons clean. They reattach the tendons and you're back dancing within six weeks." There was a pause. "What's it going to be, ribs or knee?"

Eddie tried to thrash and shout at the same time, but the two fingers closed on his throat, stifling the cry and robbing Eddie of much of his strength.

"One word, Eddie: ribs or knee. If you don't decide, I'll do both."

Eddie's response was more of a whimper. "Ribs."

"Good choice." Gabe reapplied the choke-out and Eddie slumped again. Calmly, methodically, Gabe hammered his fists into Eddie's ribs, hearing the muffled cracking. He stopped after the fourth crack and eased Eddie down onto the bricks, cradling his head until his head was resting on the pavement. Gabe stood up, his head now at street level, and waited for a moment to let the street clear. Then he bent over and tapped Eddie repeatedly on his cheeks. As Eddie stirred, Gabe walked up the stairs, turned left, and headed for the rectory.

CONFESSION

"Yesterday I put one of my parishioners in the hospital. He deserved it, but still, I'm worried about how easy it was to do. Emotionally, not logistically. As I followed him, all I could think of was what damage he could inflict on Ramona that night and in the days to come. As he kept walking, that drunken swagger of his had a sense of violence and entitlement to it, and I felt enough rage that I could have crippled him. But all that would have done is burden Ramona even further. I felt as helpless as she must feel, most nights waiting for him to come home. So when he turned the corner to his street, I knew I had to do something. So I did.

"But here's my problem: did I do this for me or for my parishioners? On my end, I won't kid you: it felt good, felt right. But if it's for my parishioners, how did what I do with Eddie help? He's not going to admit he was punished for beating his wife. Those two muggers—that got the neighborhood talking. But are people going to link what happened to them to what happened to Eddie? I don't think so. It's going to take a few more incidents like Eddie before the word gets out that if you beat your wife or take a belt to your kids, there will be consequences. And I don't know if I have them in me. This isn't what I signed up for."

Twenty-Three

THE VOICE STARTED OUT TIMID, as if the woman was swallowing each word. "Bless me, Father, for I have sinned. It's been . . ." She stopped and took a long breath. When she spoke again, her voice had a spine. "No, I haven't sinned, Father. I've been sinned *against*. And I don't know what to do."

Gabe leaned forward and said softly, "Well, let's just figure it out together. Tell me whatever you want to, in your own way. Take your time."

"I was raped. There. I've been saying it to myself for a week, but this is the first time I've said it out loud."

"Are you okay? I mean, physically? Should we be—"

"There'll be no evidence of trauma. He didn't hurt me, not like you're thinking. In fact, I'm sure the sonofabitch would say it was consensual. But he *damaged* me. And I don't know what to do."

"Where did it happen?"

"In my apartment. My own goddamned apartment, Father. How's that going to look to the cops?"

"Was it a stranger or someone you know?"

Her voice tightened. "It was my boss. My fucking *boss*, Father. My car was in the shop, so he volunteered to give me a ride home. When we got there, he said it had been a long day and could he come up for a quick drink. And like a fool, I said yes."

"Listen to me," Gabe said, his voice more firm than soothing. "I can't tell you how to feel. But I can tell you this: If you beat yourself up about this, the bastard wins. And we can't have that."

Gabe opened the door slightly and peered out. There were two more women waiting. He closed the door and turned back to the woman.

"Are you comfortable telling me your first name?"

"It's Paula, Father."

"Okay, Paula. This is a longer conversation than this room was built for. Plus, you're kneeling and I'm sitting, so that's a bit unfair, isn't it? Let's do this: I've got two more confessions to hear, then I'm closing shop for the night. Can we meet at the Starbucks over on Felton and continue this conversation?" He paused. "Is that a nod I'm hearing?"

"Yes. That's a nod. Thanks, Father. I'll wait for you there."

That night, as Gabe brushed his teeth, he thought back to his coffee with Paula and all its complications. While the sex had hardly been consensual, when Gabe asked if she'd told anyone about it and if she'd gone to either the police or the emergency room, her mouth had twisted into a bitter smile. "And tell them what? I invited him up, I'm not bruised or bleeding. Where's the evidence of rape. I did think of going to the cops, Father, but he's a neighborhood guy, born and raised. Some of the cops probably went to school with the bastard. I'd come off as a spurned girlfriend, a disgruntled employee, or a gold digger looking for a quick payoff."

"I don't know your job or your financial situation," Gabe said, "but can you find another job? Going to work and seeing him every day must be hell."

"It's not just seeing him, it's how he acts. He gives me this shit-eating smile, like it was all consensual and we've got this little secret. As if we're an office romance." She shivered. "I'll be working and he'll come up behind me and give me a slight massage. My skin feels like it grows scars the moment he walks away." She swallowed drily. "As for my financial situation, I had to put my mom in a home, and I'm her only source of support. And the bastard knows it. Plus, with everything so local here, I'd need his recommendation. Face it, Father. I'm screwed, in more ways than one."

Later that night, before he sat down to work on his novel, Gabe replayed the conversation with Paula and had to agree with her assessment. He considered what his own options might be in the matter but again came up empty. If he confronted her employer, within or outside the office, there would almost certainly be ramifications for Paula. And there was the possibility that her employer would take it to the archdiocese, in which case Gabe would have to reveal that he was acting on something he'd learned in the confessional.

He took a long shower to wash off the day, but Paula's situation stayed with him. Even after he'd dried off and settled into his chair, the most recent pages of his novel in front of him, he was unable to focus on the novel. After thirty minutes of what he thought of as empty writing, he gave up and went to bed.

Twenty-Four

FOR THREE IN THE AFTERNOON on a weekday, the bar was crowded. Every table was taken, ashtrays sending smoke up in snaky lines that dissipated before they hit the ceiling. There was a handful of women clustered at the bar, but the bulk of the bar population was males in their thirties, either out of work or at the end of the early shift.

Carla walked through the front door and looked around before walking over and badging the bartender, who cocked his ear to hear her. He nodded and indicated a table at the far end of the shuffleboard.

She ambled over and stood in front of the table and the three men it held, one of whom was bandaged and winced slightly as he drank. "Which one of you is Eddie?"

"Who wants to know?" the largest of the three asked, his voice intended to intimidate.

Carla flipped her badge, closing it almost as quickly as she opened it. "Me. Is there someplace we can talk?"

"Here's good," the wincing man said. "These are my brothers. Whatever you got to say to me, you can say in front of them."

"Okay, then." She looked around, saw an empty chair at a nearby table, hooked it with her foot, and dragged it over. She stood behind it, resting her hands on its back. "Word is that you guys have put out a reward for information on whoever beat up Eddie."

"No one beat me up," Eddie said in a hoarse, angry voice. "I was mugged."

"The distinction being?"

"Sonofabitch jumped me from behind."

"Okay. I get the distinction. But how do you explain the physician's report that it was a purely frontal assault with considerable and very precise damage, as if someone was sending you a message? And that someone sounds like a pro."

"If it was a pro, we'd know it," one of the other men said.

"Because you're connected, right? Give me a break, guys. Everyone in this part of town claims to be connected. It's like the Mob is handing out free memberships these days." She looked around the bar and then back at the men. "If you were really connected, no one would have gone after Eddie. And if they did, they'd be dead by now. So let's start over. Any idea who might do this? You owe anyone money? You piss anyone off recently?"

"No," Eddie said. "But you're starting to piss me off with all your nebby talk."

"Well, gee. I wouldn't want that. Especially since you're connected. I don't want to wake up with my cat's head in my bed."

She opened her notebook and turned back a few pages. Then she stopped and looked up. "While the hospital was calling up your files, I saw that a woman by the same last name had been treated there recently. Sister?"

"My wife. What of it?"

"You're one unlucky family, aren't you? You sure the same guy who beat you up . . . sorry, who mugged you, didn't do her as well?"

The largest of the men joined in. "Hey, did we call the cops about this? Did Ramona, when she fell? Why don't you go take care of people who can't take care of themselves?"

"I think I'm looking at three people who fit that description," she said. "Listen, guys, normally I wouldn't care less about who beat up—mugged—our man Eddie here or what you guys plan to do about it. But this is happening in my precinct, which means there are rules. And limits. Let's say I find Eddie's mugger dead, or even badly maimed. Then I'm gonna be on you guys like a cheap suit. Do we understand each other?"

She gave the men a moment to display their stubborn, tough-guy silence. When she received no response, she moved around the chair and made as if to sit down. This time, all three nodded. "Great. Here's where I think we are, guys. I don't think this guy is done with you, Eddie. I think he was sending you a message. But you don't strike me as the kind of guy who learns things the first time."

She turned to the other two men. "As much as I like him giving free lessons to folks like Eddie here, I don't like him doing it in my precinct. He's peeing in my pool, and that's gonna stop. I know this neighborhood isn't big on helping cops, but this is one case where you might make an exception. So the two of you don't wind up like Eddie. Or Eddie winds up worse than he is now. Anything comes up, you call me."

This time, the men just stared back at her with flat eyes.

Carla got up, put her chair back where she'd found it, and left without saying another word. As she passed the bartender, she handed him a ten-spot and nodded back at the table. "The next pitcher's on me. Spit in it if you want."

Twenty-Five

☩

MICHELLE HAD PREPARED and cooked a delicious dinner of scallops, couscous, and asparagus. The last item had prompted Gabe to tell her the Babe Ruth story about the Babe being at a formal dinner party during which he'd graciously told Lady Astor that he never ate asparagus because it made his pee stink. He assured Michelle he'd go outside if he had to take a leak.

They had finished dinner and were in Michelle's living room, sitting on the couch, two half-filled glasses of Merlot on the table in front of them. Michelle was barefoot and had her feet curled up under her. Gabe's shoes were off and his stockinged feet were up on the coffee table.

"Okay," he said. "I didn't say anything during dinner, but I've got to ask. That mark on your neck, the one with the make-up over it . . ."

"What about it?"

"It wasn't there at our Monday lunch."

Michelle looked at him for a moment, then her gaze shifted to the dining room. Gabe thought for a moment she was going to get up and clear the dishes, but then her eyes came back to him.

"We had an argument Monday night. He asked me how my day was and I told him about my class, about how the most recent assignment had gotten them to open up. I give John credit because he seemed interested in it and genuinely pleased for me."

"What went wrong?"

"I made the mistake of saying I'd gotten the idea from you, and that just set him off. He just lost it."

"Lost it how? Physically?" Gabe took his feet down from the table and sat up, his body taut.

"At first it was just shouting about how I find you more interesting than him. He actually used the word 'fascinating.' According to John, I find you more fascinating than him. He said, 'Maybe you should be with him instead of me. But wait. You can't be with him because he's a priest. Isn't that convenient?'"

"I'm sorry. I had no idea."

"About what? That I talk about you? That I'm more drawn to you than I am to him? Anyway, when I told him that I was going for a walk, he grabbed me by the throat. He didn't choke me, nothing like that. It was just to stop me from leaving."

"Jesus. Don't make excuses for him, Michelle." Gabe felt his feet settle on the floor, as if he were grounding himself. "What happened next?"

"Honestly, I think he was more scared than I was by what had just happened. He just backed away and started to apologize immediately. But by that time, I'd grabbed my keys and was out the door."

"Where did you go?"

"I drove around for a bit. I thought about coming over to the rectory and bunking with you for a few days." She stopped and smiled slightly. "You should have seen your face just now. I'm joking. Eventually, I realized John wasn't going anywhere and I had no place to go. So I went home and let him apologize repeatedly. Then I gave him sheets and blankets and told him I'd let him know when he was welcome back in the bedroom."

"So where do things stand now?" He held up a hand. "Note that I haven't offered a single solution."

Neither one smiled.

"He's on a business trip. We'll talk when he gets back. He's got some things to work out. So do I."

"Such as?"

"Such as whether he and I have a future. Whether Pittsburgh is a healthy place for either of us to be." Her eyes tightened on him, holding him in a way he hadn't seen before. "Such as how I feel about you." Her eyes bore in. "On that last point, it would help if I knew how you felt about me."

It was a Rubicon moment, Gabe knew, one he had thought about but never actually played through to its conclusion. It had seemed so outside his inner reality. And now that it was in front of him, he realized how unprepared he was. He had kept his attraction for Michelle in a box rather than letting it fully into his life. And he realized that the moment he was facing was larger than anything he had envisioned. All this big talk with Paul about deciding in the moment, and now that the moment was before him, and he was paralyzed. He was a fraud, and an unprepared fraud at that.

Michelle waited for a response, her eyes roaming his face, looking for any clue. There wasn't a no there but there also wasn't the eager yes she'd hoped for. His body language was equally neutral, leaning neither in nor back. His eyes were on hers and she could feel the interest there, but she couldn't tell if that interest contained desire.

"I'm going to take the initiative here, Gabe, because we both know that if we waited for you, we'd both die of old age." She took his face in her hands and kissed him. Her tongue touched his lips slightly and she felt them open. He kissed her back, at first tentatively, then eagerly.

She reached up, took one of his hands, and placed it gently on her breast. "You stop me whenever you want."

His hand moved tentatively over her breast, then with more initiative and confidence. His hand gently squeezed her bare breast, then danced slightly over her nipple and over to the other breast.

She lowered her hand to his lap and to the erection so evident in his pants. She began to stroke it gently through the cloth. Gabe leaned back, moaning gently. As Michelle started to loosen his belt, he raised his hips for a moment, helping her pull down his pants. But as she reached into the open fly of his underwear, he suddenly jerked forward. He stood and pulled up his pants in a single moment.

"I'm sorry. This was a mistake," he said, heading for the door.

"Don't go, Gabe. Don't."

He hesitated at the door, his hand on the knob but not turning it. "I have to. This isn't making sense. I know it should, but it isn't. I know how I must sound, and I'm sorry." He looked at her fallen face. "You didn't do anything wrong."

"Neither did you."

"Don't be so sure about that. This all felt . . . too good." He looked at her with wet eyes. "I'm sorry. I really am." And he left.

CONFESSION

*"You know how, in the movies, the undercover cop gets torn up by the stress of living in two worlds? And the question isn't **if** he's going to fall apart but when?" Gabe didn't wait for a response. "What the hell made me think I could play live two lives, to play with fire like that? The lunches and drinks were one thing, but I could always say we were colleagues discussing my novel or our classes. I had plausible deniability. But going to her house last night, especially knowing the problems she and John were having, what the hell was I thinking?*

"When she brought my hand to her breast, it felt natural, like something I wanted to explore further. And maybe if it had stopped there, with what Ann Landers calls 'heavy petting,' I could have gone back to the rectory and worked out how I felt about the evening and the impact it had on my calling. But when she touched my cock, everything changed. I felt a combination of arousal and shame I'd never experienced before.

"The source of the arousal is obvious, but the shame had two parts. On the one hand—no pun intended—there was the hypocrisy of the situation. On the other, I knew that if she stroked me much more, she was going to wind up with the same handful of cum that I experience most mornings. That's a sin I couldn't have lived with."

Twenty-Six

"THIS IS FATHER GABE RUSSELL. It's the evening of September 2, 2000, and I'm making this recording as a statement of evidence from the grave, should my encounter with Raymond Arkin, prove fatal." Gabe was sitting in the dark of his car talking calmly into a small recording device. "I may be overly dramatic here, but in my limited observations of Mr. Arkin, I believe he is armed and willing to employ whatever weapon he is carrying. Whether it is a stun gun or pistol, I can't say with certainty, but there is a weight to his left side coat pocket that he touches occasionally, so until I know otherwise, I'm working from the assumption that he is armed.

"Mr. Arkin is a serial rapist who thus far has avoided any repercussions for his crimes. He raped one of my parishioners two weeks ago. Since that evening, when my schedule has permitted, I've followed him in his evening rounds. During that time, I believe he's raped at least one other woman and targeted another without success."

Gabe turned the recorder off. He was sitting in his car, the engine off. Slouched down in his seat, he was able to observe Arkin through the gaps in the steering wheel. The notebook next to him was open, the page rich with ink. He sipped from his cooling cup of coffee as he watched Arkin at work. The man was dedicated, he had to give him that. There was a patience and diligence to his activities that spoke of experience and intelligence. Gabe might be in for a long night. He turned the tape recorder back on.

"Initially, I had hoped this could be a police matter, but we all know how complicated acquaintance rapes are to prosecute. And according to my parishioner, Arkin is always bragging about how many friends he has on the force. I'm not saying this to judge or condemn but to explain why she won't go to the police and why I've decided to take this route to justice."

He watched as Arkin sat patiently on a street bench, a baseball cap casually perched at the back of his head and a Boston Terrier at his feet. He gave the impression of a gentleman taking the evening air with his faithful companion. While he shifted his head every now and again as if inhaling and surveying his surroundings, Gabe could see that Arkin's eyes were fixed on three figures across the street.

Gabe brought up a small binocular and saw three girls, a blonde and two brunettes, all with long hair pulled back. It was hard at that distance to determine their ages, but the backpacks and their animated conversation had him thinking high school or maybe community college. The conversation was lively, and they occasionally threw their heads back in laughter. They gave the impression of knowing each other very well.

"Last week he followed a woman to her apartment building and gained access behind her. I was too far away to enter on my own, and if I had, what would I have done? I was forced to sit in my car, observe, and wait. I saw lights go on in a second-floor apartment. That was my only clue. Twenty minutes later, Arkin came out. There was something in his walk—a cockiness, a sense of entitlement—that convinced me he had just raped that woman.

"I crossed the street, waited for someone to enter the apartment building, and followed them in. I knocked at the second floor apartment door. No answer. I kept on knocking until I heard her come to the door, though she made no move to open it. I knocked again, and she asked who it was. But it was the voice with which she spoke—broken, torn apart—that confirmed it for me. I just knew. I apologized, said wrong apartment, and ran after Arkin. But he was long gone. After that, I redoubled my observations of his activities, leading to tonight."

Across the street, Arkin took out a cell phone and feigned a conversation as he watched the girls. The dog, which had been sitting at attention when they first reached the bench, now lay down, his chin resting on Arkin's shoes.

"In the other incident, it was clear Mr. Arkin was stalking a woman, first in a bar and then on her way home. But she met a male friend on the street and they went into a nearby coffee house. Arkin waited outside for an hour—he is nothing if not patient—then gave up and went home. I know this evidence isn't enough for you police to act, but I've heard and seen enough to believe he's a serial rapist who must be dealt with before he acts again."

Gabe now turned the binocular on Arkin. In his forties, he was high school handsome and trim for his age. His hair was freshly cut and brushed back. He appeared to use gel, which Gabe regarded as a venial sin. In addition to the baseball cap, he was dressed in light sweats and running shoes.

The girls started walking north, oblivious to everything except their conversation. One of them took out a cell phone and appeared to be reading something to her companions. Arkin waited for a moment, then eased himself to his feet and began to stroll, keeping to the other side of the street and at least a hundred yards back. His cap was now pulled down, putting most of his face in shadow from the streetlights.

Gabe reached up and disabled the interior light, exited the car, and crossed to the girls' side of the street, staying even further back than Arkin. The girls reached the next corner, and the one with the phone waved at her friends and headed west on Albert. Gabe assumed Arkin would follow the singleton, but instead, he stayed with the remaining two girls for another three blocks, at which point they separated. Gabe closed the gap by another fifty yards. Then he stopped and looked into a dimly lit shop window, his eyes on Arkin's reflection.

Arkin followed the girl with the blue backpack. She took a few steps, then stopped and turned. Arkin bent down to tie his shoe and tickle his dog under the chin, eyeing the girl from under the cap's brim. The girl called something to her friend, who answered with a laugh, and then they headed off in different directions.

Arkin's target flipped her phone open and cut across a small park, a poorly lit patch of dark green and black, chatting busily as she walked. Arkin picked up his pace and Gabe followed suit. As the girl neared the middle of the park, Arkin bent down and quickly tied his dog to a tree, giving him a treat and a parting word. He took up a jogger's pace, closing the distance between himself and the girl. When he was almost parallel to her, he dropped his left shoulder, his body shifting from a runner's posture to that of a football player about to make a tackle. He grabbed her from behind and pushed her off the path, one hand closing around her throat, the other covering her mouth. Caught completely off guard, the girl froze at first, then began to struggle.

Arkin never saw or heard Gabe, who was dressed in black and was wearing running shoes. But suddenly there was a searing pain in his kidney that robbed his legs of their strength. Arkin fell, first to one knee, then face-down.

Gabe looked at the startled girl, gauging whether she was in shock. When she blinked and gathered herself, he took hold of her hand, partly to console her, partly to stop her from fleeing. "Look around you. Get your bearings. Do you know where you are?" She did as he ordered but wouldn't look at him. "Do you know where you are?" he repeated. When she nodded, he let go of her hand. "Now go home and call the cops. Tell them what happened and where to find him. Don't worry, he'll still be here when they arrive. Go. Now."

As the girl ran off, Gabe turned his attention to Arkin, who was trying to stand. In an almost casual gesture, Gabe kicked the stabilizing leg out, causing Arkin to pitch forward onto the grass. Gabe then leaned over, so that his mouth was next to Arkin's ear.

"This is what it feels like to be helpless. Quite a turn-on, isn't it? I can see why those women you hunt like it so much." Then he pulled a ski mask down and stepped over Arkin's body, turning him over as he did so. "I don't think you want to call attention to us, given what you just attempted. But in case you do . . ." Gabe placed a thumb over Arkin's Adam's apple and two fingers pinched a nerve from the side. Arkin gave a small croak, then went silent.

"Good. Now I need you to stay still for this next part. I don't want to miss." In a sudden movement, Gabe reared back and drove his stiffened fingers, knife-like, into Arkin's groin. Arkin's eyes widened, then rolled back. A small cry slipped from his damaged throat. Paralyzed, he watched as Gabe inflicted the same damage, again and again.

Finally, Gabe straightened up. "I don't know if you're going to be able to pee again. But I sure as hell know you won't be able to get an erection for a long time, if ever." He leaned down and whispered. "But I'll be watching your recovery. And if I haven't rendered you permanently incapable of rape, I'll be back to finish the job." He delivered one last blow and then untied the dog and brought him over to where Arkin was lying. The dog licked Arkin's face as Gabe tied him off, his leash now around Arkin's ankle. Gabe reached into Arkin's pocket, found a treat, and gave it to the dog. Then he left.

Fifty yards into his departure, he stopped and turned to see if their interaction had attracted any attention, but the park was dark and quiet. He jogged back and stopped over the fallen Arkin. Reaching into the coat pocket, he closed his hand around a metal object. He took it out and examined the stun gun for a moment. Then he placed it next to Arkin's head, making sure to leave no fingerprints. "You sonofabitch," he said as he delivered one more blow before walking away.

Twenty-Seven

"OKAY, GENTLEMEN," Gabe began. "Today's lecture will be on the passion of Jesus and how the four evangelists treated it. But based on the emails I've received from some of you in the past week, I'm going to give the first half over to answering the questions some of you have raised. They centered around two topics: women in the priesthood and the recent news about pedophilia in our ranks. Compelling topics, both, and as we can discuss, they're related in certain ways.

"Let's tackle them in turn. I'll tackle the first one, though I'll be looking for a lot of input from you guys. And for the discussion on pedophilia, I've brought in a ringer." He motioned toward Michael, who was perched on a stool to the side of Gabe's desk. "I'll introduce him in a moment.

"But before we tackle either topic, I want to address something that a number of you have raised in private. And that is, why am I so tough on the Church, especially since I chose to be one of its representatives?" He held up a hand, though no one seemed about to object. "It's a fair question. And the answer is equal representation. Most of you have only been exposed to traditional Church teachings and positions, which are at the core of your calling. Which is as it should be. And outside this classroom, I hazard to say you'll receive more of the same."

He took a long swig of water and replaced the cap, seemingly in no hurry to begin. "I could say I'm just being Socratic here, challenging you with criticisms of the Church, criticisms I might not even believe myself. But the important thing I need to impart, besides the criticisms themselves, is that they're valid. Maybe true, maybe not. But since your parishioners will raise these issues—many of them as they're parting ways with the Church—I want you to be ready. Not just with the Church's answers but your own."

He waited a beat for questions or objections, then continued. "One more thing on this topic. Your parents and most of the priests at this seminary grew up with the tradition of 'Because the Church says so,' shutting down any concern or objection. That answer won't cut it anymore. Even in a traditional parish like mine, they want a Church that understands the concerns they have, whether personal, like premarital sex or abortion, or institutional, such as gay marriage or women priests. Right now, they're getting ancient proclamations from ancient priests. Your generation is going to be faced with the challenge of making Catholicism relevant, because the current crop sure as hell isn't. I want you to be prepared for that challenge. *That's* why I'm so tough on the Church."

He left his position at the front of the room and strolled among the desks. "I believe it was Mr. Gruehl who raised the issue of women in the priesthood first, so have at it."

Mr. Gruehl was an earnest young man who seemed to be intent on copying Gabe in both how he wore his hair and how he dressed. He tapped his pen on his copy of the New Testament as he talked. "It's the question I get asked the most from my friends, male and female: Why can't women be priests?

I know the official Church position, but how in the year two thousand do I defend it, especially to my female parishioners?"

Gabe nodded. "For the few in this room who aren't clear on the Church's official position, can you articulate it for us and what it's based on?"

"The conventional logic the Church employs," Gruehl said, "is that Jesus chose only men as his apostles, and thus they were the original priests. Further, there were no women at the Pentecost, when the Holy Spirit descended on the apostles, which some saw as the original ordination. So when the original set of priests gave way to subsequent generations, the Church Fathers used these two events as they established the laws of succession, which meant that women would be excluded. And even as the status of women has changed, especially in the last century, the Church hasn't. Just four years ago, Pope John Paul reaffirmed the laws of succession." He looked at Gabe, indicating he was finished.

"Excellent summary, Mr. Gruehl. And did the Holy Father say he was speaking infallibly?"

"No. But he stated that this was a ruling and practice born from the time of Jesus and that the Church could not undo it."

"And those four words—'the time of Jesus'—are why I teach this class. I've stated before that the Church is like the Supreme Court, governed by originalists who believe that the core document, whether the Constitution or the New Testament, has to be interpreted from the position of its authors. But even the originalists of the Constitution realized that the three-fifths clause, which counts blacks as three-fifths of a person, had to change to reflect the times. And that 'separate but equal' education had to go. Can someone give me an example of where the Church originalists changed their minds in line with changes in society."

A seminarian in the back of the room spoke up. "How about Vatican II?"

"Great example, Mr. Bender. And if Vatican II is a harbinger of things to come, I'm encouraged. But John's two successors are originalists who have already undone much of Vatican II's more encouraging programs, so the jury is out there. But you're right, Mr. Bender. It's more than a step in the right direction.

"Now back to Mr. Gruehl's magic words 'in the time of Jesus.' As amazing a person as he was, Jesus didn't stand outside of time. He was very much a product of his culture. And even if he were the original male feminist, his making women priests would have been viewed by his followers and those they were trying to recruit as more revolutionary than his actual teachings.

"What we do know is that Jesus had women friends and supporters, Mary of Magdala among them, which wasn't the standard practice at that time. And it's very possible that there were women present at the Last Supper and at the Pentecost, but they didn't merit mention from our four sexist evangelists. Which means we're excluding more than fifty percent of the world based on the attitudes of the time and the biases of these four men, who were writing from a severely patriarchal mindset and for a severely patriarchal audience."

"Do you foresee the Church policy on women priests ever changing?" another student asked.

"Put it this way, Mr. Loper: There are two restrooms for women in this entire building. I don't see that number increasing anytime soon."

He paused and looked around the room, but there were no more questions. "As for our second topic, the recent news about pedophilia and our priestly brethren, I admit that I was all set to come in here and be my normal pompous self, demanding that we purge our ranks of those guys immediately. But I realized I was relatively uninformed about the topic and would be talking through my ass. Then I remembered that I know someone who has had a ringside seat for this pedophilia thing—not as a participant, I'd like to stress, but as someone who's researched the issue from many angles. So let me introduce Father Michael Montgomery, a great priest and an even better friend. Mike?"

Michael opened with a brief bio, focusing on his path to the priesthood, including his time at a seminary in Massachusetts. He then shifted to his current responsibilities, including his regular assignment of following the activities of the other US dioceses, updating the archbishop whenever something of note occurred.

"The archbishop, like every archbishop, aspires to be a cardinal someday, which means he needs to be well-versed in dioceses around the country, not just his own. Tracking the competition, so to speak. So I spend a lot of time reading the local papers of dioceses around the US and following up on anything that catches my interest. Once a week—more if the news calls for it—I sit down with His Excellency, and we review the news. And recently that review has included charges and resulting investigations in the area of pedophilia."

He leaned forward in his stool until the back legs were slightly off the ground. "Before I go any further, let me be clear on a couple of counts. Then we'll get to your questions. First, I've never had a single meeting with His Excellency specifically on the topic of pedophilia. It has always been one of many topics in a crowded agenda. I don't want to give the impression that this is a topic of major and ongoing concern or that I know of any conspiracy in this area. Second, I'm not a sociologist and I don't pretend to be one. I'm happy to discuss what I'm discovering with you, but I don't presume to have theories on why this is happening. I'm a reporter. I'll leave the opinions to you guys."

He took a sip of water and let his caveats sink in. "With that said, here's what I've discovered. The number of pedophilia cases involving Catholic priests is on the rise. Whether that means pedophilia is increasing or just that victims are more willing to come forward in today's world than in the past, where it was strictly closeted, is unknown. And the trends are consistent, whether you're looking locally, nationally, or internationally.

"Take someplace like Ireland, for example. For hundreds of years, priests and nuns have gotten away with all kinds of abuse, with no reports and no police action. Nothing. And suddenly, as the political landscape over there has changed, so has the attitude toward the Church and its previous activities. And you're seeing old cases dug up—literally, since they're often excavating orphanages. There is also a new no-tolerance campaign against current abusers. So we need to distinguish between cases and the reporting of them when we look at pedophilia."

Gabe looked at the class and noted with a slight tinge of jealousy that he'd never seen them that attentive for one of his lectures.

"Now, as to the Church's response," Michael continued, "you have to look locally. Because if there's a clear Vatican-dictated policy on this issue, I haven't come across it. And believe me, I've looked. Which means each diocese has a lot of latitude in how it deals with these cases as they arise. So my advice to you guys, the ones heading into parish assignments, is do an assessment of your parish, hopefully even before you arrive there. Find out if there have been any charges and, if so, how the diocese reacted to them. In other words, know what you're getting into. And if you come up against something that bothers you, Gabe can tell you how to reach me."

Michael then gave the class a summary of his findings to date, not with the specificity he used with Gabe and the team but enough to show them the extent of the crisis as well as the lack of response in most dioceses. After twenty minutes, he opened it up for questions.

There was a long pause, broken finally by a thin voice. "What role does homosexuality figure into pedophilia?"

The classroom went quiet, a new tension filling the air. No one looked around; all eyes faced forward. "Thank you, Mr. Townsend, for addressing the largest elephant in the room when it comes to this topic," Gabe said. He looked at Michael to see if he wanted to take this one, but Michael indicated, with a slight look of relief, that the floor was Gabe's.

"Homosexuality is a topic that the Church is both uncomfortable with and in denial about. Let me give you an example. Two years ago, when I was sitting where you guys are, we had a visiting lecturer, a monk from Dallas. He joined us for dinner that evening, and the talk turned to the AIDS crisis and how, a few years back, it had decimated the ranks of his monastery. And he remarked, 'Who would have guessed we had so many intravenous drug users within our ranks?'"

There was a pause as the class digested his story. Then one student laughed, albeit nervously. As others got the irony behind Gabe's story, the laughter swelled. Gabe nodded. "Yeah. Funny and not so funny, right? But the Church has always been in denial about the number of homosexuals within its ranks. In fact, the Church has been in denial that there are any at all. This despite the sociological studies that say that ten percent of the US population is gay. And we all know that's low."

He smiled slightly. "Come on, guys, we're talking about Catholic priests here. Triple that ten percent and you'd still be low." He smiled slightly as the seminarians shifted in their seats, again keeping their eyes straight forward.

"But here's a basic question: So what? I happen to be straight, not that it's anything to crow about. Mike here is one of my best friends, but I don't know what his preference is, though I've always been suspicious of his collection of Greco-Roman wrestling tapes and magazines."

The students shifted their eyes to Michael, who raised his eyebrows at them and smiled cryptically.

"Though I'm no expert, I've done enough reading on the topic to know this: Homosexuality has no more to do with pedophilia than heterosexuality. Pedophiles, to my knowledge, are equal-opportunity rapists. Again, Mr. Townsend, thanks for having the guts to raise the issue. Next question."

"If we have a parishioner who accuses a priest of pedophilia, what should we do?" asked another student.

Michael chimed in. "Report it. Immediately. Either under your own name or anonymously, depending on your parish. But definitely report it. There needs to be a record, even if it's ignored. Worst case, report it to Gabe and me. But get it on record."

"And how should we interact with the person making the accusation?" Mr. Mandell asked.

Michael unhooked his heels from the stool and stood up. "We're getting into sensitive turf here, and I'd appreciate it if this conversation stays within this room. No one in this class—hell, in this seminary—should be proud of the way the Church has responded to this crisis. But that just puts us in the same shameful company as the Boy Scouts, the police, teachers—any collection of people who have power and influence over those they interact with. And what those organizations all have in common is that the primary loyalty of its members is to the organization, not the individual. Victims are somewhere between an annoyance and a threat."

Gabe motioned to Michael that he had something to say and took a few steps forward to the class as the heads swiveled in his direction. "Mike just asked you guys to keep this conversation within these four walls. I happen to know that this isn't happening, that some of you are reporting some of my more controversial comments to the powers that be. That's your right, though I wish you'd come see me first to discuss what's bothering or worrying you." The class was silent. This was a side of Gabe they hadn't seen before. He let the silence build.

"So here's my advice to you guys, and tell it to whomever you like. We need to change our values from 'Church first' to 'victim first.' The Church, as it's shown throughout its history, can take care of itself. The victim, by stark contrast, is usually on his or her own. We need to give that person—whether we're talking about adults or kids—the benefit of the doubt. Especially given what they're up against and what they're risking: their finances, their job, their reputation, their family relations. Who would do all that for a lie?"

When the class was over, Gabe and Michael retreated to the tavern, where they were joined by Jenny and Paul. Gabe gave Jenny and Paul a glowing summary of Michael's presentation, concluding with a salute of four raised mugs of beer.

"Aren't you worried about what Himself will do to you if he hears about what you've been doing?" Jenny asked Michael. "I mean, there's no surprise that Gabe—our little radical—has his issues with the Church. But you're an insider. Won't they feel betrayed if they hear about your involvement?"

She looked at Gabe. "I'm assuming there are at least a few spies in your class?"

"I like to think of them more as the archbishop's disciples than spies," Gabe said. "But yeah, he'll hear about today's class, probably before we're done with this pitcher."

"Why did you take this so publicly?" Jenny asked Gabe. "I mean, aren't you courting trouble? Especially now, with what we're looking into?"

"Because they asked," Gabe said, a slight irritation in his voice. "And I hate running scared on something this important. I mean, I like my job, but at what cost?"

"What do you think the response will be?" Jenny asked Paul.

"Well, Gabe is already where he wants to be," Paul replied. "And he's popular. So I think they'll leave him alone. Mike, on the other hand, they'll probably view as a traitor."

"Which is fine with me," Michael said, "because all I wanted in the first place was a parish posting. And if they try to rob me of that, I'll remind them how much I know."

Gabe shifted in his chair and rested his forearms on the table. "We can dwell on what's going to happen to Mike and me all night, but the reason I wanted to get together tonight was to update you on the playbook and what we've discovered."

"What playbook?" Paul asked.

"The playbook that it looks like the Church is using in addressing its pedophilia cases."

"Get out of here," Paul said. "An actual playbook. I mean, you all know I'm not a fan of the archbishop, but are you saying he's complicit in all of this? I thought he was just willfully ignorant and determined to stay that way." He looked over at Gabe. "Have you actually seen this playbook?"

"No, but it's clear that it exists."

"How can you be so sure?" Paul asked.

"I'm not trying to play the professor here," Gabe said, "but do you know what 'Q' is and its role in the New Testament?"

"It's a collection of Jesus's sayings, right?" Paul replied.

Gabe nodded. "Virtually every New Testament scholar believes there's a document that predates even Mark, probably more a collection of Jesus's sayings than another gospel. The similarities between the three Synoptic Gospels testifies to its existence. It's the same way with the playbook that our pedo pals have developed."

He motioned to Michael to pick up the narrative.

"It wasn't obvious at the start because we were all dealing with our own individual cases. But when I started compiling our different reports, I realized that the cases were too similar in how they proceeded—in techniques, timelines, and vocabulary—for it to be coincidental."

"If what you're suspecting is true and we can get our hands on it, it's game over," Paul said. "The Church will be culpable and have to enact major reforms." He nodded at Michael's computer "Can you show me how it works?"

Michael picked up the pen and a large paper napkin and wrote a large "1" and the word "terminology" next to it. "The first thing to know is that it's never called pedophilia. It's always 'inappropriate contact.'"

He wrote a "2" and the word "blame." "Then you put the blame on the victim. Gently at first, especially if you're talking about kids. You remind teachers and parents—whoever initiated the complaint—about how kids tend to exaggerate. You ask the parents about times when their kids have stretched the truth or even lied, not accusing them, just establishing a platform for discussion. You then move on to how easy it is for kids to form the wrong impression about a specific action or misperceive the intent behind it.

"If the parents are still adamant about what happened, you turn up the heat, reminding them that this is a man of God we're talking about and that the Church will have to investigate not only the child but the entire family. And should it go to court, the child will have to face the priest and testify in open court. Not many parents are willing to put their child through something like that."

"What about if the accuser is an adult, either talking about a recent activity or one from the past?" Jenny asked.

"If it's in the past, they use the same techniques about memory," Michael said. "If it's current, they go straight to step three. He drew a "3" on the napkin and wrote "big guns." "If it gets this far—and most cases stop at step two—the next step is to bring in a senior official. A monsignor. Perhaps even the archbishop himself. They focus on the damage a case like this could do to the Church and how their own community will react if charges are pressed. They even have anecdotes about families who were shunned to the point of having to move."

He then drew three dollar signs. "Step four, as you might guess, is money. But on the rare occasions the Church actually pays out, the money comes with major strings about repayment and possible legal action should anything about the settlement leak."

Michael took a sip of beer. His mouth pursed, as if the beer had gone bad. "One parent, a dad, was holding out not just for money but for the priest to be expelled. One of the archbishop's cronies approached the guy's employer, a good Catholic and friend of the Church, and got him to fire the dad. Then they brought the father back in and offered him the same financial package, plus help in getting his job back. But no discipline for the priest." He put down his pen. "He accepted."

"Nice company we keep," Jenny said. "I wonder who hears the archbishop's confession."

"I doubt he ever feels the need to confess," Paul replied.

"But wait, as they say in late-night commercials, there's more," Michael added. He opened his laptop and scrolled for a moment. "What I just showed you is the playbook for dealing with accusers off the record. Here's what happens in the rare instances when it winds up in court."

He read the screen to himself briefly, shaking his head. "Here's a case where, instead of arguing for the priest's innocence, the Church's lawyers took issue with the actual charge and its terminology. The priest was charged with pedophilia, the legal definition of which is sex with an individual under the age of twelve. Since the victim in question was fourteen, technically the crime is hebephilia. The case was thrown out on that technicality."

As he saw the amazement on the three faces, he held up his hand. "And then there's this. When prosecutors wised up and started to use the term 'hebephilia' where appropriate, the Church was still able to get a number of cases kicked because they involved ephebophilia, which is sex with post-pubescent kids below the age of statutory rape. Over twenty cases were dismissed on these technicalities alone before the prosecutors again wised up. From then on, the prosecutors used a dictionary as well as the *Diagnostic and Statistical Manual of Mental Disorders* before ever considering an indictment."

He closed the laptop. "I couldn't make this shit up if I tried."

Twenty-Eight

ARKIN WAS IN PAIN. With his legs suspended in slings to alleviate the pressure from his badly damaged groin, he pressed the pain button that was supposed to release the morphine, the button that had carried him through his first day of hospitalization. But for the last fifteen minutes, the press of the button had brought no relief. He pressed another button and an empty voice came out of the ceiling.

"Can I help you, Mr. Arkin?"

"Yeah. What the hell's up with the morphine? I'm pressing the button like crazy and I'm getting nothing. I'm in pain here."

"Yes, sir. We disabled your button an hour ago, but you were asleep and we didn't want to wake you."

"Whose bright idea was that, and why wasn't I consulted?"

"It came at the request of the police. That's all I can tell you."

"Well, that's bullshit. It's my pain, not theirs. Either turn my morphine back on or let me talk to the genius who turned it off."

"That would be me." Carla walked into the room, shutting the door behind her. Even though the bed next to Arkin's was empty, she closed the curtain separating the two beds and showed him her badge. "Carla Jessup. I know, I don't look like a

Jessup. More like a Hernandez, yeah? Married name, though why I keep it I don't know. Kids, I guess."

She gestured at his elevated legs. "I know you're in pain, Mr. Arkin, and I apologize for that. But when I called over today to check on your condition and find out when I could speak with you, the doctors said you were out of it, that you'd been punching the morphine button for all you were worth. As you know if you've watched any crime show on TV in the past twenty years, the first forty-eight hours are critical to solving any crime. I asked the doctors to cut back on your meds so you'd be alert enough to help me catch whoever assaulted you in such a terrible way."

Arkin straightened his shoulders and tried to pull himself up to whatever authoritative stance could be achieved in a hospital bed. He tried a peeved look on Carla, but she was fiddling with her notebook and missed it.

"The faster we get through this, the faster you can get back to your morphine and the sooner I get on with the search for your assailant." She looked up. "Can you tell me what you remember from the assault? Anything at all?"

"I'll try, Detective, but I don't know how much help I'm going to be. I was walking my dog. That's the last thing I remember."

"About that. You were four miles from your house. You always go that far to walk your dog?"

Arkin tried a winning smile. "That's a habit I've fallen into recently. Pittsburgh is such a marvelous city, Detective. I try to see as much of it as I can."

"That's admirable, sir. Me, I'm a creature of routine. Grab the leash, down to the park, lift your leg, squat if you got to, then let's head back." She looked at her notes. Without looking up, she altered her tone to a brisk inquiry. "This bastard who attacked you, did he do it from front or behind?"

"Behind. Never had a chance. I was a pretty good athlete in high school. I'd have given him a run for his money if I'd seen him coming."

She looked up. "No doubt. You look like you stay in shape. Not like my ex." She looked back at her notes. "Here's an oddity I hope you can help me with. It looks like he concentrated his attack on your groin. Normally they target the head or ribs in cases like this."

"Cases like what?" He shifted in the bed slightly, eyeing her cautiously.

"Mugging. Random attack. A guy out walking his dog, minding his own business, makes a perfect target. But he didn't take your money, and he didn't mess up your face." She looked up from her notebook. "You're a handsome man, sir, if you don't mind my saying. Many muggers would mess up a face like yours, just for spite. But this attack was so disciplined, so . . . restrained. You piss anyone off recently, anyone I should be looking into?"

"Like I said, I was just out walking my dog and—"

"Let me stop you there." Carla's chatty tone was gone. "When we found you, your dog was tied up next to you. Why was that if you were walking him? Did you tie him up or was that our oddly-behaving mugger?"

"I'm not sure what you mean, Detective. As I said, I don't remember much about—"

"What I mean, sir, is that if you're walking your dog, you don't tie it up. Not unless you're about to do something where you need both hands." She smiled conspiratorially. "Like taking a leak."

"Again, Detective—"

Her voice shifted to granite. "Do you know a Rachel Parker?"

"No, I don't."

Carla extracted a photo of a happy looking sixteen-year-old girl from her file and showed it to him. Arkin shrugged and shook his head. As he handed the photo back, she replaced it with another one. This one was of the same young woman but from behind.

"Maybe this angle is more representative, since it's how she would have looked when you approached her."

Arkin tried to sit up a bit straighter and adopted a tone of restrained outrage. "I'm not sure what you're alleging here, Detective, but I don't appreciate—"

"And then there's this." Carla took the photo back and handed him one, facedown. He turned it over and saw a close-up of the girl's badly bruised throat and mouth.

"This is what she looked like after her encounter with you. Alleged encounter, I should say." As he started to object, she held up her hand. "Let me tell you how I think it played out, since the pain has made your memory so hazy. You tie up your dog to take a leak, tuck yourself back in, and trip as you're heading back to get the dog. You reach out to break the fall and this girl happens to walk by at the same time. Your hands inadvertently wrap around—"

"For the last time, Detective, I have no idea what you're talking about. Go ahead and have fun at my expense, since I'm a captive in this bed and the drugs are clouding my mind. But I'm not saying another word without my attorney present."

Carla nodded enthusiastically. "As is your right, sir. As is your right. But when you brief your lawyer, make sure to tell him— actually, a female lawyer might play better in this case—that you were found exactly where Rachel Parker said she was attacked. I'd also work with your attorney to find a way to get in that part about loving to explore all our city has to offer."

She reached into her briefcase and took out the stun gun. She placed it on his bedside table. "I'm assuming this is yours. The first cops on the scene found it next to your head." She tapped the mechanism with her finger. "Given your habit of exploring all the neighborhoods in Pittsburgh, I can see why you have it. Unlike the Chamber of Commerce, I don't believe all our neighborhoods are crime free and safe."

She leaned forward until her face was inches from his. "Listen, you piece of shit. You tried to rape a sixteen-year-old girl. You know it and I know it. And everything I've learned in my years on the job, coupled with that nice piece of equipment you had with you, tells me this isn't your first rape." She pulled back a few inches. "But I'm a cop, and I've got a job to do here. And that's to find the guy who put you in here. Another detective is going to handle your alleged attack on Ms. Parker. As far as my investigation goes, you should want me to succeed because I don't know if this guy's done with you or not."

She got up and put away her notebook. "But when I'm done with that, I'm coming after you, motherfucker, and I'll make sure you're put away for a good long time."

She stopped at the door and looked back, giving him her own version of a winning smile. "Anything you could do to help me in my investigation would be greatly appreciated. Thank you for your time, sir. On my way out, I'll tell them to put the morphine back on. Enjoy."

Twenty-Nine

TWO WEEKS AFTER the meeting with the team, Gabe was parked across the street and one house up from the assembly hall and cottage. He had been there since 7:30, when the first priests arrived. A few had come along, some came together, and the later ones had children in tow. Two other priests waited outside the assembly hall and greeted the younger children who were brought there by their parents. One of the priests had leaned his head into the passenger window of a car in the drop-off line, exchanged a joke or two with the driver, and taken the child by the hand, guiding him toward the assembly hall. Then he rerouted him to the cottage once the parent drove away.

After the arrivals stopped, Gabe passed the time by reviewing his notes about the investigation using a penlight for illumination and placing the notes on separate piles on the passenger seat and floorboard. When he was done, he turned off the penlight and settled in.

Since their last meeting, the team's investigation into nearby pedophiles had increased, both in content and intensity. Paul was settling into a rhythm with the paper files, passing back to Michael a growing list of suspicious priests who had fallen outside the reach of the computer. Jenny and Gabe were concentrating on those priests with multiple transfers on their résumés. Some priests, it seemed, were short-timers or roamers by nature. There was nothing suspicious about them. They seemed to welcome new assignments as a chance to improve whatever parish they were sent to, moving on to the next assignment once the parish was in shape to hand to their successor. But other résumés had a stench that almost came through the keyboard. And the list of those suspicious figures continued to grow.

Surprisingly, news of Michael's presentation seemed not to have reached the archbishop's office because he found himself the target of a recruiting effort from some of the priests he had befriended in his role as the archbishop's ambassador. "The first guy to cruise me was no surprise," he told Gabe on the phone. "It was Ludlow, with his clammy handshake and rubbery lips. Hell, gay or straight, that guy couldn't get laid without roofies or a weapon. He invited me to watch Monday Night Football over at the cottage, though I'm sure the weasel doesn't know the difference between a quarterback and a shortstop. But the problem with having Ludlow invite me is that when I said no, the group didn't know if it was because I wasn't one of them or because Ludlow is such an ass. So they sent in Jefferson, with poker being the attraction."

"Jefferson?" Gabe said, the surprise evident in his voice. "Hell, he's a good guy. We went to a Penguins game together. He knows his movies, his sports. Last guy I would have picked as a pedo."

"Well, with me he was all Mr. Simpatico, talking about how this job can really get to you with its twenty-four-hour-a-day demands, difficult parishioners, and all. That's why he likes the cottage. He sees it as a refuge where you can let your hair down and relax with friends facing the same challenges."

"So did you go to the poker game?"

"Yeah. I wanted to see the inside of the place and how they might approach me. It was clear that poker was just an excuse for getting me over there. Most of those guys didn't know the difference between two pair and three of a kind. One of them mentioned playing strip poker and everyone laughed a little too hard. I could feel their eyes on me. But other than that, it was a pretty benign evening."

"How about around the cottage?"

"Jenny was right about successive approximation. On the coffee table they had a *Sports Illustrated* next to a couple of issues of *Playboy*. And someone had left a few videos out for me to see. They ranged from *E.T.* to *Debbie Does Dallas*. Nothing overt, but you could tell that the bait was there should I be interested."

"You think you'll go back?"

"I might not be invited. I decided that if I was going to waste an evening with those guys, I'd make it worth my while. I was up a hundred and twenty bucks by the end of the night. But yeah, I'll go back one more time, just to see how they move my recruitment along. By that time, I'm hoping we've got enough to go public with this."

Gabe had been casing the cottage for the past two hours. At one point he had exited the car and gone down the driveway to the left of the cottage. Dressed all in black, including what looked like a scarf wrapped loosely around his neck, he'd stopped even with the driver's door of the only car in the driveway, a late-model sedan, and slipped into the bushes on the side of the driveway where he'd spent ten minutes fashioning a small cave of sorts. At one point he'd thought about sliding along the side of the cottage and looking in through the windows, but he was afraid that if he saw what he thought was going on in there, he'd have to intervene. And what would be a one-time, feel-good hero moment for him would ruin the larger goals of the investigation. So he returned to the car and settled back into his watch.

He now watched as the children and their priest escorts left the cottage, eight participants in all. Some priests set off down the street, walking children who lived nearby home. Others delivered their charges to the waiting cars, mentioning ice cream sundaes before they shut the car doors and waved good-bye. But he continued to wait, knowing from past watches that there was one more priest to come, the one responsible for tidying up and locking the cottage.

He waited until he saw the lights go out in the cottage, first upstairs and then in the back of the house. Then he slipped out of the car and took his place in the leafy indentation he'd fashioned and waited. He listened as the front door opened and the last priest locked up, whistling to himself as he did so, a big band song Gabe recognized but couldn't name.

On his way to the car, the priest stopped briefly, took out his phone, and called someone. As soon as the call was finished and the phone was pocketed, Gabe stepped out of the bushes and drove three fingers into the priest's throat, caught the slumping figure, and dragged him into the cover of the bushes. He cradled him gently, one hand on his forehead, the other on his throat, fingers at the ready should the vocal cords recover.

Lowering his head until his mouth was next to the priest's ear, he said in a calm voice, "I know you can't speak, Father, so I'll say your confession for you. Tell me if I get anything wrong." His voice deepened slightly. "Bless me, Father, for I have sinned. My sins are: I have violated the trust and the bodies of children, damaging them for life. Including earlier tonight."

Then he went to work.

Thirty

"ME AGAIN," CARLA SAID to the floor's chief nurse. "I need to get something like frequent flyer miles or coupons—something—for all the time I'm spending here."

The nurse chuckled. "This one's interesting, Detective. We nurses have been talking about it in the break room. There's no doubt it's the same guy. The damage is too distinctive. But the victims, they're all over the place. First those two assholes. We assume they're muggers who picked on the wrong guy. Then the businessman who's a prick but a light-year away from our muggers. And now a priest." She smiled at Carla and raised her eyebrows. "If you connect the dots, let us know, please."

"I will, but I'm as stumped as you guys. But that's how most of these investigations start, with us feeling like morons. You tell me, what strikes you most about the injuries?"

"How they can be so precise and yet so violent at the same time. Violent damage is usually messy. Hell, I don't need to tell *you* that. The damage this guy is inflicting requires a large amount of force, which usually happens when the attacker is out of control: domestics, bar fights. You know the score. This guy isn't angry, he's just incredibly strong. And precise. He goes at the penis and testicles and doesn't miss. There's no bruising around the thighs, no indication that he did anything but hit his target. I've never seen anything like it."

"Neither have I, to be honest," Carla replied. "This guy's a contradiction, not just in how he attacks but like you said, in the range of his victims."

"Maybe he got the priest mixed up with someone else."

Carla shrugged. "Or maybe the priest isn't as impeccable as he seems." She put her hand on the closed door and looked back at the nurse. "But that's why they pay me the big bucks."

Once in the priest's room, she got down to business quickly.

"I know you went over this with the first cops on the scene, Father . . ." She stopped and consulted her notebook. "Mitchell. But I need to hear it in your own words. Your attacker, he came up behind you, right?"

"Correct."

"And he said nothing to you, before, during, or after the attack?" She stopped for a second. "Look at me, maligning my own gender. If you didn't see your attacker and that person never said a word, how do we know it wasn't a woman?" She smiled encouragingly, but the priest's expression stayed blank. "Did he—or she—say anything to you that would explain this attack?"

"Not a word."

"The hell with political correctness. I'm going to assume it was a he, given the damage he did. He didn't take anything from you? Not your wallet or watch? Nice one, by the way."

"A gift from my parents for my ordination."

"And he didn't inflict any damage on you except for your groin area. Any idea what that's about?"

"None, Detective. None at all."

"The reason I ask, Father, is that this attack is similar to a few others that have taken place recently. But those attacks seem to be related to issues—and to victims—that don't apply in this case. I gotta tell you, Father, I'm stumped. You know?"

When Mitchell didn't respond, she turned a page in her notebook. "The house you were found in front of, what can you tell me about it?"

He shifted in the bed, trying to find a less painful position, wincing as he did so. "It's more a cottage than a house. It's a place for priests to get together and relax."

"Huh. Like a kids' clubhouse or a country club?" When he didn't respond, she continued. "I can see the need to relax. You've got a tough job. It's like you're on duty twenty-four hours a day."

Mitchell nodded enthusiastically, the first sign of anything beyond stoic reserve. "Being a priest means you're always being observed. If I want to watch a football game at a bar, for example, I've got to drive at least two parishes over to find a place where no one knows I'm a priest so I can watch it in peace."

"Boy, do I understand that," Carla said. "That's why we cops tend to hang out with other cops. Why we have our own bars. No one else knows what our job is like. When we get off shift, we want to be able to decompress. And that sometimes means saying things other cops would understand but a civilian would find insensitive."

"It's the same for us priests," Mitchell said. "The cottage you're asking about—the clubhouse—is someplace we can get together, watch a game, shoot some pool, watch a movie. No furtive glances, no tsk-tsk from someone at the bar because we ordered a third Scotch."

"It's good to be with your own, isn't it?" She frowned and looked at her notebook. "But here's my problem, Father. The damage inflicted on you was both specific and extensive. And by leaving your wallet and expensive watch and not hitting you anywhere else—your face, for instance—your assailant was making a statement. Any idea what he was trying to say?"

"No idea, Detective. As I said, he never said a word." He motioned at his raised legs. "Believe me, I'd love to help. If not for myself, then for the next person this maniac attacks."

"You're right about this guy being a maniac, Father." Her eyes moved to her notebook, as if she'd just remembered something. "Let me read you something, Father. It came from one of the detectives in my squad, a real Bible thumper." She looked up at him. "No offense intended. Anyway, when I was in the squad room reviewing these attacks, he wrote down this passage from . . ." She squinted at the page and then put on a pair of reading glasses that hung on a chain around her neck. "Deuteronomy. 'No man whose testicles are crushed or whose member has been cut off shall enter the House of the Lord.'" She winced. Then she closed the book and looked at him. "Ouch. Looks like our mugger is an Old Testament fan. And he's out to make a statement, even if innocent folks like you get caught in the crossfire."

"As I said before, I'll help you however I can, though my input may prove minimal."

"I appreciate the positive attitude, Father. We don't always encounter that kind of cooperation in investigations of this sort." She smiled at him and peered again into her notebook. "I don't know how much you know about how detectives work, but a lot of it involves the elimination process. It's like sculpting. You carve away the pieces that don't matter, and what's left is the statue. But it takes a lot of repetition and can be a bit tedious, so bear with me, okay?"

She waited for Mitchell to say something, but he just looked at her intently and nodded.

"Let me run something by you. With all the rumors going around about priests and kids these days, could someone have the wrong idea about what your clubhouse is for? Or, and I hate like hell to say it, but the wrong idea about you individually?"

Mitchell didn't answer immediately, appearing to give the question serious thought. His forehead showed lines and the skin around his temples tightened. But then his face went blank. "I don't see how, Detective. I really don't. As I said, the clubhouse isn't a secret, and it has been in use for years."

"Yeah, but these rumors about pedophilia are more recent. I could see some asshole thinking that instead of just kicking back and watching the Steelers game—and they suck this year, don't they?" She paused. "Anyway, I can see someone thinking you guys are watching kiddie porn and pulling your puds. Or worse, that you've got kids in there with you. You know?"

"Are you hearing these rumors from parishioners, Detective, or is this a working theory?"

She smiled slightly. "Working theory. I like that term. Are you sure you're a priest and not a fellow cop? But now that we're investigative partners, you're right. It's more theory than rumor. Still, a couple more attacks like this one and it'll be a rumor that neither of us is going to be able to control."

She scooted her chair a little closer to his bed and leaned in. "Look, Father. Before I came over here, I did some research on you to see if you had anything in common with previous victims I'm investigating. And I came up with squat. From what I can see, you're a good guy who wound up the victim of either a random attack or a case of mistaken identity. Which makes your case so much harder to investigate. But that's my problem, not yours."

She lowered her voice, causing him to incline slightly toward her. "Listen, Father. As long as I'm here, I'm hoping you can help me out with a personal issue. A matter of faith."

"If I can help you, I will." He motioned at his lap and elevated legs. "As you can see, it doesn't look like I'm going anywhere for a while."

She smiled briefly at his joke and plucky attitude before plunging in. "Here's my problem. I'm Catholic and my twelve-year-old son wants to be an altar boy." She raised her eyebrows at him and waited.

"That's commendable on his part. What's the problem?"

"Come on, Father. It's just the two of us here. My concern is all the crap I'm hearing about predatory priests these days. And altar boys seem to be a prime target."

"Ah," he said, his eyes drifting off to the hospital window. "I understand now. But I can tell you, Detective, those reports are more sensational than factual. I'm sure your son would be safe, especially with a watchful mother like you."

"That's good to hear, Father, because he really wants to do it." Her voice lowered. "I got to tell you, Father, as a cop I see a lot. And most of it I understand. You're poor and jobless, so you steal. You're angry and have had a few, so you assault someone who pisses you off. Maybe a family member, maybe a complete stranger. But this pedophilia thing—I can't get my head around it. Especially when it involves . . ." She made air quotes. "Men of God. Tell you the truth, if I were investigating pedophile priests instead of chasing down your assailant, I wouldn't even know where to begin looking. Because from what I hear, these guys are as normal on the outside as you and me."

She waited for a response, but he maintained a fixed expression of professional interest and sympathy. Carla's voice rose slightly. "Have you ever met one of these bastards? I'm not looking for names, just trying to get my hands around this whole pedophilia thing. Anyway, have you? Met one."

"None that I can say with certainty. Maybe a doubt here or there, but nothing actionable."

"And by 'actionable' you mean?"

He shifted again in the bed, looking for a new position to ease the pain. "If I were certain about one of my fellow priests,

I would report him to the diocese. Or to you. You can count on that. But I'd need to be certain. I haven't given the topic much thought, Detective, but before I made a charge against a fellow priest, I'd have to be certain. I'd need hard evidence, not just doubts or suppositions."

"You'd make a good cop, Father. But here's the deal about my job. You usually don't start with hard evidence. You start with, to use your words, doubts and suppositions, and you see where they lead. Which is why I'm asking you if anyone comes to mind. Perhaps someone our attacker mistook you for."

"You say my assailant attacked others in the same vicious way but that the others weren't priests."

"Correct."

"So was I a mistake? Or should I be worried?"

"My take? Too much planning went into this for it to be random. But based on what I've learned about you, both before I came in today and now in this interview, the guy made a mistake." She smiled at him. "Unless you want to confess to me that you're a pedophile."

Father Mitchell chuckled lightly, and Carla's voice dropped again. "But I've got to tell you, Father, I hear rumors as a cop. And ever since my kid said he wanted to be an altar boy, I've wanted to just throw my arms around him and keep him home. But I know that's not fair to him. Or, to be honest, to the priests I've met over the years."

"That's good to hear, Detective. Many people just can't get past a rumor here or there, which at times can be as damaging as the sin itself."

"Let me stop you right there, Father. I agree with you about the danger of rumors, but from what I can see, some of these accusations have substance. My God, think what these people— these *kids*—are risking. And for what? To be bullied and ostracized within their own fucking church?"

When Mitchell made to respond, she raised her hand. "Sorry about that little outburst. I wasn't speaking as a cop right there, but as a mom. But cop or mom, Father, I'm having a hard time getting a starting point here, visualizing how something like this can even happen. I mean, how can anyone, much less a man of God, think it's okay to bend a twelve-year-old boy or girl over a desk, rape them, and then send them back to class? And then have that poor kid just live in hell, waiting for the next time, knowing there *will* be a next time. And meanwhile, these bastards go about saying Mass, hearing confessions, and baptizing babies. These aren't men we're talking about, they're monsters."

Father Mitchell shifted slightly. "Well, not having known any of these men personally, I can't say what they—"

"Look at me, putting you in an impossible spot. I'm asking a good man to try to explain a living, breathing asshole to me. But these assholes stump me. They call themselves men of God, and yet they're serial rapists. Do they go to confession, and if so, is it only with each other so that they can be granted forgiveness, then go back to raping one day and saying Mass the next."

She paused and looked at Father Mitchell, letting the silence grow until he shifted his gaze from the window to her. But he simply raised his eyebrows in a 'don't know' gesture. It was clear his cooperation was nearing an end.

"In my job," Carla continued, "when things go south—on the job or off—we've got therapists we can see. And anything we say to them about our jobs, ourselves, our excesses is all sacred. Just like your confessional. Do you guys have the same kind of resources?"

"I believe we do, though I've never had to avail myself of their services." He shifted his posture, sitting up more erect. "How about you?"

"Once. I shot a perp, which is an automatic referral." She corrected herself. "Not the shooting, but if the perp dies, it's automatic. Which was the case here."

"Do you mind my asking the circumstances?"

"Not at all. He had killed his wife—in front of his kids, no less—and was holding one of the kids hostage with a knife to his throat. I was first on the scene and had to make a judgment call, then and there. The muscles on the guy's arm, the one with the knife, were pulsing. I had no idea what the bastard's next move was going to be. Luckily—for me, not for him—the backup cops made some noise coming up the stairs and he turned his head. I shot him in the temple."

"And afterwards, did it help to talk to the therapist?"

"Tell you the truth? Not a damn bit because I didn't have any second thoughts or doubts. Not with his wife on the floor dead and those muscles twitching on his knife hand. I know I shouldn't say it, but I slept like a baby that night. The therapist was a required six sessions, but after the first session she could see that I was fine. So we just chatted for a couple of sessions and she pretended I'd attended all six and cleared me for work."

"Still, it must have been traumatic."

"It's nothing compared to the victims' traumas. I look at their faces and I know—I just know—they won't be able to un-see or undo what they've just seen or experienced. Maybe for the rest of their lives. And those are one-time events. In the case of the kids you and I are talking about, I can't imagine anything more traumatic than a child being raped by someone they trust. And knowing that it's probably going to happen again, by a man of God, no less. That child is going to be scarred for life." Her voice rose. "I'll tell you this, Father. If that priest can sleep the way I did that night I shot the wife killer, he's one seriously sick fuck. Excuse the language."

She stood up. "I've taken up enough of your time. I need to let you get back to healing. Let's do this so I can clear you and your fellow priests and let you guys get back to your football and pool. You provide me a list of everyone who was there the night you were attacked. I'll interview them, clear them, and then put the word out in the neighborhood that there's nothing about that cottage they should worry about. How's that sound?"

Without waiting for a response, she put her notebook in his hands. "Print their names so I'm not having to keep calling you for the right spelling. I'll be out in the hall on the phone. Take your time."

Mitchell looked at the door through which Carla had just exited, then down at the notebook. Then he reached for the phone by his bedside and asked for an outside line.

Thirty-One

"I DON'T KNOW IF THIS . . ." Carla stopped and shrugged her shoulders. "We don't know what to call him down at the station. 'Vigilante' is the current favorite, but some guys like 'Pilgrim.' Either way, they admire him. Part of me does too, but that won't keep me from doing my job." She looked around the table. "The reason I'm telling you about this guy is that he might be related to our investigation. I don't know how, but when you're a cop, if something tickles your mind, you don't ignore it. Anyway, I thought I'd keep you guys in the loop."

It was four o'clock and the group had gathered at the tavern for what had evolved into a weekly update. When it was her turn, Carla added Father Mitchell to her growing list that included the two muggers, followed by Eddie and Raymond Arkin.

"And you're sure it's the same assailant? Or vigilante?" Jenny asked.

"No doubt about it," Carla replied. "I talked to the nurses at Good Sam. You want the truth, always go to nurses, not doctors. They agree. The damage to these guys is so precise, so professional, it has to be the same guy. Like I said, I wouldn't have even brought him up except for this latest attack." She looked at Gabe. "You know him? I mean, that cottage is on your turf."

Gabe shook his head. "That cottage is on diocese property, which means it's open to priests throughout the Pittsburgh area."

"Have you been inside?"

"Once. I was new in my parish assignment and was invited to join poker night there. So I went, lost my obligatory ten bucks, and cashed out early. Said I had an early morning. What I remember is how forced the banter was, like everyone was trying too hard to not be a priest for the night."

"You?" Carla asked Paul.

"Same as Gabe. Once. A Monday night Steelers game. I've been gone for over twenty years, and I still knew more about football than those guys." He took a sip of beer and looked at Carla. "What was your impression of the good father?"

"My initial take was that he was a victim of mistaken identity. But as we talked, I started to get this vibe from him—call it police intuition. So I went with the mistaken identity approach, telling him how shitty it was that a good guy like him could be taken for scum like those pedo priests. I saw his eyes squeeze a little at that, so I just lit into pedophilia and pedophiles from a cop's perspective. Then from a mother's perspective, telling him my kid wanted to be an altar boy and asking if I should encourage or discourage it."

"What was his reaction?" Michael asked.

"He tried a sympathetic face at first, but I think he was smart enough to know that it probably didn't look genuine. And it didn't. So he shifted to the blank poker face, which he maintained until I started in on pedos, turning up the heat about how they were the scum of the scum. It wasn't obvious, but I could see that some of my punches were landing. So if I had to say right now, I'm leaning toward dirty."

"What did Mitchell do when you returned for his list of priests who use the cottage?" Jenny asked.

"He referred me to your office," she said, turning to Michael. "Said you guys were the only ones who could give out that kind of information. So I guess I'll be seeing you soon. Don't worry, I'll pretend I don't know you."

"Don't worry, I'm used to it. Especially when it comes to women."

Carla put a hand over his. "Honey, if you weren't a priest, I'd be all over you."

Michael brightened. "Really?"

"No," she said. "You're too young." She turned to Paul. "You, on the other hand . . ."

Thirty-Two

EVEN THOUGH HE WAS in the street behind the cottage, Gabe still disabled the interior light of his car. He had sat in the dark car for the past twenty minutes assessing the foot and car traffic. Now, with dinner over in most houses, the inhabitants had settled into their routines. Windows flickered from televisions, both upstairs and downstairs. Other rooms stayed dark.

Checking to see that his phone was on silent, he eased the car door shut behind him. Dressed in dark clothes, he walked casually up the street. When he was even with the house that backed up to the priests' cottage, he slipped into the darkened driveway and walked briskly but quietly down the driveway and into the small backyard.

He had cased the cottage earlier that night, driving by at normal speed, checking if there was anyone there and whether security had changed in light of the attack. His first trip along the street had yielded an empty driveway and equally empty porch. Half an hour later, there was a diocese-issued car in the driveway and a heavy-set black man in a nondescript blue uniform sitting on a chair on the porch. Involved with the magazine in his lap, he hadn't looked up as Gabe eased past.

Gabe had then driven to the block behind the cottage, stopping just down from the house that backed onto the cottage. Having cased the house earlier that afternoon, he now knocked on the front door, ready with a confused excuse about being at the wrong house should anyone answer. But the house was quiet, and there was no car in the driveway or out front. He slipped around to the backyard and found a wooden fence that he scaled easily, bringing him into the cottage backyard.

Comfortable in the dark and silence, Gabe crouched and observed the cottage from his new vantage point. After five minutes of sustained silence, he moved quietly but quickly to the back porch. To his surprise, the back door was unlocked, so he pocketed the flat-edged tool he'd bought an hour earlier at a hardware store. With a gentle, silent pull, the door opened, bringing him into the kitchen. The sound from the television drifted into the kitchen, covering any noise he might make in traversing it. He glided through the darkness, his fingertips touching the stove and the refrigerator as he moved toward the lit doorway.

He knew from Michael that the chairs and couches would be facing away from the kitchen and toward the television. Easing his head around the doorway, he saw the back of two priests' heads. On the television screen was a shot of a child that could not have been more than ten being anally raped. The priests' pants were open, their cocks out, and they were masturbating. Gabe recoiled unconsciously and took a step back, almost falling over as he took in the scene.

Muffled by the sound from the television and propelled by his own fury, he closed the distance between the kitchen and the couch quickly and noiselessly. He disabled the two priests with jolting blows to their necks, then stood back and watched them slump noiselessly together on the couch. Confident that the silent attack hadn't alerted their hired security, he shrugged out of a small backpack cinched tightly to his body and brought out duct tape and zip ties. With the priests secured—hands behind their backs and tape over their mouths—Gabe pulled a thin black mask over his face and tapped them lightly on the cheeks, bringing them back to the reality of their situation.

His plan had been to calmly face the men down, explain what punishment they were facing, and demand that they then spread the word to their fellow pedos. Instead, he found his throat choked and his eyes rich with tears. "Goddammit," he said in a croaking voice, "aren't you guys getting the message? Don't you realize the damage you're doing?" He looked at them with hard, probing eyes. "This shit has got to stop. You're damaging an entire generation of believers and violating your oaths in the process. I can't let it keep happening. I can't."

He stepped back and gathered himself, feeling the tears sinking into the fabric that covered his face. "You think I like doing this?" he asked, whispering at them harshly. "You think I get pleasure from damaging you? Do you really think that?"

He rubbed the fabric beneath his eyes with his palm. "Can't you guys just stop? You see what's happened to your pedo pals, and yet you . . ." He was embarrassed by his imploring tone and gestured at the television. "Has this got its hooks that deep into you?" He stared imploringly at the men, searching for any sign of remorse. But all he saw in their eyes was fear.

He looked at the door and kept his voice low. "You and your pals have turned me into someone I don't like. But what kind of man would I be if I just stood by and did nothing, now that I know what you do to these kids?" He took two steps and turned the TV sound up slightly. Returning to the men, he stood there for a second, flexed his hands once, then stiffened the three middle fingers and slid the thumb and pinkie under them. "So this is on you." He began to sob quietly, but it didn't prevent him from going to work on the two men.

When he was done, Gabe reached into the backpack and withdrew a small bottle of battery acid. He walked quickly over to the VCR, tilted it slightly, and poured the acid into the slot. He poured the rest of the acid over the perforated top of the television. Then he left the way he'd entered.

Thirty-Three

CARLA THANKED THE RECEPTIONIST, took the proffered glass of water, and sat down on the couch. Across the room, seated behind a large, beautifully carved desk, Archbishop Francis Cafferty was finishing up a phone call. Putting down the receiver, he stood up and moved around his desk to greet Carla. A large man with an impressive mane of snow-white hair, he was clad in a black cassock trimmed in black silk with a silk sash around his waist. He strode confidently and regally toward Carla, and as he approached, she got a whiff of expensive cologne. He held out his left hand, which was dominated by a large ring.

Carla rose and shook the extended hand with her own left, which momentarily flustered the archbishop. But he quickly regained his bearing and motioned with an elegant turn of his wrist for her to retake her seat. He sat across from her in a plush wingback chair, and she noted that the seating put him slightly higher than her.

"I'm seeing you without an appointment, Detective, because I was told this was a matter of some urgency."

"And some delicacy as well. I was told to call you 'Excellency.' Do you prefer that or something less formal, like 'Father'?" She tried a smile. "I'm assuming 'Frank' is out of the question."

The archbishop didn't return the smile. "'Excellency' is traditional."

"Okay, Excellency. Are you aware that six of your priests have been assaulted recently? Grievously assaulted? And all in the same manner?"

"As you're probably aware, Detective, there are more than four hundred priests in my archdiocese, which extends far beyond Pittsburgh."

"But six of that number—three just this past week—have recently been rendered modern-day eunuchs, Father—I mean, Excellency. I'd have thought that would have captured the attention of your head of security."

He smiled with more than a touch of condescension. "We have no one by that title in this archdiocese."

"Then maybe you should. Because someone is targeting your priests. And unless I miss my mark, he—or she—is just getting warmed up."

"This sounds more like your province than mine, Detective."

"Not from where I sit, sir. The occupation of the victims and the type of punishment lead me to believe a vigilante of some sort is exacting revenge for the recent upsurge in pedophilia within your ranks. Perhaps not your archdiocese specifically, but the Church in general. And your priests are getting caught in the crossfire."

"That's a serious accusation, Detec—"

"It's what I call a working theory, Excellency, not an accusation. How would you explain it, then? Six of your priests attacked in the same manner at the same venue. No theft, no damage to any portion of their body except their groin. And all of them taking place at a cottage that some of your flock believe to be a site where sex between priests and minors takes place."

The archbishop shifted in his chair. "The Church takes any allegations of sexual impropriety very seriously these days, as I'm sure you know."

"Which is why I'm here to ask for your help. I'd like to shut down this working theory and the rumors it's generating before they gain a life of their own and reach the press."

"And how do you propose to do that?"

Carla held up her index finger. "First, I'd like to examine the house in question and see what kinds of materials—magazines and videos—are there. If it's just *Sports Illustrated* or *TIME*—hell, even if it's *Playboy* or *Penthouse*—then we're good."

"And if I were to grant you that access, that would satisfy you?"

"Satisfy? No. Because that house could have been sanitized already. But it would be a start. And a nice show of cooperation and support on your part."

"And beyond access to the house in question?"

"Beyond that, I'd like our computer guys to have full access to the email and browsing activities of the priests who have been assaulted. Not only can my guys determine these men's viewing habits, they can also see if there have been any attempts to purge or disguise their online activities."

The archbishop peaked his fingers in front of his lips and closed his eyes, as if he were giving her request due consideration. Without opening his eyes, he said, "Do you realize the lack of faith in my people I would be demonstrating if I acceded to your request? And the validation I would be giving to your working theory?"

"I do. But let me be clear, Excellency. Let's forget the perpetrators for a moment and consider the victims. We're talking trusting children here, possibly even members of your diocese. And if these rumors are true, these kids are being scarred for life by men who have no sense of decency and no business being anywhere near the public, especially children."

Her eyes bored in on the archbishop, who remained blank-faced. "The people who commit these crimes are scum. The only people worse are the ones who know of their activities and enable or protect them." She paused for a moment, shifting her face from anger and outrage to an open, relaxed posture. She held up a hand. "Now, I'm sure this judgment doesn't apply to you and your lieutenants, Excellency. In fact, I came here today hoping you'll partner with me in this effort—work with me to clear the good guys and put away the bad guys." She leaned forward slightly. "Are you that partner or should I be looking elsewhere?"

The archbishop opened his eyes and stared at her evenly, letting the silence grow. Carla stared back, equally comfortable with the silence.

The archbishop spoke first. "I admire your diligence, Detective—" He looked at her card. "Jessup. And your passion. But I won't violate the privacy of my priests. We are a family here and—"

"With all due respect, sir, these are not family members we're talking about. They're employees under your command. If this were a Walmart and we wanted access to the records of—"

"Surely you're not equating the Roman Catholic Church with a Walmart."

"No, I'm not. Walmart doesn't have a history of pedophilia among its employees. Or of transferring its morally and legally repulsive employees from one store to the next."

The archbishop's face reddened and he stood up. "This conversation is at an end. And if it continues, it will take place at a level high above your pay grade, Detective."

"I would hope so, sir," Carla replied, remaining seated. "Because the changes that are needed, within both your ranks and mine, need to take place at that level."

The archbishop took a step forward, almost looming over her. Carla stood up, leaving the two uncomfortably close to each other.

"I learned recently that this network of pedophilic priests is larger and more organized than I—and I hope, you—could believe. And that it reaches directly into your diocese. And here's another gem I just learned. To make it easier for their peers to identify a child who's already been raped—though they use the term 'converted'—these priests give that child a silver cross and tell them to wear it at all times. A cross, Father. How sick is that? It's like they're branding their cattle."

The archbishop fell back into a silence that grew to over a minute. Carla looked at him, the disgust evident on her face. She let the silence build, then spoke to him in a low voice. "But back to why I'm here: the assaults on your priests. If you're not going to assist in this investigation, I'd appreciate it if you don't try to hinder it. Because if you do, remember this: You may have the Chief of Police on speed dial, but I've got four reporters from the *Gazette* on my phone who'd kill for a story like this."

She moved to the door, then turned back to him. "Thanks for your time, Frank."

Thirty-Four

"WELL, THAT CONVERSATION was like something out of an O. Henry short story," Michelle said. "You come over here worrying about how to let me down easy—that you're staying a priest—and I'm worried how you're going to take the news that I'm leaving." They were sitting on the couch in Michelle's living room. Gabe had brought their favorite red wine, and the bottle sat on the low-slung table, half empty.

"I kinda fucked things up, didn't I?"

Michelle took a long moment to respond. "Yeah, you kinda did. But I'm a big girl. I knew what I was getting into. Or thought I did." She tried a smile, but it fell flat. "Getting hung up on a priest is new ground for me."

"Well, at least we made it through the entire conversation without either one of us saying 'It's not you, it's me' or 'I hope we can still be friends.'"

"Little victories." She smiled and curled a leg under her. "I hope you don't expect me to wait around for five years while you figure things out."

"Well, while I do, I hope we can still be friends." This time they both smiled. "Is the seminary okay with you taking the rest of the year off? You kind of sprang this on them."

"I hinted that it was medical." She lowered her voice and cupped a hand around her mouth. "Female issues. The good fathers couldn't sign the leave form fast enough. I've found over the years that there are certain terms men either don't understand or run screaming from. They're my go-to phrases whenever I need something."

"Such as?"

"Well, anything that contains the word 'vaginal' is a winner. Periods and associated problems are also a mystery to you guys. My go-to word is 'yeast.' But these are priests we're talking about. 'Female issues' was enough to get immediate approval for an indefinite personal leave."

"So where are you going?"

"Phoenix. To begin, at least. I'll stay with my sister awhile, then I might travel for a bit. Get away from everything—starting with you and John."

"Speaking of which, how's he doing with your decision?"

"Hard to say. He stormed out of here last week when I told him I didn't love him anymore. And he hasn't been back. I've left him voice and email messages, but he hasn't responded."

"Well, I'm sorry you're leaving, but I'm glad you're taking care of yourself."

She looked at him over the rim of her wine glass. "What about you? You good with your decision to stay?"

"Depends on the day. When it comes to decisions like this—tough decisions—I find that if I'm really stuck or indecisive, there's a technique that always works. I go somewhere comfortable, sit, and have a beer. Just one. Two makes me sloppy and overly sentimental. When I finish that beer, I usually find I've got just the right balance of head and heart. And the right decision becomes obvious."

"And what did your one beer tell you this time?"

"To have another beer. It was like one of those old cartoons where you've got an angel on one shoulder and a devil on the other. The angel whispers, 'You're born to be a priest. This is just a bump in the road. You're going to do a lot of good someday.' Then the devil chimes in, 'You're a fraud. You've got no fucking business being a priest.'"

"So did either voice make more sense than the other?"

"I'm going with voice number one. For now. Mostly because it's what I know. But I've got a lot of thinking to do."

She leaned forward, her face growing serious. "Listen, Gabe. This is going to sound callous, but when you're trying to make sense of this past few months, keep this in mind. Whether we intended to or not, we each took advantage of the other to find out something about ourselves. I used you to see if I wanted to still be married. You used me to figure out whether you wanted to be a priest."

Gabe tried a smile. "You sound like someone in one of those movies where one of us tells the other, 'Go on, get out of here. I never liked you in the first place.' Even though it breaks their heart to say it." When Michelle didn't return the smile, he dropped the jovial tone. "That sounds a bit clinical, Michelle. This wasn't some science experiment. At least not for me. At this point, we both just need to—"

She reached over and put a hand on his arm. "Gabe, listen to me. There's no 'we' in this equation. There never was." She tightened her grip on his arm and her eyes on his. "In all the time we've known each other—from teacher/student to good friends to whatever we are now—did you ever go beyond the moment?" Seeing his confusion, she continued. "For example, did you ever think of us being married or having kids? See? Neither did I. This was an opportunity that came along, a chance for both of us to deepen what was obviously a meaningful relationship and learn important things about ourselves at the same time. An experiment, if you will. And we grabbed it. So don't beat yourself up about—"

Michelle was interrupted by a sound of a key in the front door lock and subsequent click. She looked over at Gabe, her face full of fear. "He hasn't been here in two weeks," she said, her voice tightening. "This can't be a coincidence."

The door opened and John stepped in. "Lucy, I'm home," he called out in a bad Cuban accent. He stood in the doorway for a moment. Just under six feet, he had a slight paunch and a military-style crewcut atop a large bullet-shaped head. He surveyed the room slowly, letting his eyes come to rest finally on Gabe and Michelle, then he strode into the living room. "And who's your young friend, if I may ask?"

Gabe stood and extended his hand. "Gabe Russell. I'm one of your wife's colleagues."

John ignored the hand, his eyes taking in Gabe for a second then settling on Michelle. "I know who you are. I was using irony, one of my wife's favorite teaching tools."

Michelle stood up. "What are you doing here, John? You disappear for the past ten days and now you show up?"

"Ironic, no? It's almost like I've been keeping an eye on my own house since our . . . change in status . . . waiting to see who shows up. And now here we all are."

"What do you want, John?

"Since I'm a player in this little drama, I just want to see how this story—sorry, this narrative—plays out."

"There's no narrative here, John," Gabe said. "We're just—"

"Hey, Father. Shut the fuck up. I want to hear from my wife."

"You're not entitled to another word, John," Michelle said. "From either of us."

"Oh, I think I am, honey. That's my couch you guys are sitting on. That's my bed in there that you two may have recreated in. So, yes, I'm entitled to an answer."

"*My* couch. *My* bed. *My* wife. If you ever listened to yourself, you'd already have your answer."

"And what might that be, hon?"

"That we're over, and we have been for a long time. Or, since you're so fond of writing metaphors, we're in the past tense. I can't pretend any—"

John's hand flashed out. There was the thin sound of flesh on flesh. It was a dismissive slap with no force behind it. Michelle started to raise her hand to her cheek, then lowered it and glared at John, her cheek reddening.

"You've got a pretty limited vocabulary these days, don't you?"

John stood there, his hands dangling at his side. Gabe let his own hands hang loosely at his sides, but his thumb and little finger had slid beneath his palms, leaving the remaining fingers joined and stiff. John took a step toward Michelle, but there was no threat to it. When she cringed and shrank back, he stopped.

"I didn't mean to . . ." His voice was small and unsure of itself. He put his hands behind his back and took a step backward. "I'm sorry, honey. I'm so sorry." He hesitated. "I don't know who I am or what I'm doing these days." He looked around the room, as if the answer were somewhere there. "We've gone from being us to two people I don't even recognize."

He turned to Gabe. "Listen, Father—Gabe—I apologize. Not just for tonight but for . . ." He left the sentence dangling. Then he grimaced and shrugged, shrinking into himself.

"I'm not the one you need to apologize to," Gabe replied.

John turned back to Michelle, his eyes pleading. "Hon, I'm so sorry. Ever since we started falling apart, I imagine things.

Maybe they're not true—they're probably not—but they feel so true when I'm thinking them." His chin dropped. "I'm fucked up."

He turned back to Gabe. There was no longer anything threatening in his stance, expression, or voice. "Again, Father, I apologize if my suspicions are wrong. And even if they aren't, Michelle can make her own decisions. But right now, even though I have no right, I'm asking a favor of you." He gestured weakly at Michelle. "I'd like to talk to my wife. Alone. There are things I need to say to her, and I'm sure there are things she needs to say to me."

Gabe frowned, his eyes assessing John before moving to Michelle, who was also looking at John. The left side of her face still glowed from John's slap, but she was composed as she assessed her husband. Eyes still on John, she said, "He's right, Gabe. We've got unfinished business. Every time we've tried to have this conversation, it's led to one of us walking out. We need to see it all the way through."

"I'll do whatever you want," Gabe said, "but from what I just saw . . ." He motioned at the mark on her face.

John bowed his head. "Ask Michelle. She'll tell you that in all the years we've been together, I've never done anything like what you just saw." He stopped. "Correction. There have been a couple of incidents in the past few months that I'm not proud of. And I take full responsibility for those. But they're not who I am, and Michelle knows it." He looked imploringly at Gabe, whose eyes were still on Michelle.

"I don't think I'm going to like what Michelle has to say," John continued, "but I need to hear it. And she needs to hear me. I'm asking for an hour, that's all. And when we're done, she can call you and you can come back over here. What do you say?" He extended his hand.

Gabe ignored the proffered hand and looked questioningly at Michelle, who nodded. "The storm's over," she said. "We need to take advantage of the calm. Go back to the rectory. I'll call you later."

Gabe regarded her for a long moment. He flexed his hands once, nodded to her, and turned to leave. John stepped into his path, his hand still extended. Gabe hesitated, his eyes searching John's, then he shook his hand. He walked slowly toward the front door and turned back one last time. "Give me a call when you guys are done," he said to Michelle, his voice covering the sound of his unlocking the front door. "Just so I can quit worrying."

Gabe stood by his car and looked back at Michelle's house. His body leaned toward the house subconsciously, as if he could pick up something amiss from that distance, and his hands dangled at his side, flexing. But Michelle was right. This was between her and John. He thought back to the encounter he'd just witnessed, his first exposure to John. On the one hand, there had been that sudden flash of violence, though it had been more a slap than an assault. But the violence in the air had been evident, and it was why Gabe was hesitant to leave. On the other hand, John had looked truly contrite after the slap. More importantly, Michelle looked to be in control of the situation. Besides, there was no way he could stay there with both of them asking him to leave. So he got in his car and drove off.

Returning to the rectory held no appeal, nor did hitting his favorite bar and watching what was left of the Penguins game. He drove idly, taking corners for no apparent reason. After a few minutes, he realized that the turns had a purpose, ensuring he stayed within a mile of Michelle's house.

He'd been driving for ten minutes when his phone rang. Leaning over, he punched the hands-free button to answer. The panicked voice came through the phone, a tinny sound that grabbed at him.

"Don't, John. This isn't you."

"But it is, darling. It is." There was a scuffling sound that Gabe couldn't place. Then he heard, "This is nice. You on your hands and knees. No, don't try to get up. Get used to being down there. It's going to be a long hour before your priest pal comes back. Then I'll take care of both of you."

Gabe swung the car around in a burst of speed and complaining tires and headed back, swearing to himself—and at himself—as he drove. Two minutes later, he pulled into Michelle's driveway.

He opened the door silently and stepped into the foyer, taking in the scene in front of him. Michelle was on the floor, crawling in an attempt to escape John, seeking to get under the dining room table. She was bleeding from her mouth and nose, the blood and mucus hanging from her nose, swaying like a crazy pendulum.

John looked up as Gabe started over. If he was surprised or afraid, he didn't show it. "Join us, Father," he said, waving Gabe over the way boxers taunt their opponent, trying to draw them into range. "Let's have a different kind of ménage à trois."

Gabe moved in deliberate steps, his eyes fixed on Michelle, giving the impression that his attention was solely on her. At the same time, he assessed John and the situation at hand. There was no gun or knife in either hand. Emotionally, John seemed very much in control of himself as he followed Michelle, kicking and slapping at her as she crawled.

Reaching Michelle, Gabe bent down, turning his back on John. As Gabe placed his hands on her shoulders, as if to help her to her feet, John reared back and fired a kick at his head. Anticipating the move, Gabe whirled and swept his arm up, knocking John's leg to the side. John staggered sideways, trying to regain his balance, and Gabe rose quickly from his knees and drove the palm of his hand into John's face. There was a soft crunch as John's nose collapsed under the blow.

Furious, John gathered himself and lurched forward, swinging wildly. Gabe ducked a punch and drove the heel of his hand into John's exposed solar plexus. John let out a harsh grunt as the air left his lungs and put his hands on his knees, his head dangling helplessly at waist level, trying to gather himself but coming up empty.

Gabe looked over at Michelle, who was now sitting on the floor, collecting herself. Her face was a smear of blood, tears, and mucus and her eyes were unmoving and vacant. Gabe snapped his fingers, which made her look over at him. He nodded at the helpless John and raised his eyebrows. "I can end this all right now, Michelle. No more threats and no more beatings. Ever. But it's got to be your call." He watched as her eyes broke their trance, but there was no indication that she'd heard Gabe.

He motioned once more at John, whose gasping and wheezing were easing. He was beginning to straighten himself, moving with deliberation now. The next attack wouldn't be so frenzied. Gabe looked at Michelle in frustration. "What do you want to do?" he asked, almost growling the question. But Michelle's eyes wouldn't acknowledge him or the decision at hand. No longer glazed, they were alert but gazing at something only she could see.

Gabe looked at her one last time, then reached over and roughly pinched John's carotid nerve, sending him to the floor. "Go grab some things and take yourself somewhere safe. I'll stay here and make sure he doesn't follow you."

"You won't—"

"No. But tomorrow I'd file for a restraining order. I don't know when you were intending to leave for Phoenix, but the sooner the better." He reached over and helped her to her feet. "Call me when you're ready to pack for Phoenix. I'll come over and make sure you get off okay."

CONFESSION

"That thing the other night with John scared me. My emotions took over. That's never happened before. The one thing Benni, my Krav Maga teacher, instilled in me was to go calm when you're under attack. Don't react until you've considered your options. Easier said than done, but he drilled it into me and we practiced it every session. But something kicked loose in me as I watched Michelle crawling like that, dripping blood and drool onto the floor, John kicking at her like she was a misbehaving dog. This curtain of red came over my eyes. And when lifted, John's head was hanging in front of me, like a piñata. What if that curtain of red had stayed there until I brought my hands together, locked the fingers, and swung up, driving his broken nose into his brain? Or what if Michelle had looked at me and simply nodded to go ahead and finish things? Could I have followed through? I think the answer is yes. Could I have lived with myself afterward? I honestly don't know.

"But if I think of John's death as removing a violent bully from the world, I'm ignoring my own Church's teachings on forgiveness and redemption. Any chance of John changing into a loving husband for the next woman in his life—or even Michelle, for that matter—would have vanished as I swung my hands up into his face. Still, as Benni says, if you're guided by 'what if' thoughts, you'll never act. It all comes down to whether I think bullies, pedophiles and rapists can change. I don't think they can, but then, I'm not God."

Thirty-Five

IT WAS TWO WEEKS after the final evening at Michelle's house. Safely arrived in Phoenix and ensconced in her sister's guest room, she had sent Gabe a six-page letter, something, she said, to tide her over until she could find a therapist. She had recounted their relationship and how it had developed, at least for her, from first impressions in her classroom to the first failed draft of his novel to subsequent drafts, charting her growing interest in and attraction to him as things went along. There were no amazing insights or illuminative moments, she said, editing her own letter. She just wanted to let him look at their relationship through a lens other than his own to appreciate how wonderful he was on so many fronts.

She hastened to assure him this wasn't a Dear John letter, though she had sent one, she said with a written wink, to her husband. Divorce proceedings were already underway, and she didn't expect John to contest. No, she just felt unmoored and wouldn't be returning to Pittsburgh or corresponding with him any further until she felt more stable earth beneath her feet.

They had seen each other one more time since that night with John. Gabe had helped her pack, both for her protection and for the opportunity to say whatever had been left unsaid.

But there were no further explanations or revelations. Together, they had built and filled boxes that Gabe then carried out to the car. When it became clear that there were more boxes than the car could accommodate, Gabe took the already-packed boxes out and laid them all next to the car. Michelle prioritized what was going with her, and Gabe offered to bring the rest of the boxes back to the rectory. He would forward them when she was settled in at whatever her final destination might be. Their parting had been dry-eyed, a surprise to each of them.

Once Michelle was gone, Gabe had rejoined the investigation with a fresh enthusiasm and perspective, helping Paul with his paper backlog and Jenny with the computer searches. Carla had taken Michael's completed searches and matched the Church findings with both closed and open criminal investigations. It felt like déjà vu, she said, with many of the records reading like her Ferguson investigation: a promising start with solid evidence and testimonies, then an abrupt stop and handoff.

Michael, who had emerged as the unspoken leader of the group, had said in their last meeting in Gabe's classroom that he thought they were nearing the point where they should shift from information gathering to assembling their findings for possible reporting and distribution. They'd make a final decision about schedule and recipients at their next meeting.

It was 7:30 in the evening, and Carla and Gabe were parked down and across the street from the clubhouse in Carla's unmarked squad car, a two-year-old Taurus that fooled none of the criminals on her beat but fit this neighborhood nicely. Carla had a long-lens camera that she had put to liberal use during the past hour chronicling the arrivals of the priests and their guests. The older ones, mostly teenage boys, arrived on their own, usually on bikes. The younger ones, both boys and girls, were accompanied by priests, who held their hands as they crossed the street to enter the house.

The previous two weeks had seen two more priests hospitalized, along with a cop with a reputation as a wife abuser. Carla knew the cop. She also knew that despite multiple trips to the ER, the wife always refused to press charges in the end. The precinct had been of two minds about the attack. Some thought the cop in question had it coming, but the majority seemed more offended that the pilgrim had the temerity to go after one of their own.

Carla lowered the camera and dabbed angrily at the single tear that rolled down her cheek. "God, I wish these guys and that cottage were my assignment instead of this goddamn vigilante." She motioned angrily at the cottage. "These guys are operating in plain sight, and no one's doing shit about it. Certainly not your Church, and my side's pretty much sitting on our hands. These poor kids are on their own with no one to fight for them. Except for maybe this vigilante."

"How's that going, by the way? We're normally talking about our pedo targets when we get together. I forget sometimes that you've got a day job."

"I'm on the clock tonight. My lieutenant approved overtime in case the vigilante shows up. Which means we wait until the events in there break up and there's only a couple of priests left. That's when our boy will strike, if he shows at all. If he does, I plan to let him administer his punishment before I arrest him."

"You think he'll show?" Gabe asked. "I've staked this place out a couple of times at Mike's request and I haven't seen anyone other than the participants. Also, weren't you saying he's all over the place, both with his victims and his locations?"

"Until recently. He seems to have shifted his focus from regular citizens to priests. Which helps me some, though I still can't figure out how he selects the victims who aren't priests, how he knows about them." She paused. "Unless he's a cop."

"You think that's a possibility?"

"A long shot, but one I need to consider. Every cop has a touch of vigilantism in him, especially after you've seen your cases get screwed up by a shitty lawyer or a legal technicality. You see those assholes walking free and you just want to take them apart, piece by piece. But thinking and doing are two different things. Whether it's loyalty to their oath or a fear of being discovered, I don't see it being a cop."

Gabe picked up a small binocular from his lap and surveyed the cottage. "What did your lieutenant say when you told him about the pedo network?"

"I didn't have a chance. I walked in to update him and he said the captain wanted to see me. Now. Cap took my head off the moment I walked through the door. Turns out he and Frank are golfing buddies, on top of everything else."

"Not that it's any of my business," Gabe said, "but you seem pretty relaxed about how much shit you're stirring up. You're not worried about keeping your job?"

She shook her head. "First, I'm a cop's daughter. That buys a lot of cred and probably a bit more rope than I deserve. And second . . ."

She looked out the window. Her jaw was set so hard it tremored. Gabe knew there was nothing to be gained from urging her on. So, as the confessional had taught him, he waited through the silence.

"My first year on the force, I was recruited by a group of cops running a protection ring for a drug cartel. When I declined, they made it clear what could happen if I talked. They fire-bombed my place and killed my dog. I kept my mouth shut and acted intimidated, but for three months during my off hours, I followed those bastards and documented every step of their operation.

"Then I went to my lieutenant and told him I didn't know if he was in on it or not and that I didn't much care either way. I didn't even tell him it had to stop or that I'd grown up with the Blue Wall and knew that some cops were always going to be dirty. I told him I didn't want to change the world, or even his precinct. I just wanted to do my job in peace.

"He listened to me with a stone face, like one of those heads on Easter Island. I could see him running through his options: fire me, transfer me, or set me up for an accident. Finally, I opened the box and showed him the photos, meetings, and ledgers. I told him they were his to keep, that I'd made two copies of everything he'd just seen. One was in a safe deposit vault and the other was with my lawyer, along with the names of three reporters who were to receive their own copies in the case of my mysterious disappearance or death."

She looked over at him through the darkness. "So between the cop's daughter thing and my safe deposit box, I've got a little more latitude than the rest of the squad."

"Jesus, that's rough," Gabe said. "And you still have to work with these guys?"

She shook her head, her eyes straight ahead. "Two of them had mysterious accidents that kept them out of action for six months." She turned and looked squarely at Gabe, holding his eyes. "The other two got the hint and transferred out."

They sat for a few minutes in silence, then Gabe asked in a lighter voice, "So who's watching your kids tonight?"

Carla smiled slightly. "Yeah, about that. Can I confess something to you, Father? I don't have any kids. Never been married, either."

"But I thought that—"

"Yeah, everyone thinks that. And I let them. Single mother with two kids. It makes me look spunky. People like spunky. It also chases off those cops who like to hit on anything with two legs. Also, it gets me out of stakeouts, except for the ones I want. Like tonight."

Gabe sat there for a moment. "You're a devious little thing, aren't you?"

"Yeah, well." She picked up the camera and focused on the front door.

"First Friday of every month, huh?" Carla said, putting down the camera since there hadn't been a new arrival during the past half hour. "I get what you mean about the helpless feeling, just sitting out here when God knows how many felonies are going on less than a football field from where we're sitting." She waved her hand dismissively in the dark. "But you're right. We barge in tonight and we get a few minnows. And the sharks, including our two bosses, swim away."

Carla reached behind her into the back seat, which was littered with files and empty soft drink cans, and grabbed a video camera. She handed it to Gabe. "It's showtime. You know how to work one of these things?"

"This button is on/off and that one is zoom. Anything else I need to know?"

"You're a natural. Okay, I know we've gone over this, but I'm a bit OCD when it comes to preparation." She nodded at the camera. "Take it and hide behind that bush over there. I'm going to go knock on the door and identify myself. Get a shot of whoever answers the door. Close in on him if you can and record whatever transpires there, even if the sound doesn't carry. There's no way whoever answers is going to invite me in, so he'll probably ask me to wait on the porch while he consults the others."

She pointed to the back of the house and the stand-alone garage. "As soon as he shuts the door, you hustle around back and hide behind that big oak near the garage. Then focus on the back door. The moment it opens, start shooting and don't stop until the last person—priest or kid—leaves." She pointed at one of the buttons. "Use the zoom when you can to get close-ups of the exiting priests."

Gabe left the car, checking out his hiding place for the first shot as he approached the property. He passed the cottage then doubled back and crouched behind the bush about twenty yards from the front door and nodded to the dark car. He saw Carla get out, secure her gun on her hip, and head across the street.

Twenty minutes later, Carla and Gabe were back in her car viewing footage on the fold-out screen on the video camera. They watched as Carla mounted the steps and knocked on the door. A casually dressed priest answered. Carla showed him her ID and gestured behind him, into the house. The priest listened politely, nodding helpfully, then held up a hand, gesturing for her to wait, and shut the door.

The camera stayed on as Gabe left his hiding place in the bush and walked carefully down the path, the screen showing a combination of his feet and the gravel on the path. "Nice camera work," Carla said. "Especially the shots of your shoes."

"I was petrified that I'd turn it off and wouldn't be able to get it back on in the dark."

The action on the screen stopped and then jostled slightly as Gabe settled in next to the oak. He had steadied the camera, focusing on the back door and experimenting with the zoom function while he waited. Suddenly, the back door flew open and a priest hustled out, dragging a young girl behind him. For the next ninety seconds, the camera recorded a constant exit of priests and children, over a dozen in all.

"They stayed behind the garage until you left," Gabe said. "What did Father Merchant say when he finally came back to the front door?"

"That he'd love to help in any way he could, especially if it would help quell the vicious rumors I'd been hearing, but he had to check with the archdiocese. And sorry about having me wait so long on the front porch, but it was tough to reach anyone there at night. In fact, it turned out he couldn't raise anyone by phone. He hoped I understood, but he couldn't let me in without permission of the owners. Said he'd talk to them tomorrow and meet me back here, once he'd gained their permission. Great guy. Very helpful."

Gabe nodded at the screen. "So what next?"

"Next, I drop you off at the rectory. Then I'm heading to the precinct to make five copies. One goes to my lieutenant, one to the captain, one goes to my new friend, the archbishop, and one goes to each of us. Call it insurance."

Thirty-Six

GABE'S EYES MOVED from Michael to Jenny, then back again. Neither was looking directly at him. Ever since they had sat down on the couch in the rectory, they had found things to look at or fiddle with. Gabe had never seen either of them look so serious. Or so nervous.

They looked up as Dolores entered the study with three glasses of wine. Nodding their thanks, their eyes followed her to the door.

"Can you give her the rest of the night off?" Michael asked. Gabe cocked his head and looked at Michael, then Jenny.

"It would be better if she weren't here," Jenny added.

"No problem," Gabe said. "Dolores," he called out, "you can go home early tonight. I'll see these two out and then lock up."

"It's not a bother, Father," came the voice from the hallway. "I've still got any number of things to do."

Michael shook his head and pointed at the door. "It's okay. Looks like we're going to be late. You can head home."

"Make sure she leaves," Jenny said, her voice almost a whisper.

Gabe frowned his confusion before standing up and going to the study door. He opened the door to find Dolores standing in the foyer, her coat over her arm but making no move to leave.

He took the coat and helped her into it. Then he walked her to the door, thanking her for the day's work. Once she'd gone, he locked the door and returned to the study. He took a seat in the wingback chair and leaned forward, his knees touching the low-slung table.

"Okay, you've got my interest. What's up?"

Michael looked at Jenny, who took the lead. "I'll set things up, and then Mike can tell you what we've found." Michael nodded to her to continue. "We were working late tonight at the diocese offices. Mike was compiling the general searches and I was working on those two Cleveland priests you and I were tracing." Her voice rose at the end of the sentence, as if seeking recognition from Gabe. When he nodded, she continued. "Anyway, my search led me into a new area of the files, a place you and I haven't been before. I was locked out, so I went into the next room and got Mike to come over and give me access." She nodded at Michael to continue.

"I was logging in on Jenny's computer as administrator when I saw something odd. Paul had logged in earlier in the evening."

"So? You gave him access, didn't you?"

"Yeah, but he logged in using 'A' commands." He looked expectantly at Gabe, who shrugged. "I forgot. You don't have A command authority, so there's no reason for you to know about it. But here's the thing. Jenny doesn't have A authority. And Paul sure as hell doesn't."

"Okay," Gabe said tentatively. "But I'm still not following."

"I made sure the three of you were locked out from anything A related so you could only read the files, not manipulate them. Meaning edit or delete," Michael explained. "I did it for a reason. If the archdiocese tries to move against us at some point, we can show that anything we found was available to anyone in the public—reporter, cop, concerned citizen, lawyer—as long as they knew where to look. In other words, these files could all be considered the Church's version of public domain."

"Got it," Gabe said. "So how did Paul get access to A files?"

"Someone in the archbishop's office had to give it to him. Or he knows a helluva lot more about computers than we gave him credit for."

"All right. I think I'm following you, but I'm not sure what the crisis is."

"How he got access to A files is worrisome," Michael said. "What he did with that access is why we're here. Michael fixed his eyes on Gabe's. The darting eyes and hesitant voice were gone. Anger spread across his face and into his voice. "Once Jenny alerted me to Paul's new status, I went in as master administrator to discover what files he'd accessed. And I saw he'd deleted four files, four active investigations where it looked like we had the priests in question dead to right." He looked up. "I didn't undelete them because that would have alerted Paul or whoever he's working with. Instead, I noted the files by number and gave them to Jenny for a paper search."

"I went into the paper archives," Jenny continued, "and found them. And Mike and I took them apart."

"And what did you find?" Skepticism and impatience were there in Gabe's voice, but so was a tinge of worry.

"The first two were charges against Paul for pedophilia. From 1972. A twelve-year-old girl named Audrey Keller. The third file was the results of the internal investigation, which deemed that the charges had merit. The fourth was the decision to transfer Paul to Rome."

Michael and Jenny sat back, giving Gabe room to absorb the news. The silence in the room was brittle and uncomfortable. Gabe leaned back in his chair, stunned. "It's not that I don't believe you, but—"

"We were as stunned as you are," Jenny said. "We've just had more time to digest the news." She looked at him, the sympathy evident on her face. "I was so staggered, I had Mike show me everything, step-by-step. It all checks out."

Michael picked up the narrative. "I went back into the archives. There were three other complaints about Paul during his tenure here. Attached to one of them was a note from a church psychologist with the assessment that Paul was a serial offender with no signs of remorse. The last file recommended his transfer to Rome."

Gabe looked down at his hands, now held tight on his knees. Michael and Jenny both sat back, giving him room. Gabe stood up and walked around the room, his feet shuffling aimlessly. He looked over at his two friends, his face pale and drawn. "I feel like my brain's on fire."

Thirty-Seven

GABE RANG THE DOORBELL and took a step back. He heard voices from within, followed by feet on the other side of the door and the release of locks. Then the door opened. A pleasant looking woman in her late thirties or early forties looked out. "Father Russell? Is anything wrong?"

"Audrey, I'm sorry to be calling so late, but it's important. Do you have a few minutes to talk?"

She looked over her shoulder and took a step back. "Sure. Come on in. I was putting the kids down, but Gary can take over. Have a seat and I'll be right back."

He stayed where he was. "Do you mind if we take a quick walk instead? I don't want to bring this topic into your house."

She looked at him for a moment. Then the welcoming smile disappeared. "You're right. Wait here. I'll get my coat."

Thirty-Eight

GABE AND PAUL were in the rectory, facing each other in the matching wingback chairs. A small fire, more for atmosphere than warmth, cast a flickering orange tint on the men's faces. Gabe had an untouched beer on the side table. Paul sat comfortably, a snifter of brandy in his hand. He swirled it gently, took a sip, and sighed his appreciation.

"I haven't been back to this room in years. It's pretty much the same as when I was here. The only thing that's improved with age in this place is the brandy." He swirled again and smiled.

When Gabe didn't return the smile, Paul leaned forward. "I won't ask you about your dreams—unless that's why you wanted to talk so urgently."

"That's not it," Gabe said in a tight voice.

"If it's okay, can I ask how things are going with the subject of the dream. Michelle, right?"

"We had a bit of a hiccup recently. Nothing I want to go into."

Puzzled by Gabe's reticence and tone, Paul sat back in the chair and let the silence grow.

"By the way," Gabe said finally, "I ran into an old friend of yours. Audrey Pasca. She said to tell you hi."

"Audrey Pasca." Paul's forehead crinkled. "Don't think I know anyone by that name."

"That's right. You would have known her as Audrey Keller back then."

Paul shifted his expression from puzzlement to that of someone reaching back into the past, trying to reclaim the name. Then he shrugged. Gabe registered the shrug, but also noted how Paul's neck had gone tight, coupled with a small pulsing at his temple that hadn't been there when he sat down.

"C'mon, Paul. Audrey Keller. Seventh grader at St. Mary's. Do you seriously not remember her, or were there so many that you just lost track?"

"I'm not sure where you're going with this, Gabe. It's been twenty years since I was—"

"This is a girl who said you raped her repeatedly during her junior high years, here in our parish."

He saw Paul's face shift from benign forgetfulness. Now his jaw, cheeks, and forehead were hardened.

"Maybe you're confused because they call it middle school these days," he added, "but it was called junior high back then."

"Normally I appreciate your sense of humor, Gabe. You know that. But something like this? There's nothing funny there."

"I agree. Tell you what, let's move on from the easily forgotten Audrey Keller and let's go straight to the bonus round question. Have you ever had sex with any underage kids? Male or female?"

"Where's this coming from, Gabe? Making accusations like this. This isn't like you."

"You're right. But that old Gabe, the one who'd be stunned to hear accusations of this sort against someone he regards as both a friend and spiritual counselor, *that* Gabe took a hike tonight. And I don't think he's coming back." He took his first swallow of beer, which was now at room temperature. "But hey, enough about me. Let's talk about you. And just for the record, I'm not hearing a denial."

Paul put his brandy down and gathered himself. He was trying to regain a congenial, relaxed posture, but the tension in his bones and tightness of his skin wouldn't let him. "You've been a priest for what? Ten minutes?" he said, his tone vacillating between outrage and a controlled snarl. "And you dare to make accusations like this of people who've given their entire lives to the Church?"

"You're right, Paul. I'm new at this priest thing. But I've been a human being all my life. And any human being will tell you that abusing a child is the lowest of sins. I don't know which level of hell is reserved for people like you, but I hope it's scalding hot. And let me remind you, I still haven't heard a denial."

"I'll ask you again, Gabe, where the hell is this coming from?"

"From you, Paul. It's coming from you. You probably could have kept on fooling us until your year here was up, but you had to erase your files, didn't you? Even knowing that we'd never go back that far in our search and that you were safe. After all our meetings, don't you appreciate how good Michael is with computers?"

Gabe regarded his beer bottle. Then he began to peel the label with his fingernail, his eyes focused on this new task instead of Paul. "Those are the files. The testimony is another matter. Audrey is willing to come forward, if it comes to that. But I don't think that will be necessary now that we know where to look. Jesus, Paul . . ." He was silent for a moment before whispering, "Kids."

"You're going to take the word of one troubled woman— and I *do* remember Audrey, though it's not my place, even after all these years, to discuss the problems at home that plagued that poor girl."

The skin around Gabe's eyes pinched into little lines. "And you pretended that you didn't know what the playbook was. But there you are, going straight to rule number one: Blame the victim." He nodded earnestly. "But I'm with you on this one. I could see how she could confuse a loving priest she trusted with a rapist who violated her body over and over. Happens all the time. Ask any therapist."

"I don't appreciate your sarcasm, Gabe. Not about something as serious as this. Accusations like this can . . ." His voice sought a reasonable tone. "We're talking about events from twenty years ago, son. More. It was a different time."

"You're the historian, Paul, so I'm at a disadvantage here. You tell me the era when it was both legal and morally acceptable to bend a twelve-year-old girl over a desk and rape her. Or have an altar boy suck you off because God commanded him to drain your sins from your body." He held up a hand to stop a response that wasn't forthcoming. "By the way, you're in the clear, legally, though I'm sure you know that. The statute of limitations expired on Audrey's charges years ago. So it's just us, two old friends talking. Tell me about it. For example, how did you get started?"

"Listen, you little shit. I don't owe you an explanation or an apology. You're a kid, taking events of a lifetime ago and—"

"You know what I did after I heard Audrey's account, Paul? I left my car where it was and walked back to the rectory. I didn't trust myself to drive. I just walked, trying to come up with defenses or explanations for you, my mentor—"

"You know I've always hated that word."

"Okay, my *friend*." The word dripped from Gabe's mouth. "How's that? When I got back to the rectory, I realized I had nothing to defend you with. No answer, no excuse, no explanation. Nothing. And I threw up."

Paul glared at Gabe, trying to take control of the moment. But Gabe refused to give ground. He stared at Paul, his eyes empty of sympathy or understanding. The silence and animosity grew until Paul's mouth twitched slightly and broke into a grin.

"You slipped, didn't you?" The grin turned into a full smile, all teeth with nothing behind them. "You screwed up, didn't you, Gabe? Thought you could play with fire and not get burned. Now, whether out of shame or guilt, you want to wash out your sin by—"

"You're right," Gabe interrupted. "I slipped. And it was one time—actually, not even that. But my mistake, my sin, was with an *adult*. A fucking adult, Paul. And a consenting one at that. You, on the other hand—we're not talking about adults or consent. We're talking about kids. Kids, you sonofabitch. Kids who are scarred for the rest of their lives because you and your pals needed to get your rocks off."

Gabe's right eye clouded and began to leak. He rubbed the eye and cheek with the heel of his hand. "Have you ever listened to any of their confessions, Paul? How these kids—whether twenty or forty years old—still sleep with a light on? How even after everything you and your pals did to them, they still go to church every Sunday and wonder what they did wrong or what they could have done differently all those years ago? That doesn't weigh on you? Or do you go to sleep every night with a clear conscience?"

Paul said nothing, but his glare was rich with contempt. Gabe mirrored the contempt, but it was mixed with anger. With neither yielding, the air between them felt combustible. Then the lines around Paul's eyes—the eyes the parish women still swooned over—quivered. His face slackened and collapsed, and he seemed to age as his vitality failed him. It was such a radical transformation that Gabe sat back in his chair and regarded him skeptically.

"You don't understand what it's like, Gabe. This job. This calling. How perfect you have to be. All the time. How approachable you have to be while floating above everything at the same time. You're not a person. You're God's representative, and you can send others to heaven or hell with a flick of your finger—or so they believe. You can't have normal relationships of any type because you're their *priest*." He drew the word out bitterly, as if it were an illness. "The normal forms of contact— the hugging and kissing—are closed off to you, so you need an outlet."

· "Paul!" Gabe's voice knifed the air. "Listen to yourself. You want an outlet? Join a fucking gym. Don't rape innocent kids."

"What the hell are you talking about? Rape? These are will-ing participants we're talking about."

"Can you hear yourself?" Gabe shouted. "Have you ever lis-tened to your own words?" "Or have you become deaf to any-thing except your own needs? How the hell can a kid be a willing participant? Are you that delusional?"

Paul's eyes filled with tears, and his voice softened as he looked down at his knees. "Just wait. You'll learn, Gabe, just like I did. You'll stand back from it for a while—years, maybe. But the need for some form of human contact will become too strong. It creeps up on you. Then one day it leaps. I know it's a tired phrase, but it's a sickness, like alcoholism or . . ." He looked up, his eyes wet and pleading.

Gabe lowered his voice. "You're right, Paul. I don't under-stand. Maybe it's because I'm so new to the job. Maybe in five years or so I'll have experienced things that make me think it's just fine to rape a kid and then pass him or her around the room like a bag of potato chips. But that's in the future. We're talking about now, about you. When you felt these temptations creep up on you, why didn't you leave the priesthood and join the rest of the world, where you could have normal relations with consulting adults, male or female?"

"Because I'm a *priest*, Gabe. I was *called*. Just like you were. And are. I take my vows seriously—probably more than you seem to, based on our conversations. It's what I know. Hell, it's *all* I know. And it's what I'm good at."

"And being a priest gives you license to demand sex of kids as young as eight?" Gabe was trying to control the rise of his voice, but he was failing.

"The young ones, that's not me. And I never forced anyone to do anything they didn't want to do."

"Yeah, twelve-year-old girls are so capable of making reasoned decisions. Why don't we give them the vote, as long as we're at it? Are you listening to yourself, you sick fuck?"

Paul looked down at his feet for a long moment. Then he looked up with beaten eyes. "So where does this leave us?"

"Other than done as friends?" Gabe's eyes bored in. "I don't know. What do you think should happen, Paul? Or to put it another way, if you were me, what would you do with everything I know?"

"I'd confront the person. Which you just did, and I'm not blaming you for doing it. Then I'd give that person another chance and see what they did with it."

"I thought that's what they did when they sent you to Rome. Are you still active?" When he saw Paul's confusion, he added, "Do you still have sex with children?"

"No. That was a brief period in my life. I was—"

"It couldn't have been that brief. Audrey said it was all three of her junior high years. And she can't have been the only one.

Was she?" Paul looked away. "I shouldn't have asked that question, not because it was rude but because I'm not going to believe whatever your answer is going to be. But here's the deal. Now that I know what you've done—and what you are—I'm complicit. But I'm not going to look the other way and let you keep on abusing children. And I'm not going to believe you've changed, so don't ask me to."

"Then what are you going to do, Gabe? This is my life we're talking about. Not just my reputation, my *life*."

"What I'm going to do depends on what *you're* going to do. Right now, all I know is that I want you gone from my parish and from my seminary. I'll let you finish out the semester—not out of fairness to you but out of fairness to your students. After that, you're going to announce that you're retiring to a life of contemplation. Whether that involves repentance is up to you. But you're done training future priests and you're done being anywhere near kids."

"And if I don't do what you're asking?"

"Then think about this as you huddle with the archbishop and his team. What we've found is now a permanent record. It's not going to vanish. Not if the archbishop transfers us to Timbuktu. Not even if the three of us should meet with untimely deaths. Every night Mike sends an updated copy of our research to an off-site location. It's got a simple instruction: If it hasn't heard from Mike for seventy-two hours, it forwards its files to two addresses. One is a reporter Mike trusts and the other is a cop Carla trusts."

He leaned forward. "And then there's this. You know that vigilante who's been doing such damage to your pedophile pals? Well, thanks to the confessional, I know who he is. As you've informed me, I can't act on anything he's told me. But that doesn't mean I can't tell him about *you*. Keep all that in mind as you consider your response."

"You snot-nose punk," Paul said, his voice rich with brava-do. "You're so far out of your depth, it's ridiculous. Go to the press. Go to the police, while you're at it. See who they believe: the new kid who's over his head and sleeping with his former teacher or the beloved pastor everyone remembers so fondly. Go ahead. I'll just deny this entire conversation ever took place. And I've got friends in the archbishop's office that can make your files look like forgeries."

"You mean the conversation I've been taping?" Gabe picked up a stack of papers on the table next to his chair, revealing a small tape recorder. He stood up and faced Paul. "And now it's time for you to go. You've got some thinking to do."

Paul stared at the recorder and sat back, his entire body a defeated slump. "Why are you doing this, Gabe? After all I've done for you, for this parish, for the Church. Why are you doing this?"

"You wonder why I'm trying to rid my community of a serial rapist who targets children? Jeez, that's a tough one. But if you're wondering why I'm like a dog with a bone when it comes to peo-ple like you, let me explain. Remember the bullying in high school I told you about? Well, I didn't tell you all of it. When the football team found out I'd quit, they hassled me at first. Then there were the beatings. And when those didn't work, they thought they'd turn up the heat. The linemen held me down and the quarterback and running backs took turns sodomizing me with a relay baton. Everyone took a turn. And when they were done, they told me to be grateful it wasn't a baseball bat."

Paul's face lost its defeated look. His slump vanished, his body putting its bones, muscles, and blood back in working order. "God, Gabe, that's awful. I wish you'd told me about this a long time ago." He raised himself from the chair and walked toward Gabe, his arms extended.

His vision compromised by the tears that had welled up as he recounted his rape, Gabe stepped back, waving his arms for Paul to keep his distance. But Paul kept coming, and as he passed Gabe's chair, he picked up a heavy glass ashtray, kicked Gabe squarely in the balls, and slammed the ashtray into the side of Gabe's head. Gabe's body shuddered once, then he sank to a knee, his head bleeding from the temple.

Paul stepped back and assessed the situation. Eyes still on Gabe, he reached over to the table and picked up the tape recorder. He glanced down for a moment, found the eject button and pressed it. Eyes back on Gabe, he put the cassette in his pocket.

"I'm sorry I had to do that, Gabe. And I'm sorry about what happened to you. With the team, I mean." His mouth twisted into a mean smile. "But in the future, if you find yourself in a similar position, try to relax. It will hurt less, and who knows, you might find you even like it." He straightened his hair and clothes, preparing to leave.

The blow to the head had surprised more than injured Gabe. The kick to the groin was what worried him because the intense pain had robbed him of the strength he needed to surprise Paul. He stayed down on one knee to let the pain dissipate and to calmly consider his options, as Benni had taught him. He took a quick inventory of his condition. The pain was lessening, the bleeding didn't bother him, and he didn't think he was concussed, though he didn't know how steady or forceful any response would be. To buy time, he looked up at Paul with unfocused and vacant eyes, as if he were dazed. Then he blinked, hard and fast, as if trying to bring the world into focus.

Paul leaned in and hissed, "For the record, my friend, I've never forced any of my converts to do anything. They know they're performing a service that makes us better priests and that a little suffering in this life will reap God's generosity in the next one. And to answer your question, no, I've never stopped. But these days in Rome, it's mostly young men—altar boys and seminarians."

He leaned in even closer. "But I come back here and the girls are in such a hurry to become women. So sometimes I help them in their pursuit. There's this one girl I've had my eye on. Thirteen going on twenty. I'm thinking that—"

Gabe drove up off a knee, the top of his head slamming into Paul's chin. Paul's teeth issued a loud clack, which was followed by a low cry of pain from his throat. Gabe slammed his elbow into Paul's nose, breaking it and flooding Paul's eyes with pain. Paul charged at Gabe, swinging his arms wildly. Gabe ducked under the wild punches and drove his knee up into Paul's groin.

The kick took all the life out of Paul. He started to fall, then steadied himself by placing his hands on his knees. Gabe stood over him for a moment and watched his blood and Paul's mingling on the floor, the pool of red starting to expand. He lifted his gaze from Paul to the ceiling and raised his eyebrows for a second, fixed his eyes on the top of Paul's slumped head, and took a deep breath. Then he joined his hands together, fingers locking, and drove the muscle and bones upwards, catching the broken nose perfectly and driving the shattered cartilage up and into the brain. Paul stayed upright for what seemed like forever, his stance steady and strong. Then he toppled over.

Thirty-Nine

CARLA AND THREE OTHER DETECTIVES were in the break room drinking coffee. It was nine o'clock and the day shift was wrapping up what had proved to be a long day all around. Gentry, the longest serving of the detectives, took a flask from his coat pocket and topped off his coffee. He raised his eyebrows at the other detectives, all of whom pushed their cups in his direction.

"I hear our boy attacked two more priests this week," Peterson said to Carla. A beefy man with the spider veins of a drinker, his face sagged into his neck. He had a crew cut that had grown out, needing to be either cut or combed. His eyes were bright blue and alert as he spoke. "What's that bring the total to?"

"Priests? He's up to eight," she said. "Factor in rapists and abusers and we're at a baker's dozen."

"I hope you're not trying that hard to catch this guy," Garcia said. "It seems like this pilgrim is doing us all a favor."

Carla nodded. "I know. But the lieutenant is getting heat from the diocese, even though they won't acknowledge why their boys are being attacked."

"Any of those priests back to work?" Gentry asked. "That was some pretty serious damage our boy inflicted this last time." All the men around the table unconsciously winced at the mention of the injury.

"You boys and your privates," Carla said, nodding her thanks at Gentry for the second top off. "Some are out of the hospital but not back to work. Some are still in. None of them are going to be the same, I can tell you that."

"You know what stumps me about this guy?" Peterson said. "The complete lack of forensic evidence. He's up to what, nine separate attacks, some with more than one victim?" Carla nodded. "And still nothing? This guy is good."

Carla looked back over her shoulder, gesturing at the bulletin board filled with the photos of the priests and other victims, along with columns of text accompanying each assault. "After the first few, when this guy was making no mistakes, I started thinking he might be one of us—a cop. Maybe he cleans up after himself when necessary, but most of the time it seems he's just in and out, leaving no trace of any kind. And the street justice. Tell me there isn't a cop who hasn't thought about going rogue at least once in his career."

The men nodded in unison.

"But most cops I know can't keep a secret. They might be disciplined in tidying up the crime scene, but afterward, they'd either brag about it to their pals or try to recruit a team to expand their reach." She nodded back at the board. "I'm not eliminating cops from my thinking. I'm just saying it doesn't feel right."

"What about someone with a medical background?" Jensen asked. "To be that precise with the damage, this guy obviously knows his way around the human body."

"I thought about that too," Carla said. "Again, I'm not eliminating anything or anyone. But if it's a medical person, my money is on a nurse. They're the ones, not doctors, you read about mercy-killing over fifty terminally ill patients. They're the ones who see something they don't like and do something about it. But again, I'm not feeling it. My guess is that when we catch this guy, we're going to find it's not their profession that's behind this but some event in their life we don't know about—and couldn't know about. Something they're making up for now. Hopefully, it's something recent we may be able to figure out, because if it's something from way back, we're screwed."

"What are the factors in your search?" Peterson asked.

"I've focused on two areas: recently released cons and recent victims of homosexual rape. The first group is easy enough to trace, and sometimes the records hint at a rape. For the second, I've been discreetly going to the heads of the rape crisis center in the city, not asking them to betray a confidence but to let me know if they think I might be on the right track. But so far, nothing on either of those fronts."

"Any idea on what kind of equipment he's using to inflict the damage?" Gentry asked, putting his empty bottle in his desk drawer.

"According to forensics, all the damage is manually inflicted."

"What's he doing, kicking them in the balls? I know we've all used that technique to subdue perps at one time or another. Even our gentle Carla here."

"It's not feet," she said. "The damage is too precise and too narrowly applied. This guy is painting within very specific lines—not just physically but psychologically as well. From what I gather from his victims, he has them completely at his mercy. It feels like he could kill or cripple them without breaking a sweat. But he seems to have limits he won't go beyond." She took a sip of her liquored coffee. "Like I said, I kinda like the guy, though I'll be damned if I can figure him out."

Laughlin spoke up. "I saw you calling around to the different martial arts studios. Anything?"

"Not so far. Most martial arts are kick-based, and while a series of karate kicks could do the kind of damage we're seeing, they'd do a lot of peripheral damage in the process, especially since the foot is turned so that they strike with the entire foot, not just the toe of a shoe like we do when we kick someone in the cojones."

"You know, I heard something recently you might want to look into," Peterson said. "My brother-in-law is into these bizarre martial arts, like Thai boxing where they use their knees and elbows." He looked around the table but got a collective shrug. "Anyway, he was working out at the seminary where he teaches, and he said he watched a guy just destroy one of those martial arts practice dummies. I mean *destroy*—just with his hands."

"What do they call it? Do you know?"

"Yeah. I remember it because it sounded so different from the Asian versions. It's called Krav Maga. It's Israeli."

"I like it already," Garcia said. "Those Israelis don't fuck around."

"You remember anything else your brother-in-law told you?" Carla asked. "About this Krav Maga guy?"

"Just a couple of things. The first was that he was a priest, which my brother-in-law didn't believe at first, based on the level of violence this guy was inflicting."

"What was the second thing?"

"Huh?"

"The second thing that bothered your brother-in-law. You remember it?"

"Oh, yeah. How young he was. He said the guy looked like one of the students."

Carla put down her coffee and stood up. She grabbed her shield and gun from atop the table. "Fuck. Me," she said and bolted from the room.

Forty

CARLA KNOCKED ON THE RECTORY DOOR, three hard raps, then stepped back and waited. After a brief wait, the door opened slightly and Dolores peered out.

"Dolores. It's so nice to see you again. Is Father Russell in?"

Confused by the pleasant tone, Dolores frowned. "He is, but he's with someone."

"Well, I need to see him on official police business. Could you tell him it's urgent? Interrupt him if you have to. Tell him we need to talk. Now."

Dolores opened the door, allowing Carla entrance. She scurried down the hall and knocked on the library door. After a few moments, Gabe opened the door slightly. Dolores stepped back at the sight of his face.

"Father, you're bleeding," she said, aghast at the sight. "Can I get you something?"

"One of those plastic bags filled with ice would be nice. Thank you, Dolores."

"Detective Jessup is here. She says she needs to see you and that it's urgent."

Gabe looked past Dolores. Then he turned and looked back into the library. Stepping out into the hall, he closed the door behind him. As Dolores headed for the kitchen, Carla walked over to him.

"Do I want to see the other guy?"

Gabe grimaced. "Normally I'd appreciate the joke. But you're about to see the other guy. And you'll see why I'm not laughing."

There was a long pause as each assessed the other. "Are we going to stand here and play twenty questions, Father Krav Maga, or do you want to tell me what's behind door number three?"

"Listen, Carla. There's something you need to know."

"That you're the vigilante? Gee, thanks, but it's a bit late to confess. Goddamn you, Gabe. You played me for such a—"

"There's a dead man in the library. It's Paul Reynolds. I killed him. I was just about to call you."

Carla started toward the door, but Gabe stood in her way. His hand was on the handle, his knuckles white with Paul's blood stark against them.

"I know I'm in no position to ask a favor, but before you go in there, I need to tell you what happened. And then play you something."

"Make it good. Because I'm not in a listening mood. Especially from you."

"Five minutes. That's all I need."

She stared at him, her face a stone mask. "Okay. Let's hear it."

Paul's corpse lay facedown next to the wing chair. The blood beneath his face had pooled and stopped its spread. Carla reached into her jacket pocket, took out a pair of thin blue gloves, and put them on. Bending over the body, she felt for a pulse. She lifted Paul's head, looked closely at the face, and lowered his head back to its original position.

She straightened up and stood there silently, looking down at the corpse. "You're lucky you're bleeding. That'll count in your favor. And hope that his kick landed, because I'm going to have forensics check your balls for bruising."

"There should be damage. He nailed me straight on. I never saw it coming." He hesitated for a moment, his eyes fixed on the corpse on the floor. "What kind of trouble am I in?"

"From a legal standpoint, you should be okay. Between your head injury and the tape, there's justifiable cause. But you and I both know, given your skills—that I'm just discovering, by the way—this man would still be alive if you wanted him to be."

Gabe nodded. "Maybe. But he isn't." He looked at her with solid eyes. "And if you had been in that room instead of me, we'd still be looking at a dead man."

"Maybe. Maybe not. What I do know, my Israeli friend, is that you've got a rough road ahead of you." She nodded at the body. "This guy was a legend around here. Even I know that. I don't think your parishioners are going to forgive you that easily."

He nodded. "How about criminally? What should I be prepared for down at the station?"

"Like I said, the blood and the confession are your friend's. But there's one thing you better get straight before we officially question you. You know what it is, don't you?"

"The killing blow. And how it came about."

"The coroner on duty tonight isn't the sharpest knife in the drawer, but even he knows that this kind of death requires two blows, not one. You break the nose with one blow, deliver the killing shot with another. So get your story down now, memorize it, and stick with it. He came at you, you swung wildly and hit him in the nose. He kicked you in the balls, then clocked you in the temple with the ashtray. You went down and he bent over to choke you. You kicked at him and suddenly he wasn't attacking you. You scooted away, then looked over and saw him lying there, facedown." She looked over at the corpse. "Anything beyond that, if the investigating officer—and it won't be me—gets too aggressive or too inquisitive, your answer is always, 'I can't be sure. It all happened so fast.'" She glared at him. "Say it."

Gabe nodded, but she persisted. "Say it."

"I can't be sure. It all happened so fast."

She checked his eyes, making sure he was registering what she was saying. "I'm taking you in now, Gabe. And I'm going to keep my yap shut on the way so you can rehearse. Keep your answers short, but don't be too in control. Remember, you're confused and semi-concussed. And don't let the conversation go anywhere near Krav Maga. Whoever's questioning you finds out about that, all bets are off. You'll probably be looking at second degree murder; manslaughter at the least."

"Got it. Why are you helping me, if you don't mind my asking?"

She nodded at Paul. "Because this piece of scum deserved to die. And because I want the pleasure of bringing you down myself, partly for your taking the law into your hands and partly because you made me look like a fool. Regardless of how it goes at the precinct tonight, my advice is to lawyer up, pal. Because I'm coming for you."

CONFESSION

"I'm a pariah in my own parish. Paul was a saint to these folks, and they don't give a shit that the cops labeled it self-defense. The priest they grew up with is dead. And the one who killed him is saying Sunday mass. Attendance is down, no surprise, though I do see a few new faces each Mass. But I think they're only there to get a glimpse of the killer priest.

"According to Mike, the Church's going to send me to a monastery in upstate New York for a month to let things calm down. If I'm still persona non grata, then I'm off to another parish, one so desperate for a priest they'll take anyone, even me.

"If this is my last confession in this box, I want to get one thing straight. I'm not looking for absolution. I did what I've done because of the damage I've seen—most of which will warp the lives of so many people—kids, especially—for as long as they live. But there's also the damage pedophilia is doing to the Church I love. It's like a rot that's in the foundation and the floors. If we don't expose and rip it out, it'll bring the entire structure down. And I can't stand by and watch that happen. The Church is flawed, fucked-up even, at times. But then, so am I."

Gabe stood up. He turned the door handle gently, peering out to make sure no one was walking by. Confession hours weren't scheduled to start for another ten minutes. He bent over, picked up his water bottle and exited the penitent side of the confessional, closing the door behind him. Then he walked the three paces to the confessor side of the box, opened it, and settled in.

Forty-One

A MONTH HAD PASSED since Paul's death. The confusion, the rumors, and the way the parish had divided its loyalties between Gabe and Paul had combined to lead the archbishop to send Gabe to the upstate New York monastery for a month of silent retreat and reflection. In reality, Gabe took his Walkman and books along and did a lot of gardening and writing during that month. He alternated between his Krav Maga practice and hiking in the nearby Adirondacks in the afternoon.

The rumors abounded in his absence. One had Gabe as a spurned lover who had turned on Paul when rejected. Another had it as the end of a highly intoxicated evening. A cop who was also a member of the parish created his own version of the fight in which Gabe had been the aggressor against the much older man, hinting that the only reason Gabe wasn't in jail was that the Church didn't want to lose two valuable assets in one evening. But with the mood of the parish shifting decidedly against Gabe, it looked like his hiatus was going to be a permanent one.

But then couriers delivered two heavy boxes to the editor of the *Pittsburgh Post-Gazette*. And someone sent tapes of Paul's and Gabe's confrontation to Channel 8 and the *Post-Gazette*.

Overnight, Gabe went from killer to hero, and his parish clamored for his return.

The archbishop waited two more weeks to show he wouldn't be dictated to by his own followers before announcing that Gabe would be back the following Sunday. Mass that Sunday saw the largest attendance in parish history, though Gabe acknowledged neither the newcomers, including the press, nor Paul's death.

Four days after his return, Gabe, Michael, and Jenny met with the two reporters the *Post-Gazette* editor had assigned to the story. In return for a guarantee of total anonymity, they answered a wide range of questions that the two boxes of evidence had generated. Michael pulled out his laptop and walked them through the network, the playbook, and the Church's role in protecting the priests and intimidating their accusers.

When Carla told the three that she had been named by her captain to assemble a task force to pursue criminal charges, they agreed that their days of amateur sleuthing were at an end, though they also agreed to continue the weekly meetings at the tavern.

Forty-Two

A WEEK AFTER his return to the parish, Gabe finished up his Krav Maga workout, grabbed a quick dinner, and settled into the confessional for the seven to nine shift. Business was slow, and by 8:30, he decided to close shop and head back to work on that week's class lecture. He was bending down to gather the detritus from the confessional floor—two empty water bottles and a *Sports Illustrated*—when he heard the confessional door open. He gave a slight sigh and settled back into his chair.

"Bless me, Father, for I have sinned," said a familiar voice. "It's been forever since my last confession." The penitent waited for a response.

Gabe didn't acknowledge her by name. He waited to see where she was going to take the conversation. "Forever's a long time. What brings you in today, my child?"

"I'm facing a dilemma, Father. A big one. Part legal, part religious. So here I am."

"So here you are. Why don't you tell me a bit about this dilemma?"

"Before we go any further, I want to make sure I'm in the right place. You're the one who killed that pedophile priest, right?"

"The confessional is supposed to be a place for anonymity, yours as well as mine. But since this doesn't sound like your standard confession, let's say yes."

"And the Church sent you away. But your parish—*our* parish, I should say—led a noisy campaign to bring our reluctant, modest hero back. And now here you are."

"Here I am. So how can I be of assistance?"

"Here's my dilemma, Father. I'm a cop, and there's a violent criminal at work in my precinct. Which is also your parish, by the way, so maybe it's your dilemma too." She waited for a response, but there was none. "I had a partner in this investigation, or someone I *thought* was a partner. But he let me down. Big time. Know what I mean?"

"Perhaps. But these sound like two separate issues, this criminal you're chasing and your partner. Let's take them one at a time. What kind of criminal are we talking about?"

"The worst kind. A smart one."

"And what is the nature of his—or her—alleged crimes?"

"Oh, it's a he, no doubt about it. And there's no 'alleged' here, Father. I know his identity, and I believe I know his motive. He's a good man trying to right some wrongs. But he's also a violent person who, in my view, is acting as cop, judge, and jury. Or to put it in your terms, he's acting like he's God. And that's a dangerous role to assume, as we both know."

"I agree. It sounds like he might be delusional. Do *you* think he's delusional?"

"No. I think he's as sane as you or me, Father. That's what scares me."

"Is it possible that this man has justifications for his activities?"

"Absolutely. From the outside, I'm sure a lot of folks would approve of what he's doing. But you and I are both insiders,

Father. And we know how dangerous it can get when people start thinking they're above the law. Or above the Church."

After a full minute of silence, Gabe said, "Tell me something. If you weren't a cop, how would you view this man?"

"As someone who does what others, including the law and the Church, won't. Or can't. He's administering justice to people who might escape it otherwise. Yeah, if I weren't a cop, I'd probably be cheering him on. But I *am* a cop, so instead of cheering for him, I need to take him down."

"Given what you've told me, maybe for the purpose of this conversation we should call this person a vigilante rather than a criminal." He waited for an agreement or objection, but neither was forthcoming. "One more question: Does this vigilante's punishments fit the crime or is he being violent for the sake of violence?"

"Until recently, I would have said the former. But he crossed the line about six weeks ago. He killed a man for activities that in the past would have merited a harsh beating, no more. And in my experience, once you cross a line like that, you erase it in your mind, making it much easier to cross in the future. Do you understand what I'm saying, Father?"

"I do, but in my world, we believe in forgiveness and in fresh starts."

"Yeah, well, in my world, we believe in recidivism, in the past repeating itself."

"This vigilante. Does he know you suspect him?"

"I'm sure of it."

"Then why wouldn't he simply stop? Or at least lie low until your attention turns elsewhere?"

"First off, I don't think he wants to. His work, as he sees it, isn't done. Hell, it may never be done, given the people he's targeting. And second, I don't think he *can* stop. This guy has a taste for it—both for the violence and for the justice he believes he's achieving. He's going to keep pushing his activity up a notch, administering as much justice as he can before he's caught or killed. It's called 'decompensating.'"

She leaned closer to the confessional screen and lowered her voice, which made Gabe lean forward as well. "And here's the thing about decompensation, Father. At first the perp is in total control of his actions. Then, as the acts of retribution increase, both in number and violence, he'll get sloppy. Our vigilante may be smart, but he's also an amateur. He may have gotten away with his activities so far, but now that I know who he is, I've got a much larger arsenal of tools I can use to bring him down. I'll get him, Father. If I want to."

"And why wouldn't you want to?"

"Because, to put it in your terms, and as one of my fellow detectives put it, he's doing the Lord's work."

The silence grew until it was like a third participant in the confessional. At one point, Carla started to speak, then she kept her mouth shut and waited.

"What if this individual isn't decompensating?" Gabe finally asked. "What if he's completely rational and just had that one event that was out of character?"

"Then I'm conflicted. I don't know whether to arrest him or to . . ."

"Or to?"

"Partner with him."

"Can you clarify what you mean by 'partner'?" Gabe asked.

"I know you hear some awful things in this box, Father. But I see those same things every day. *See* them. A child with cigarette burns all over his body. A woman with layers of scars, fractures, and bruises. *Layers*, Father, from years of abuse. And girls fourteen and fifteen years old strung out on smack who won't say word one to me about the pimps who get them addicted and then sell them on the street like handbags."

She realized her hands were together, fingers interlocking, in front of her face. She uncoupled them and let them dangle at her side. "Some of the time I put the bastards away. But some of the time they walk. And when they walk, it's not just how smug they look on their way out that gets to me. It's that I know—*I know*—they're going to go right back to burning their kids, beating their wives, and stringing out young girls."

"So what are you saying?" Gabe asked guardedly.

"I'm saying that if I knew I could trust this vigilante to work with me and apply his skills only in those situations where we both agreed it was a last resort, then we might make a good team." She paused, and when she resumed, her voice was harder and lower. "But that's only if I could trust him. What's your take, Father? Do you think I could trust this man?"

"From what you've told me, I'd say you could. But only if this partnership were a two-way street."

"What do you mean by that?"

"It sounds like this individual has targets—or cases—of his own. I'd think he'd like to see how the two of you could work together to bring these sinners to justice. In one way or another."

Carla waited for more, but it was clear that the ball was in her court. She nodded in the darkness. "I could see that working. We bring each other our individual cases and review them together. And we agree to take extraordinary action only after we've exhausted all possible solutions. Do you think he could live with that?"

"I would think so. Acting as judge, jury, and executioner, as you put it, must take its toll. I could see him wanting a partner."

Carla stood up, straightening her slacks and tucking in her shirt. "This has been very helpful, Father. I'm going to go back to the precinct and finish some paperwork. When my shift ends, I'm heading over to The 3-Spot and order a pitcher and two mugs. Do you think my new partner would want to join me?"

"I'd say you can count on it."

She opened the confessional door. Then she closed it and knelt back down. "I told you it has been forever since my last confession. What's my penance?"

They sat together in the semi-dark. Gabe couldn't tell if Carla was serious or jerking his chain. But when she gave no sign of leaving, Gabe gave her request some thought. "As you're sitting there in the bar with that first beer, waiting for your new partner, say this to yourself. It's something a wise person once taught me: One and one don't make two. One and one make one."

"Don't take this the wrong way, Father, but for a smart man, you're lousy at math."

"Perhaps. But that's your penance. 'One and one don't make two. One and one make one.' Now go in peace, my child. And sin no more."

"Yeah, right," she said, using the prayer shelf to hoist herself from her knees.

She opened the door again, this time to find an elderly woman sitting in the closest pew.

As Carla stepped out, the woman rose unsteadily from her seat and started toward the confessional. Holding the door open, Carla reached to take the woman's elbow, but the woman shook off the helping hand and made her way in small but strong steps into the confessional. Then the woman reached over and closed the door, not acknowledging Carla in the slightest.

A smile crept onto Carla's face as she started down the central aisle, gliding past all the empty pews. Reaching the back of the church, she paused before the massive entrance doors. She put a hand on the outsized handle and started to push. With the door partially open, she turned slightly to her right and saw the font, half full with holy water. She released the door and reached over to dip her fingers into it. With wet fingers, she made the sign of the cross—forehead, heart and each shoulder. "What the hell," she said in a low voice. "It can't hurt."

She leaned her shoulder into the door and pushed it open. Stepping out into the night with the water still damp on her forehead, she headed to the bar.

Acknowledgments

ONCE AGAIN, the fun part of writing a book is thanking the people who either helped it or me along during what was at times an arduous process.

I used to wonder why every writer thanked their early readers so effusively. I mean, wasn't the book fully formed by the time it reached them? But this book showed me the real value of assembling a group of people who will: a) take the time to actually read the book (sometimes multiple drafts); and b) critique the work honestly. In the case of *The Empty Confessional*, that criticism included discussions about what was and wasn't working but also suggestions on how to fix those items. Most of those suggestions wound up in the finished work, so a special thanks goes to my early reading team: Jenny Overstreet, Elaine Cummings, Amanda Iles, Jim Decker, Larry and Cindy Loper, and Elizabeth Cvetic.

As with my earlier book, Melanie Mulhall, a gifted editor, helped make for a much better book than she was handed, and hopefully made me a better writer in the process.

If the book looks and feels good to you, thank Bob Schram, our designer. And a special thanks to my daughter, Maya Hogan, for the cover design.

A special thanks is due to Cheryl Callighan, my right and left hand in negotiating the world of publishing, including marketing *The Empty Confessional*. This book couldn't have gotten into your hands without her efforts.

Finally, a thanks to the women in my life. My mother, Peggy Hogan, passed away as I was finishing this book. She lived to be 102 and died in her own home on her own terms. I miss her every day. But she was able to hear/read the first two drafts of this novel, for which I'm very grateful. And as always, to the three women who make my life immeasurably richer: Pamela Pearson, my best gal and best pal, and our two wonderful daughters, Rachel and Maya.

Pedophilia within the Catholic Church is an ongoing problem. Until the Church faces up to it, starts cooperating with authorities on complaints against its clergy, and dismisses those priests guilty of pedophilia, this sin will continue to stain the Church. Survivors of pedophilia deserve our understanding, support, and admiration for coming forward and holding accountable those who stole their innocence and faith. They are true heroes. To support these survivors and their efforts to not only heal but to seek accountability, half of the proceeds of this book will go to SNAP (Survivors Network of those Abused by Priests). They can be reached at www.SNAPnetwork.org.

About the Author

TOM HOGAN IS THE AUTHOR OF three novels: *The Empty Confessional*, a crime novel about pedophilia and the Catholic Church; *The Devil's Breath*, a thriller based in Auschwitz (Amazon Best-Seller 2021), and *Left for Alive*, a crime novel (2019). He is also the coauthor of *The Ultimate Startup Guide* (2017). His screenplays have won awards (the PAGE competition, and the Austin and Napa Valley Film Festivals). He has also written on politics and history for *Newsweek*, *The Jerusalem Post*, and *The Bulwark*. Prior to joining Silicon Valley, where his agency, Crowded Ocean, launched over fifty startups, he was a Lecturer of Holocaust and Genocide Studies at Santa Clara University and UC Santa Cruz. He now lives in Austin, Texas, with his wife, the lovely Pamela Pearson, three dogs, and three cats.

Connect with the Author

THANKS FOR READING. If you enjoyed this book, please consider leaving an honest review on your favorite store.

Connect with me on:
WEBSITE: https://tom-hogan.com/
BLOG: https://tom-hogan.com/blog/
FACEBOOK: https://www.facebook.com/tomhoganauthor
TWITTER: https://twitter.com/hogcom
GOODREADS: https://www.goodreads.com/author/show/15211235.Tom_Hogan

Sign up for my newsletter and learn about upcoming/future books.
https://tom-hogan.com/books/

CPSIA information can be obtained
at www.ICGtesting.com
Printed in the USA
BVHW052119220522
637751BV00015B/764